FORREST WOLLINSKY: BLOOD MISTS OF LONDON

LEONARD D. HILLEY II

NOCTURNAL TRINITY PRESS

For Christal, as always, my love

CHAPTER 1

*E*vening had settled over London. Thick, grayish-white mists crept over the cobblestone streets, slowly swallowing and darkening the Whitechapel district. Uneasiness made me shudder. I sensed something sinister moving within the fog, possessed by its restless need to shed blood. The evil seemed familiar, quite similar to Baron Randolph during his ruthless hunt upon his innocent victims in Bucharest. While such culprits like the baron can be killed, the evil that possessed them continues, lurking to inhabit new hosts to feed and fulfill its bloodthirsty cravings.

From what some London residents had told us, this summer had been oddly cold. Prior to my father, cousin, and I arriving in late August, reports of snow had fallen upon most of the region a month earlier. Snowfall in July? I found myself wondering if the weather had followed us from Bucharest since I had learned about vampires during one of the worst winters ever. The cooler temperatures in London might have explained the sudden fog on a midsummer night, but the weather wasn't a correlation for the evil presence approaching along with it.

My father stood silently at the edge of the damp street, smoking his pipe, watching the fog approach. His beard was a wiry bush and his uncut hair stuck wildly from the sides of his worn top hat. He looked more like an animal than my cousin Jacques, but Father didn't seem to care about his gaunt countenance anymore. His inner pain remained tender and unhealing. His unkempt appearance dissuaded folks from approaching and made him fit in with the other folks living in the slums. In spite of his frightening defense to ward off unwelcomed outsiders, his haunted eyes spoke volumes while he focused on the sweeping fog. He shoved his hands into the pockets of his thick overcoat and sighed.

Few people ventured along the streets this dismal night, and those who did, noticed the drifting mists and warily increased their steps to get home or inside one of the pubs. They possessed the common sense to get indoors.

I marveled at the slow moving wall of fog. The consuming veil prevented us from seeing beyond its fringe and what traveled within. Not even the gas streetlamps were visible once the sweeping fog congealed past them.

Jacques met my bewildered gaze. "You sense it, too, Forrest?"

I nodded, adjusting my hat. I transferred my Hunter box from one hand to the other. During our long journey to London, I had learned it was wise to always keep the box near at hand. This night was no different, actually reinforcing my pacifying connection to my arsenal, but I wondered if my box even contained a weapon capable of destroying what lurked within the mist and shadows. I pondered whether this unseen enemy was even a vampire at all.

Father regarded me with a side-glance, expelled smoke from the side of his bearded mouth, and motioned with a slight nod toward the door of The Britannia. I walked up the steps and pulled the door open, allowing him to hobble past me with his stiff legs. He offered a small smile, something he seldom did after Momma's death, but the gesture was probably more for over-quenching his thirst to temporarily numb his mind from remembering the loss of my mother, his wife.

Lately, he drank far more and talked a whole lot less. Often he seemed a mute, incapable of saying anything. I had lost my mother in death, but oddly, my living father I had known and loved was no more, either. I doubted he'd ever recover from his heartache or that his compassion for life could even be rejuvenated. No matter how much love and support I offered, it was limited. Once he succumbed to his drunken stupors, it became the matter of keeping him from harming himself or others, or worse, seeing him jailed in a village or city that viewed us as common street ruffians or traveling gypsies, which we were not. Nonetheless, he was freed but usually at a high cost or risk to my own wellbeing.

Once a magistrate discovered the tools of my trade inside my Hunter box, father's bounty for release changed from monetary fines to me slaying a vicious demon of the night—as most Catholics termed vampires—for his pardon and release. Mind you, not all were vampires I had to kill. Some were actual demons or zombies. A time or two I had faced ghouls, which I increasingly despised since they traveled in small packs around cemeteries and fire seemed the only way to destroy them. Those were the times when I missed Dominus the most and wondered how he fared.

Jacques felt no loss in Dominus' absence. I understood why. Dominus had teased Jacques, who was more serious, and Jacques took the jests more as insults and belittling than anything else. But during the past few months, Jacques had been a great help in training me when he wasn't roaming the forests in his werewolf form.

"You okay?" Jacques asked.

I nodded.

"You appear lost in thought."

I shrugged.

"It's understandable." Jacques smiled and steadied the tavern door with his hand. "Go ahead."

"Aren't you coming inside?" I asked.

He glanced toward the rolling fog. His hand tightened on his silver cane.

"Not yet. I'm curious."

"So am I, but I don't think it's best for us to linger outdoors in a city we know little about. Besides, almost every city has viewed our arrival with ill intentions." I placed my thick hand upon the door and pressed my back against it to hold it open, hoping he'd step inside to join my father and myself, but he didn't.

Jacques flashed a brief smile, straightened his hat, and tightened the collar of his coat before tapping his silver cane against the stone steps. "Tend to your father. Keep an eye on him. I shall return before he's too sloshed to stand."

With that, he headed down the street where the fog was destined to engulf everything within its path. Even though I had traveled with Jacques for months, I occasionally forgot that his senses of hearing and smell were far greater than my own. It was quite an adjustment having a cousin who was a werewolf.

Wafts of fog expanded, rose, filling the streets and alleyways, and clinging to the cobblestone and walls like a smoky entity. As the thick cloud grew, so did my apprehension. Nothing good would come of this night. I was only a novice Vampire Hunter, pushing close to two dozen kills, but even that was not enough expertise to quality me for what I was about to encounter.

A young couple joined hands, laughing and running ahead of the fog, playfully pretending that the fog intended to devour them. I shook my head and entered the tavern, allowing the door to close behind me. If they only *knew* how accurately close their little game was to the truth, they'd have no laughter, only fear.

I turned and looked out the window. A few seconds later several dirty-faced lads ran from the fog with evident fear in their widened eyes. Something within the shadows was pursuing them. They had seen it, and they were too frightened to attempt a scream. I considered stepping outside in the fog, but not without Jacques. And Father . . . it was never wise to leave him alone to drink.

Leaving Bucharest behind had been more painful than I had anticipated. The forests surrounding our former cottage had been the only home I had ever known, but without my mother . . . I thrust the painful memories away.

The thin barkeep, dressed in a white shirt with a bowtie, noticed my Hunter box, gave me a quick glance over, and shook his head with a narrow brow. With his thick handlebar, his lips looked comical when he spoke. In spite of his appearance his voice was deep, gruff. "I don't allow the trading of wares in here."

I shook my head, setting the box against the bar. "What I carry isn't for anyone else."

"We're not an inn, either, Gypsy."

I ignored his statement and the bitterness in his tone. While my accent was similar to the Gypsies in my home country, my heritage was far different. It did no good to argue the point with someone who already held preconceived judgmental ideas about a culture he didn't understand.

Sitting on the stool beside my father, my long overcoat draped to the floor, partially concealing my Hunter box from curious onlookers and prying eyes. Due to the injuries Baron Randolph had inflicted upon my father, he no longer carried his Hunter box. It was difficult enough for him to walk on stiffened legs without any added weight, so he kept two stakes and a cross inside his overcoat, in case we encountered one of the undead. But lately, he was seldom sober enough to combat a feral cat, much less a hungry vampire.

I ran a hand through my thickening beard while Father told the barkeep what he favored. I suppressed a grin while looking around at the patrons. None would ever have guessed I was a boy because I was larger and more muscular than anyone else in the pub. My deepened voice backed the façade.

Like my father, I ordered a tankard of large dark ale. The first big gulp was bitter with a horrid aftertaste, almost like the foam had transformed into a coat of dingy fur on my tongue. Turning slightly on the stool, I gazed across the tables.

This boisterous bar was no different the dozens my father and I had entered during our journey. Folks laughed, swore, or slammed their mugs upon the table, buttressing their arguments with vigor. Near the midnight hour, after too much ale and whiskey were consumed, brawls broke out. Such were easier to predict than the weather. Where men gathered for strong drinks, destiny dictated that some would ensue fisticuffs.

A few women walked from table to table with blushful smiles, hoping to engage the attention of a one-night suitor for money. Jacques had been the one to warn me about them and not my father. In many ways my cousin took Father's destined role to inform me about society and how to deal properly with people.

Father spent his time staring into a bottomless tankard, slipping into his nightly oblivion and shutting everyone else out. And while I was the size of a grown man, I wasn't ready to complicate my life with unfamiliar emotions, especially when improper affection and infatuation might be mentally misconstrued as love for a young mind like mine.

In addition to Jacques' advice, I continued gaining the knowledge and insight from each vampire I had slain. So I understood things that other eight-year-old children might not otherwise know. I longed to keep my childlike innocence, but the more undeads I killed, the less my mind tarried on ignorant naivety. My body was mature, and although my mind was catching up, I still chose to shun the ideas of infatuation and love. When I entertained such intimate thoughts, my curiosity dwelt on Rose and my guilt for never properly telling her goodbye in Bucharest troubled me. My actions had been childish. Often I wondered if she resented me for exiting the way I had, or if she occasionally thought of me.

Distance had not shaken her from my memories, but I wasn't ready to face her or her father yet. She had bewitched me, unknowingly and without magic. But, I knew being near her while wrestling with my affection for her prevented me from doing my ordained duty in slaying the undead demons of the night. It didn't help that she had begged me *not* to pursue my destiny, and I knew if I chose to love her and settle down, she'd have nothing less from me. To be with her required me to deny my Chosen status, which I couldn't do. I was certain if I did, awful things would happen to her for being the obstacle blocking my destiny.

Daring another gulp of the bitter brew, I placed the tankard on the bar and wiped the froth from my beard with the back of my hand. A woman seated alone at a corner table met my gaze. Unlike the couple of women sauntering from table to table, she didn't offer a hint of a smile. Her eyes narrowed, not from anger it seemed, but from unsatisfied inquisitiveness.

Her complexion was dark, as were her eyes and bunted hair beneath a tight bonnet. Her dress was plain gray without frills. She didn't wish to draw additional attention to herself. There was nothing fancy about her, and to everyone else she was invisible much like a ghost. She looked out of place, slightly uneasy, but bold enough to acknowledge me with an unflinching gaze. With an even smile and a slight nod, she motioned me with her eyes toward the empty chair across from her, an invitation that made me leery.

Her eyes held no contempt, nor did they gleam of sorrow, betrayal, or mischief. She offered a slight plea, perhaps, for a person to take a moment to notice her, which I had, and now she had bid me to join her. I sensed a tendril of power flowing around her, different from what had moved in the mists outside, and the mysticism surrounding her was refreshingly familiar like an old friend, and not an enemy.

Father turned up his tankard, downing the contents. He tapped the bar twice and the barkeep brought him another.

Shaking my head, I stood and clasped his shoulder. "I'll return in a few minutes."

He didn't nod or reply. He simply stared at his frothy ale. I wasn't even sure he had heard me.

I grabbed my Hunter box and walked to the woman's table. Her eyes reflected slight fear as I towered over the chair across from her and set the heavy box on the tabletop. Perhaps she had underestimated my true stature, but her alarm might have been due to my natural unfriendly facial expressions. I looked angry and unpleasant most of the time, which often stopped confrontations before they even had a chance to begin. Nonetheless, after I seated myself, she became more at ease.

"You're a traveler, aren't you?" she asked.

I nodded.

"Peddler?" Her curious eyes fastened on the box.

"No."

She looked disappointed. "Ah, I see. I thought you might be a refugee from Russia."

I shook my head.

"No matter. Why carry such a large box if not selling fine merchandise?"

"I have my reasons." Offering nothing more, she took my silence and stoic expression as hostility.

"My apologies."

"None necessary," I replied, adjusting the hat Dominus had gifted me. "For what reason did you invite me to sit here? What is it that you need?"

She shrugged slightly. "You seem different than the other men that frequent the pubs. What name do you go by?"

"Forrest. And yours?"

"Matilda," she said softly. She offered her hand tilted toward me. "It's nice to meet you."

I took her hand in mine and kissed it in the manner Jacques had told me polite gentlemen did. "The pleasure's mine."

She blushed. "The old man with you . . . Your father?"

"Yes."

Matilda eyed me suspiciously. "You're a bit old to be following your father around, aren't you?"

I held a slight grin, studying her eyes for intent. What did she want, and why all the prying questions? "We're close."

Usually terse replies informed a person the conversation was over, or unwelcome at the very least, but she remained persistent.

"If you're not from Russia, where is your homeland? Your accent is strange compared to ours."

I laughed deeply. "I imagine it is as I've thought the same about those in London. We are Romanian."

An amused smile curled her lips, but not in an attractive way. She straightened in her chair. "Then my premonition concerning you was correct."

I frowned. "About what exactly?"

Matilda glanced across the room without turning her head. She leaned closer and whispered, "You travel with a werewolf."

I held an even gaze without flinching, which was a mannerism I was getting much better at performing. It had taken a lot of practice to prevent disclosing a tell whenever a person challenged me about facts or events that weren't their business to meddle in. I gave her a confused expression. "A werewolf? What is that?"

Her eyes narrowed, this time stirring with slight anger and agitation. "Don't offer ignorance, Forrest. Any child in Romania could describe such a beast. Or a vampire as well."

Folding my hands atop the table, I cocked a brow. "Even if I understood what a werewolf is, what makes you think I'd be traveling with one? I assure you that my father isn't such a monster."

"Not your father. Your father is prey to his own demon. Misery has caused him to drink to escape his reality. It's not him. You must travel with another as well?"

I sensed power leap from her and brush against me. Still I refused an outright answer. "What makes you think that?"

"Because his scent is on you."

"And you would know this how?"

"Their kind roamed London's streets before. They were part of our general population until things got out of control. Lots of people died. You were a fool to bring him to the city."

How did she know? I wasn't certain, but enough with my charade. I grinned.

"I didn't bring him here. *He* brought my father and I."

"This isn't a jest, so don't take my caveat lightly. The police have been sworn to kill any such creature since the city magistrate has strictly ordered immediate death to any werewolf found within London. The constables are equipped with silver bullets and silver daggers."

Nothing displayed in her voice or on her facial features indicated that she was lying. I found myself concerned about Jacques, especially with the rolling wall of fog. She must have noticed my slight anxiety.

"Don't worry," she said. "I would never betray him or you."

"You don't know us. You owe us no protection at all."

"Perhaps not. But tell me why you ventured to London?"

I scooted back in my chair. My jaw tightened.

Matilda offered a warm smile. "You have difficulty placing your trust in people."

"There are few outside my immediate family that I confide in."

"I understand," she said. "I'm the same way."

"And yet you call me, a complete stranger, to sit with you in a pub?"

"Only because I was told to," she replied.

"By whom?"

Matilda glanced nervously around the room. "I cannot tell you here."

"Why not?"

She swallowed hard. Again, she looked around, fearful someone else might hear our conversation. With the clattering of tankards, boisterous laughter and talk, it was doubtful anyone could hear if either of us shouted. She leaned across the table and I copied her movement so she could whisper. "Because of what I am. Should I reveal that and be found out, my fate would be equal to that of your . . . friend. But trust me, my wisdom doesn't come from books or other humans. It is more . . . spiritual, I suppose you could say."

"A witch?" I whispered with a slight grin while folding my hands on the table between us.

Her eyes widened as though I had betrayed her. She gripped my hands and squeezed. She shook her head and whispered fiercely. "How dare you!"

"It was obvious before you invited me over."

Matilda cocked a brow. "How?"

"You have a veil of invisibility protecting you."

She studied me with renewed curiosity. "You know magic?"

I shook my head. "No."

"How did you know?"

"I discern things, much like you, but in other ways as well."

"Then you need to know that witches aren't tolerated here, either. It's a death sentence though not done publicly anymore."

"Your secret is safe with me," I replied.

She trembled with obvious relief. "Thank you, and I shall keep secret about your traveling companion. May I ask something?"

I shrugged.

"Why did you come to London?"

"It was my cousin's request. He has an interest in going to America."

"He'd be safer there than here. When you said that you can discern things, what did you mean?"

"It's difficult to explain."

"An example?"

I took a deep breath and thought. I didn't want to expose that I was a Hunter, but if she knew what Hunters were, she might already know because of my Hunter box.

Matilda patted my hand. "It can be anything."

"Before my father and I entered the pub, a heavy fog was sweeping down the streets and alley. Something evil lurks within those mists. I detected its presence, perhaps it did mine."

She nodded. "It had been here a few months ago. It has recently returned."

"It is what my cousin is seeking to find."

"You had best hope he not find it."

"Why not?"

"He might be outmatched."

My eyes narrowed. "What will he face?"

"No one knows. But Death follows closely. Bodies have been discovered soon after the fog dissipates."

A customer pushed open the door to leave and outside a woman screamed in the darkness. It was such a hideous sound to come from a human. Silence filled the pub. Eyes widened with horror as the patrons turned their attention to the door. No one rose from his chair or stool. Father never even acknowledged the high-pitched sound.

The man at the door stiffened, hesitant to exit or allow the door to close.

I stood, grabbed my box, and stepped away from the table.

"No, Forrest," Matilda said.

I ignored her. Something tragic had occurred and as a Hunter it was my duty to help. Jacques was out there with whatever lurked in the darkness. In spite of my better judgment, I left Father to his drinks and pushed past the man holding the door.

CHAPTER 2

*C*harging through the dark fog, nothing was distinguishable. I slowed my pace until a woman sobbing and heaving deep breaths caught my attention. With caution I walked in her general direction. My hand slid into my coat pocket and gripped a sharp wooden stake. Distraught deception was a vampire's keenest bait to lure a compassionate spirit into its snare.

Shrouded in the heavy dark veil of swirling mists, my vision prevented me from seeing the crying lady.

"Who's there?" I asked, still warily approaching.

"Emily," she replied in between sobs.

"Were you the one who screamed a few moments ago?"

"Yes."

"What's the trouble?"

"There's been a murder."

"Where?"

"Back down the street," she said, pointing. "Not too far from here."

"When?"

"Not long ago."

Leery that this might be a vampire waiting for an opportunity to rush me, I hesitated going any closer. A streetlamp glowed faintly in a dim circle enclosed by the fog. A part of me doubted her story. As shaken as she displayed herself, I didn't think she'd have run through these soupy dark streets.

Whistles blew farther down the street.

"What's that?" I asked.

"Police."

"Have you talked to them?" I braved a few more steps toward her bent form.

"Yes. They told me to go home."

"You live nearby?"

"No."

"Why are you here?"

Emily dried her face with a handkerchief and looked at me. Her face seemed normal. She didn't bear fangs, nor did she appear hostile. She was just visibly upset.

"I can't go home."

"Why not?"

"The killer might go there to kill me."

"What makes you believe that?"

"Because the woman he killed was my roommate."

"I see."

Lightning flashed, brightening the fog around us like windblown white linen sheets. Thunder rumbled and she jolted. My hand held the hidden stake even tighter.

She stood and took a deep breath. "They're trying to catch the man responsible. He left something at the crime scene."

"That's good news," I said. "What was it?"

"A silver cane."

My chest tightened. "If you're too afraid to return home, I suggest you go inside the tavern. You'll be safer there than on the streets."

She nodded.

I bolted down the shrouded street into deeper darkness. More thunder echoed. A light cold drizzle pelted the street, the roofs, and the occasional awning. These backstreets were empty of streetlamps.

While I held no doubt that Jacques would never kill an innocent person, I also knew he'd never leave his cane for someone else to find. It was as sacred to him as my box was for me. I needed to find him, but I had better hope for him to find me by using his senses after I had entered the unlit streets and alleys where the police whistles shrilled.

I couldn't see any farther than a few inches ahead. I was almost running blind. Without a lantern or a light source, Jacques could use his wolf abilities to see me or track my scent, but I relied upon the dumb luck of accidentally running into him. Being swallowed by complete darkness unnerved me.

Two swinging lanterns approached my direction swiftly. When the two Police Constables noticed me, they slowed and stopped to question me. They wore long thick overcoats and odd helmet hats strapped around their chins. In height I stood almost a foot taller than them and was nearly as broad in the shoulders as both of them pressed side by side.

One raised his lantern and held it close to my face. "State your name."

"Forrest Wollinsky." I offered a kind respectable smile, no doubt strangely obscured by the lantern's glow.

"What brings you here?" he asked, cocking a brow. His hand rested on a small club attached to his belt.

I shrugged. "I heard the commotion and came to see what was happening and if I could help."

Recognizing my accent to be quite different than theirs, he stared at me with a suspicious gaze for a few moments. "Sir, I'd advise you to get indoors unless you wish to be taken to headquarters and questioned, which might take hours of your time. This is a matter for metro police."

I gave a simple nod. Both men fashioned thick handlebar moustaches and maintained calm polite manners, which I respected. But neither could hide the fear in their eyes. They had seen something dreadful and perhaps sought to warn the others roaming the streets to seek shelter. I truly wished to offer my services, but being a foreigner, I was considered more suspect than alliance. And what I sought to destroy wasn't what they probably expected to find.

Sadly, I might have been more equipped with whatever stalked the dark recesses of the streets and alleys than they were. But should they arrest me, there wasn't anything I could do to find the sinister murderer from inside a prison cell.

The other PC glanced at my Hunter box with keen curiosity. "What are you carrying?"

"Wares." I figured since everyone else kept arriving at that conclusion, why not go with the lie? It was less likely they'd ask me to open the box. Explaining the mallet and wooden stakes would be difficult. In Romania, few ever questioned my weapons or my methods.

The PC eyed me shrewdly for several seconds. "The streets are too dangerous this time of night to carry such things. I suggest you get back inside."

"Yes, sir." I smiled, turned, and headed back toward The Britannia. Jacques was somewhere in the streets. For the moment I could only hope for his safety since the PCs were equipped to kill werewolves.

When I entered the pub, Matilda wasn't there. She had gone, which didn't surprise me. Father glanced toward me. His eyes were red and his head bobbed slightly side to side. My guess was that he had probably lost count of how many tankards he had drunk.

I placed a hand on his shoulder. "Let's get back to the inn."

He placed his hands against my chest to hold himself steady. His breath reeked of beer and something stronger. Gin, I supposed and some type of pickled meat. Beer was cheap in London, and more plentiful than clean water. His slurred speech indicated he had gotten more than his money's worth in a very short amount of time. "Wh-where's Jacques?"

"Still roaming the streets," I said softly. I hefted him off the stool and set him on the floor, holding his elbow so he didn't embarrass himself by falling.

"Wh-wha-a-t happened?"

"A woman was murdered."

Father tilted his head back and nodded. His eyelids hung heavily while he tried to focus on me, and his tongue hung partway out of his mouth. His eyes kept rolling back, and he was near passing out.

"You need to get some sleep, Father."

He leaned against me, and I opened the door. I carried him more than he walked. My heart grieved for him. He was another reason I was determined to shun love and destined myself to live a solitary life. Nothing was worth such inner turmoil. Perhaps finding love wasn't a bad thing, but the loss of what was considered true love had to be the worst pain imaginable.

Wind blew and heavy rain fell. The fog was thinning, making it easier to see the streetlamps. I propped my father against me for several blocks in this poverty-stricken area, which wasn't so much different than the common areas of Bucharest. Whatever presence I had sensed earlier in the evening was gone.

Without knowing the full details of what the murder entailed, I imagined whatever it was had been satiated by the killing. Blood had been spilled. Death had come. In this area of the city, potential victims were countless, and like vermin they had found places to hide away from the part of society that despised them.

Although we had earned a fair amount of money during our journey to London by slaying and collecting the bounties off a few vampires, Jacques had insisted we venture into the poorest sections of Whitechapel because we'd blend in easier. This certainly seemed true enough because we were mistreated in the same manner as the lowest class.

At our small rundown room, I struck a match and lit the oil lantern on the crude table. My father dropped onto the rough straw-filled mattress on the floor. He was snoring seconds later. I worried about Jacques. Surely he'd be back by now. Thinking of the information Matilda had given me about werewolves once being a part of society, I couldn't help but wonder what events tarnished such a previous coex-istence?

Father snored facedown. I removed his hat and boots, hoping to make him a bit more comfortable, and then tossed a ratty old blanket over him. I was exhausted and wanted nothing more than to lie down and sleep until morning. But I couldn't. Not until I knew Jacques' welfare.

A gentle rap came at the door. I stared and frowned at the door, as if I did so long enough I'd be able to see the person on the other side. I cautiously approached. I didn't believe it was Jacques because he would have knocked bolder. The person outside was timid and uncertain.

"Yes?" I asked, standing at the side of the door.

"Forrest?"

"Matilda?"

"It is I."

"How did you find me?"

"I followed you."

I unlocked the door and pulled it open. "Why are you here?"

She didn't make eye contact. Sadness and embarrassment was in her voice. "I have nowhere to stay tonight. With the rain and cold night, I will catch a deathly cold or die before morning should that predator of the night find me."

"You have no home?"

A glum expression seized her face. "Not a permanent one. Besides, this evening I don't even have enough coins to even enter one of the poor houses where people stand in a line against the wall and a tethered rope holds you upright throughout the night."

I frowned. "You sleep standing up?"

She nodded. "Not well. And seldom a few minutes at a time. It's hard to sleep when you feel like you're going to fall."

"I imagine it is. We have room here. Find yourself a place to sleep until morning."

"Thank you. Are you not going to sleep?"

"Not until Jacques returns."

Matilda sat in an old rocker and pulled a thin blanket over her. She eyed my Hunter box on the table beside the lantern. "May I see what you have in the case?"

I shook my head. "I'd rather not. These are personal items."

"Do you always dash off into the thick of night chasing danger?"

"Whenever necessary."

"What about tonight was necessary? You're not a Londoner. A

murder here should have little concern to you. Besides, what makes you think you could do a better job than the constables?"

I smiled. "Because they don't know how to fight it."

"And you do?"

"Possibly."

Matilda frowned.

"You said that you sensed something evil, right?" I asked.

"Yes. Something I've not felt in several months."

"It's been here before?"

"And left dead women behind then, too."

"How did you know a woman died this time?"

"I listened when you spoke with the victim's roommate."

From where, I wondered. I had not seen her, but the streets were opaque when I had sought the sobbing lady and my focus had been on the crying woman and not anything behind me. I had foolishly made myself vulnerable by not keeping check on my surroundings. "So they've never caught the murderer before?"

"They've had their suspects, but they've never outright accused anyone of the crime. It's quite possible the actual killer was taken into custody at one time and released. But he is careful and too intelligent not to leave any obvious evidence to tie him to these murders."

"You think it's a he?"

Matilda nodded. "That's the feeling I get. What do you think?"

I had never focused on the gender. I sensed something much darker than ordinary humans though. Undead or possessed, perhaps? Premonitions from the intellect of the vampires I had slain indicated something with supernatural powers, so being male or female didn't register with me. It didn't really matter.

Evil came in various forms, always seeking to destroy whatever good it could find or to cripple a town or city with fear.

"I don't know," I replied. I peered out the window but couldn't see anything except my reflection off the glass. "Get some sleep."

She bundled up part of the blanket, making a small pillow, and leaned her head against it. She closed her eyes.

I returned to the table, placed my box on my lap, and watched the door until dawn, hoping Jacques made it back safely. When the sun rose, he still had not returned. With morning's light, I decided to see if I could find him.

CHAPTER 3

I awakened Father, which wasn't a good thing after a night of heavy drinking. He was more than cranky. When he rolled over, his hand rose to backhand me. Once recognition stirred in his eyes, he lowered his hand. His sad eyes offered an apology that he never worded.

"Jacques never came back last night," I said.

Though Father's eyes held concern, he shrugged. "He's a grown man."

Matilda looked in the crude mirror and hand combed her dark hair. "You never slept?"

I shook my head and glanced toward my father. "He's also a were-wolf and Matilda informed me that the PCs are armed with silver bullets and daggers. He might be dead."

Sitting on the edge of the mattress, Father grabbed his boots in haste and pulled them on. He stood and grimaced, placing his hands at his temples and grumbled curses under his breath. Wincing, he put on his top hat, pulling it tightly around his head to combat his agonizing hang-over. It was the same each time he had overindulged. I didn't under-stand why he continued to drink heavily when he hurt so badly the next morning. For me, once would have been enough to dissuade me from ever getting drunk again. Father would grumble for most of the day until he was able to find another drink to combat his headache and heartache.

I opened the door and let Matilda exit first.

"Thanks for allowing me to stay here last night," she said.

I shrugged. "You're welcome, but I have no idea where we'll be tonight."

She smiled and headed down the outer hallway. "I'll find a place by then. Thanks for your hospitality. I hope you find your cousin."

After she was out of sight, my father stepped outside the door. I locked the door and turned to follow my father to the innkeeper's desk.

I placed the room key on the desk and glanced over to see the morning paper's headline: **Buck's Row Murder. Suspect Being Held**. The sketch of the perpetrator was clearly Jacques. I read enough to find where he was being held, grabbed my father's elbow, and hurried toward the door.

Father gave me an odd side-glance. "What's wrong?"

"Jacques is in jail."

He frowned. "Whatever for?"

"He's a suspect in last night's murder."

"Nonsense."

"That's what the post reports."

Father shook his head. "He'd never do something like that."

"I know, but we're foreigners and suspects first. From what I've noticed the Londoners don't take too kindly to outsiders. Either we're outcasts or victims, but in Jacques case, he's being blamed for something he probably didn't even do."

"No probably about it, son. I've known him far too long. The only time he kills is if he encounters a vampire or an undead. I've never known him to kill another human or his own kind."

I gave an incredulous stare at my father.

"What?" he asked.

"Nothing," I replied. But, it was the most he had spoken in weeks. Granted, it had taken our cousin getting arrested to pry his mouth open, but I'd take it. Whenever our family had been faced with injustice,

Father had never been silent. He'd fight with words and physically should the need arise. "How's your head?"

"Like a grape being stomped by an elephant. Multiple times."

I clasped his shoulder. "It will pass."

He nodded, winced. "It always does."

"Until the next morning."

He regarded me for a few moments. "Yes. And I'm sorry."

"No need to apologize."

"Yes. It's necessary," he said, gruffly. "I've allowed myself to be consumed by my loss and have abandoned you in the process. But no more. It's time I accept that Olivia's gone. But a part of her lives on in you. The last thing she'd have wanted is for me to wallow in self-pity for the remainder of my life. And since you're a Hunter, I can offer some advice and training to you, but not if I'm incapacitated."

"Although it's been hard for me to watch, I understand why you've gotten drunk so often."

"That's no excuse."

"In ways, it is. You simply weren't ready to deal with the pain. The question now is, 'Are you willing to face it?'"

Father nodded. "I am."

"Well, there are some things that you can accept to make the process of healing a little easier."

"Like what?"

"The baron didn't turn Momma into a vampire and force us to have to kill her undead form. And the baron and all those responsible are now dust."

Father thought about it for several minutes while we walked down the side of the cobblestone street. "It would have been better if the baron had outright killed me."

"No," I replied, shaking my head. "Don't think like that."

He pointed a stern finger at me. "Yes. Then she'd still be alive. The baron would have had no reason to pursue you or her."

"All of the events were destined, like it or not. Had you died and never returned, I doubt Momma would've even told me that I was a

Hunter. She didn't like that you took me to get this Hunter box and supplies. So don't allow your guilt of being alive blind you."

Father's jaw tightened. He hobbled, trying to keep pace with me. "Blind me? Guilt?"

I nodded. "That's exactly what you've been doing. You keep thinking if you'd done something differently, she'd still be here. Believe me, I miss her sorely, but nothing we could have done would have had a different outcome."

"Fate?"

"Her time, like ours, is destined. We're allotted a certain amount of days on Earth."

He eyed me shrewdly. "You're becoming religious, aren't you?"

I shrugged. "Not necessarily, but it makes sense."

"How?"

"Father, when you arrived at our doorstep in the condition you did, I didn't see any possible way that you'd survive, but you did. Against incredible odds, you survived. You're alive. I doubt anyone else could have recovered from the injuries you did."

He winced as he walked. "Every day is filled with pain from those injuries. Some days I'd accept death as a blessing."

I held my silence. I recognized that each step he took brought pain. He was never able to hide the agony from his facial expressions, but he persevered. He kept pressing forward. That had to wreak havoc on his mind. I believe that was another reason he drank so much. To ease his physical pain as well as his memories of heartache.

"Instead of wishing for death, think about killing more vampires."

"Believe me, I think about that every day. But, when the night falls, all I've been able to do lately is find a tavern."

"I've noticed."

"Again, son, my apologies. But I give you my word. Last night was the last time I allow myself to become enslaved to drink."

"Good to hear." I pointed. "There's the jailhouse."

CHAPTER 4

*F*ather and I entered the small prison office. A PC, Constable Shields, sat at desk and eyed me for several moments, partially in fright, after I stepped through the door with my heavy box in my hand. He glanced from me to my feeble father before finally greeting us with a slight smile and standing. "Morning, chaps. How might I help you?"

I pointed to the newspaper on his desk. "We'd like to speak to the man you are holding about last night's murder."

"You know him?" Shields adjusted his hat. His cheeks were plump like a chipmunk. He had a neat thin moustache and short sideburns. He wore tiny-framed glasses that made his brilliant blue eyes brighter.

"He's our cousin."

"Ah, I see. He's hardly said a word since we took him in last night. By your accent . . . where are you from?"

"Romania," I replied.

"Ah."

Father's jaw tightened. "Are you charging him with this murder?"

Constable Shields shook his head. "Not yet, we haven't. No. We just wanted to ask him some questions. He's in holding."

"May we speak to him?" Father asked.

Shields nodded and took a ring of large metal keys. "Of course, since no charges have been made. Perhaps the two of you could persuade him to answer our questions?"

"We can try," I replied. "He tends to get moody at certain times each month."

"He seems like a marvelous chap. Nice and tidy, well reserved, but stubborner than an old ass."

"That would be him," my father said.

The constable led us down a hallway with locked gated cells on each side. The iron bars were thick. Steel plates reinforced the corners of the cell walls. They seemed impassable, even for a werewolf. When we reached the cell where Jacques was, the man placed the large key into the lock and turned it. "You have visitors."

Jacques gazed toward the door as Shields pulled it open. He didn't seem angry but probably perturbed. He forced a half grin. "I suppose you read the early post?"

I nodded.

The constable glanced at Jacques. "Look. We only brought you in for a few questions. If you could provide us with the answers, you're free to go."

Jacques stood and sighed. "I told you last night why I was on that particular street."

"Buck's Row," Shields said.

"Yes."

"Did you see anyone else?"

"Yes. I saw the man who killed that woman. I tried to stop him, which is why my cane was left behind in the street. After a brief struggle, he fled, and I went to pursue him."

"And then you lost him?"

Jacques nodded. "Only because I was struck in the back of the head when I darted past him. I have the knot to prove it, if you'd like to examine it."

"Then why didn't you simply tell us this last night when we found you? We'd have let you go."

Jacques rubbed the back of his head and winced. "I had quite a headache and was suffering from embarrassment, mostly. I'm usually a more resourceful fighter. I thought I had him, and then . . . I lost consciousness."

"Ah, I see. Could you describe what he looks like?"

"His face?"

"Yes."

"There isn't any light on the street, so no."

Constable Shields frowned. "You said that you saw him?"

"*Encountered* would be a better word. He wore nice clothes, not like the poorer people in the slums."

"How could you tell if you couldn't see him?" Shields asked.

"I grabbed for him. His shirt and tie were silk. Even in the darkness I can distinguish silk from any other cloth. Can't you?"

Shields offered a slight shrug and pressed his glasses against the bridge of his nose.

I gave Jacques an inquisitive stare. With his abilities, he could've seen what the murderer looked like in the darkness. I flicked my gaze to the constable.

"How did she die?"

The constable's cheeks puffed, and he released a long sigh. "She was butchered. Two slashes across the throat. Her abdomen was all cut up. She probably died quickly. The weird thing was how little blood was found where she lay. We think that maybe she had been killed elsewhere and then brought and left where we found her."

I gave a side-glance toward Jacques when Shields mentioned how little blood was at the scene. Jacques nodded slowly.

"If you would, follow me back out front and sign a few papers?" Shields said, looking at Jacques. "Then you're free to go."

Jacques stood. "Sure."

"So was Jacques ever a suspect?" Father asked. "The post indicated that he is."

The constable shrugged and shook his head. "Headlines sell. But a real suspect? No. A person of interest as being a possible witness, yes. From how she was murdered, he'd have had a lot of blood on him. A slashed throat is a messy way to kill someone. We found no traces of blood on him."

We followed the constable to the desk. Shields lifted the silver cane and studied it for a few moments. "Interesting. Splendid, actually. I've never seen such a cane."

"It is an eye-catcher," Jacques said, taking it.

"Indeed."

Shields slid Jacques a few forms to fill out. Once he finished with them, we left. Outside, I stared at him. "What are we dealing with? A vampire?"

Jacques shrugged. "Right now, I honestly cannot tell you."

"How could you not know?" I asked. "You can see in the greatest depths of darkness."

"That's true. But I don't know that he's a vampire or if he's something else. He never flashed fangs, but he moves as swiftly as any vampire. He has supernatural abilities, and he was drinking her blood when I happened upon him. But not from biting her. He used a jagged long knife to gash her open and drank from her wounds."

"A knife? Have you ever known a vampire to use a weapon instead of biting his victim?" I asked.

"Never. But I suppose I wouldn't put it past one."

"Why's that?"

"Teeth marks on the neck immediately identifies the killer as a vampire," Jacques replied. "But the man responsible is a wealthy aristocrat, a man of prominence somewhere."

"Like the baron?" I asked.

Jacques nodded. "He's a man with a lot of influence or at least, he poses to be. The woman he attacked had been at ease with him just moments before he slashed her throat."

"You witnessed the murder?"

"Unfortunately, I did. I don't think he realized I was nearby."

We walked along the street. Awnings hung over numerous tables of produce and goods. Last night, the streets had been empty, barren, but this morning, people milled along the sidewalks and along the cobblestone by the hundreds. Never had I seen such hopeless faces like these of the merchants and potential customers. In Bucharest, we had slums, too, but these ragged folks looked more depressed.

Dirty-faced children trotted in small groups, some causing mischief and others stealing whatever items they could in hopes of trading their loot for food elsewhere. Either the parents had abandoned these children or the children had forsaken their parents, having decided to fend for themselves. Parents didn't seem to hold any concern for their children and perhaps this was due to how difficult it was for one human to feed him or herself. It didn't matter what part of the world one resided, social classes all seemed to display identical traits, whether good or bad. Utopias only existed in the pleasantest of dreams. It was far unlikely the world we lived in would ever achieve such a plateau, and London certainly wasn't at the top of the list to eat from the table of plenty.

"I met an interesting lady last night," I said to Jacques.

"Oh?" he replied with a teasing smile. "Seeking romance so soon after our arrival?"

I blushed and shook my head. "No. Nothing like that. She . . . she knew a lot more about you than I expected."

"Meaning what exactly?"

"About what you are."

Jacques cocked a brow and straightened his tie. "My inner beast?"

I nodded.

"How?"

"She's a witch."

"So?" Jacques replied. "You could have denied it."

"Believe me, I did. But she persisted. She said that she smelled your scent upon me."

Jacques stopped walking. Concern narrowed his eyes. "Did she now?"

I nodded.

"That's not a trait a witch would have. She's something else."

"Like what?"

"What makes you think she's a witch? Did she do anything to prove it to you other than tell you she was?"

Father frowned. "Are you referring to Matilda, son?"

I nodded toward him and then I faced Jacques. "She was under a partial invisibility spell."

He grinned. "How would you know that?"

"I can sense magic. I have ever since Rose's father handed me this box. Just like you were able to sense the magic on my dagger. She had a veil of invisibility cast because the majority of people in the pub didn't notice her. When she noticed that I had, she motioned for me to sit with her."

"That may be, but magic alone would not enable her to know that I was around you. There must be more that she's not telling you."

"Like what?" I asked.

"She might have seen us together and somehow come to that conclusion. But she couldn't have known by scent. Not unless she is a demon or some type of shifter herself."

"Regardless of how she knows, cousin, she knows. She told me that you're in great danger by being in London. Werewolves are put to death without any real need for a trial. The constables are armed with silver bullets and daggers. I think we need to find another city to reside in."

Jacques shook his head. "Not until we find the man who killed the woman last night."

"Do you have proof he's a vampire?"

"No. But if we don't stop him, he'll kill again."

"How do you know that?"

"You felt the evil yesterday when the fog approached, didn't you?"

I nodded.

"He's not finished. He thirsts for blood. His hunger hasn't been satisfied. I've been around his kind before. He's just getting started. And look around you. He has a bountiful supply of poor people who are better off dead and won't be missed by the rest of the area."

As a Hunter, I couldn't simply abandon the situation, not if the murderer was, in fact, a vampire. At the moment we didn't really know. My biggest worry was placing Jacques into danger. The longer he stayed in London, the more likely it became for someone to discover that he was a werewolf and if that person was one of the constables armed with silver bullets . . . it simply wasn't a risk worth taking.

"I suggest you leave London and allow Father and I to go after this man."

"No, Forrest. You've matured over the past few months, but you're not ready to face this man."

"Did he really knock you unconscious? He'd have had to hit you quite hard. I'm surprised if he did that he didn't simply kill you afterwards."

Jacques rubbed the back of his head. "He fled because the PCs were approaching, but no, he didn't knock me unconscious; although he did rattle me badly though."

"How? I've seen how fast you are."

Jacques smiled. "There's always someone faster or stronger. You'll learn that the older you get."

"He's that fast?"

"Last night he was."

The expression on his face indicated that he wanted another chance to fight this man or vampire. He wasn't about to retreat. "Okay, so if you're too stubborn to leave, what do you suggest we do to find this man?" I asked.

"We learn the streets, especially here, near where he killed her."

"You really think he'd kill close to where he did last night?"

"I cannot rightly say. It won't hurt to look for clues that might be overlooked by the constables."

"He's right, son."

I took a deep breath and looked at the people. I wasn't about to stand idly by and let another poor soul be food for something else. The eeriest thought was that one of these people might actually be the person we were looking for. "Then let's get started."

CHAPTER 5

The three of us walked past a pub on our way toward the murder scene. My father's eyes looked at its door longingly for several moments. He swallowed hard, and already his internal struggle for sobriety challenged him, trying to overpower his will. Sweat beaded his brow. He paused in step to wipe his brow with his handkerchief, even though the morning air was quite cool.

"Fancy a drink?" Jacques asked.

Father shook his head and turned his gaze from the door. "No. I'd rather find a place where we can get some breakfast."

Jacques flicked his gaze toward me.

I smiled and gave a slight nod.

"Good," Jacques said. "But if we're going to find something more suitable and filling, we need to head out of this area nearer to the heart of London. By the time we find a place to eat, it will probably be closer to lunch. Once we've eaten we can come back and look for evidence."

"Where might a vampire hide during the day in Whitechapel?" I asked.

"That's what I hope to find out. My guess is that the small gangs of boys would have a better idea of the Underground. Their curiosity stems greater than the adults. They're more apt to explore and find places to hide during the day."

"Especially the thieving little brats," Father said.

I frowned.

"What?" he asked, gruffly. "You've not seen them pickpocketing?"

I chuckled. "I have, but I didn't expect that you would have noticed."

"And why wouldn't I? I'm about my full senses this morning, regardless of my intense headache and uncontrollable shakes."

Jacques squeezed Father's shoulder. "It gets easier, John."

Father rowed his shoulder to shake loose Jacques' hold.

We walked to Whitechapel Road where the social class was better off than those in the back alley slum districts and found a nice little dining club. We entered, and even though most were better dressed than ourselves, we weren't shunned or shown the door. Most seemed leery of me, but since the outside of my Hunter box was adorned with polished silver, most assumed us far wealthier than we actually were. With our few vampire kills along our journey up the Danube River, we had earned an adequate amount of money to eat and sleep at the fancier establishments. However, due to the bloody nature of our slayings, Father and I never invested a lot in new clothes. Jacques, on the other hand, had exquisite taste and dressed in finer suits. When the three of us were together, he was like a peacock traveling with two pigeons.

We were seated at a round table that was covered with a white tablecloth embroidered with rose patterns. Two lit candles burned softly. The place settings were dainty and more like art than something food should be served upon. Before our order was taken, we were served black coffee. The aroma was far more appealing than the sharp bitter taste.

While we ate, Jacques kept his attention focused on the table where Constable Shields sat alone, drinking his coffee. A copy of the East London newspaper lay on the table beside his saucer. Shields frowned, deep in thought it seemed, but his attention never turned toward us. At least not immediately. He was troubled and his mind held him elsewhere. He cocked a brow and tilted his head to the side while rubbing his chin. A few moments passed before a server walked by and interrupted his gaze. He shook his head, blinked, and suddenly regarded us. His brow rose and he offered a polite smile and nod. Jacques motioned him to sit at the empty chair at our table.

Shields grinned, rose from his seat, tucked the paper beneath his arm, and brought his teacup and saucer with him. He promptly sat and set his cup and saucer on the table. Without a lessening of his smile he glanced to each of us and placed the paper on the table. "I've been thinking about you chaps."

"Oh?" Jacques said.

Shields nodded. "What brings the three of you to London from Romania? That's quite a long journey."

Jacques sipped his coffee and set his cup down. "We love to travel, see new places, but I'm interested in sailing for New York. From what I've heard, London often hires crew to work in exchange for the fare."

"Some do. That's true. New York? Ah, ever been before?" Shields asked.

"No."

"I visited once last year. Lovely city. Almost any nationality resides there. It's like a great set of cities within one city. London seems to be that way here of late."

I crossed my massive arms, cleared my throat, and eyed the newspaper. "Constable Shields, have you learned anything more about the murder last night other than what the post reported?"

Shields nodded. "Ah, yes. She was known as Polly. Poor woman. Went from workhouse to workhouse for the past several years. Also, she worked as a prostitute, which might have played a part in her death last night."

"You think so?" I asked.

"At this point we can only assume," Shields replied.

Jacques shook his head. "I don't think it mattered."

"How's that?" Shields said with a frown. His glasses slid a bit on his nose. He took his teacup by the handle and sipped more tea. His eyes never shifted from Jacques.

"My guess is she was a convenience, an opportunity."

"Like being in the wrong place at the wrong time?"

"Exactly," Jacques replied. "You see, constable, this man was dressed in fine clothes unlike the poorer population that dwells in that area of Whitechapel."

"Sort of like yourself?" Shields asked with a shrewd stare.

Jacques' eyes narrowed. "We're only here trying to help."

"I'm not accusing, but . . . Yes. About that, you wanting to help . . . Why does this poor woman's murder interest a trio from Bucharest? She's a commoner that had nothing overly special to offer society. In a week few will even remember her. You're not officers in your own country, are you?"

"No, we're not," I said. "We investigate—"

"Forrest, no," Jacques said in a low voice. "We're not constables, but we have been paid to track murderers though."

"Bounty Hunters?" Shields asked.

"In a manner of speaking," Jacques said, nodding. "We are."

"I see. And is that what you're hoping from this situation? That we'll offer a reward?"

Jacques replied with an even smile. "Someone will, especially if this man kills again."

Shields studied Jacques for several long moments. "You think this person might kill someone else? Why?"

"From what you told me about how he killed this woman, he did so with incredible violence."

"He did," Shields agreed.

Jacques nodded. "He's unleashed his need to shed blood. It will be much easier for him to kill again."

"So, you've seen similar cases?"

"Constable Shields, we're from a war-torn country undergoing reconstruction and recovery. The hostilities of war spill over into some men's personal lives after peace has come. If ever there's a time when people are granted proper permission to kill other people, ever how viciously, it is during mandated war. Murder twists the mind, and once that lever has been flipped, some cannot turn off the need."

Shields took a deep breath and held it. The information Jacques had given alarmed the constable. He sighed. "Are you suggesting this man might have been a soldier?"

Jacques shrugged. "It's possible."

The waiter returned and filled our cups.

Shields nodded his thanks. He glanced toward Jacques. "I would've never considered such."

"You've not been exposed to as much death as we have, constable," Jacques replied.

"No, I suppose not."

I said, "Do you think there's a connection with last night's killing and that of the other two women killed some time back?"

"The modus operandi of those murders isn't the same. How would you even know about those two? You haven't been in London that long. Those murders happened nearly six months ago."

"A woman mentioned them last night."

Shields folded his hands atop the table. His face became solemn. "You need to understand about the various newspapers. They tend to go overboard in delivering every sordid detail of these brutal murders. Like you, Jacques, they were ready to pin last night's murder on you without any facts at all."

"They tried," I said.

Anger hardened Shields' face. He tapped his index finger on the newspaper while he spoke. "The reporters would do better to write mystery novels with all the exaggerated details they add to sell the news."

"That's probably true," Jacques said. "But we still offer our help in any way possible."

"We have hundreds of constables," Shields replied. "Do you honestly think the three of you can do a better job?"

I smiled. "In some ways we can."

"How's that?"

"We keep being called Gypsies, so in appearance we blend in with the lower class. We don't wear uniforms that announce who we are. I believe most of them will better trust us than you. What do you think?"

Shields grinned. "I never thought of it like that, but you're probably correct. But tell me about the types of cases you've worked on?"

"One case in particular," Jacques said, "was the most unexpected discovery in what we were hired to do."

"Being what exactly?"

"The serial murderer was a baron. A man of high prominence in Bucharest."

Shields was intrigued. "Really?"

We all nodded.

"More than that, we cannot tell you," Jacques said.

"But you stopped him?"

"We did."

Shields leaned back in his chair and crossed his arms. "How long will you three remain in London?"

Jacques looked at me. I shrugged. "Until we find this murderer."

"Even though no guarantee of a reward is being offered?"

"It's not about the money," Jacques replied.

"I won't dissuade you, but I will caution you. I'm not empowering any authority to you. None. Is that understood?" Shields asked.

We nodded.

He sighed. "And, that means you can't take suspects into custody. I do insist that you keep me informed of whatever clues you might discover along the way though."

"Not a problem," Jacques said. "We're simply the eyes and ears that your uniformed constables won't have."

Shields stood, took his paper, and regarded each of us. He placed enough money on the table to pay for our coffee and meals as well as his own. "Most importantly, don't get yourselves killed."

"That's not part of our plan," Jacques said.

Shields offered a curt smile. "I'm sure it wasn't Polly's either. Be safe, gentlemen."

CHAPTER 6

*A*fter we finished eating at the dining club, we journeyed into the depressed heart of the slums. A young lad with crooked yellow teeth attempted to yank my Hunter box from my grip, so I let it loose. The box was too heavy for him to carry, and he dropped to the cobblestone beside it. His panicked eyes gazed upward into mine. I offered a sinister grin with a harsh frown. He crawled and scurried on all fours until he was able to stand. He darted through the crowded streets, still looking at me over his shoulder.

I hefted my box and shook my head. The boy was small like Bodi, immediately reminding me of him. I couldn't help but think about my school friend with a tinge of remorse and regret; even though there hadn't been anything I could have done to prevent him from being turned into a vampire at such a tender age.

The would-be thief slowed at the corner of a vendor's table and stopped to observe us. Another larger boy slugged his arm and yelled at him. I assumed his abuse came because the boy had failed to steal my box. While the boy rubbed his arm, three more grimy, soot-coated lads joined them. All of them fastened their gazes toward my Hunter box, which was still on the cobblestone. I leaned lower, grabbed the box's handle, and stared at them in a daring manner. The greed in their eyes didn't have the bravery to back a second theft attempt.

"I never imagined a gang of thugs being so young," I said, nodding in their direction.

Jacques studied them for a few moments. "Let's see where they lead us."

Jacques and I turned, walking in their direction. All of the lads bolted. "Wait here, Father."

I didn't expect him to argue, and he didn't. Running was the last thing I'd ever ask of him.

Jacques and I ran after the kids. They ran much faster than I ever could for my clumsy height and large feet, but Jacques was swifter. We didn't need to actually catch them. We only needed to see if they knew a way to get beneath the city streets.

In most of the larger major cities, underground tunnels and passage-ways exist that often mirror the streets overhead and most people never even know they exist. For the few who do, they have an advantage over the surface-dwellers because they can seemingly vanish whenever they're pursued. Since these lads were frightened, they'd seek the quickest escape route.

As Jacques sprinted ahead of me down the next side street, the boys zigzagged through the congested street, causing folks to sidestep and some nearly tripped, trying to allow the boys through without getting knocked flat. Even though the boys were short and difficult to see in the crowd, they were easily followed by how the pedestrians reacted to their erratic running patterns.

Jacques cut across the street where one boy yanked a chain to raise a metal door outside an old leather shop. The boys hurried down the metal rungs with the last one pulling the door flush with the walkway. From what I could tell, once I got closer, the door appeared to lead into an underground storage room for the leather shop, but after Jacques and I followed, we discovered something more.

Because of Jacques' unique night vision, he found an unlit oil lantern hanging on a long rusted nail. He struck a match and lit the wick. The glowing light revealed a hole in the wall that led into a deep dark tunnel, which was manmade and possibly destined to be expanded. The thieving boys had apparently entered through here many times before.

Jacques and I peered through the hole. A lit lantern swayed side to side as the boys ran along the cleared narrow path. I thought it odd for any youth at their ages to have the gall to venture through a tunnel that would make the bravest adult hesitate. After all, the worst, most evil things in this world hid in the darkness, waiting for the opportunity of a misfortunate passerby to enter into their territory. Crafty predators used numerous traps to snare their prey. Spiders were the most tactful masters in trapping their victims, but so were vampires, demons, and unidentified monsters. A dark tunnel such as this one held endless possibilities for what lurked in the shadows, waiting to feed or to transform.

A set of rails split the path's center. An old rusted hand-operated rail car was positioned on the track. In the distance a rumbling rocked the ground and shook the walls as a train engine roared.

"An underground railway?" I asked.

Jacques nodded. "Yes, but nothing runs along this tunnel except these small supply carts for the shop owners. This one doesn't seem to have been used for some time though."

"How far do you think these tunnels go?"

"We'd have to ask." Jacques climbed through the hole with the lantern.

I didn't even attempt to squeeze through. My shoulders were too broad. I pushed at a couple of the rocks. Loose mortar spilled like draining sands in an hourglass. After a couple of minutes of rocking the stone back and forth, it dislodged and fell from its place. I repeated the procedure with several more stones until I opened the hole wide enough to crawl through.

"It wouldn't need to be far though. Just a quick way underground."

Jacques shrugged. "For a quick escape, that would only be a luxury. But if this killer has a hiding place down here, and the tunnels are long intersecting mazes, we could spend weeks hunting and never find him."

"That's true."

"We don't have that kind of time."

The lads with the lantern disappeared around a turn in the tunnel. We pursued, only to discover where they were going. Since they had not actually stolen anything from us, sending a sliver of fright into them might discourage them from attempting theft from me again. They seemed to know the tunnel system quite well, so they held the greater chance of losing us than our continued tracking of their position. Depending upon how long the tunnels were, there might be hundreds of places for them to return to the surface while losing us in the process. But with last night's murderer, we needed to become familiar with these tunnels. If he killed again, he'd most likely resort to fleeing here to lose the constables and us, which he might have done to escape the previous night.

Several bats chirped and flitted from the crevices near where the boys had turned. Jacques slowed at the corner of the tunnel, allowing me to catch up.

High-pitched squeaks echoed from behind us and around the corner, reminding me of how Baron Randolph had first appeared as a cloud of swirling bats and assembling into human form before me. We had seen a few bats flee the tunnel as the boys entered, but these squeaking sounds were eerily different than those bats made. The nerve-grating shrills increased from every tunnel opening and crevice in the crude tunnel walls.

With only one lantern in the impenetrable darkness, our vision was greatly limited. We were outnumbered. By what exactly? I wasn't certain.

A bad feeling set upon me. Inside my mind came a stern warning, a premonition, perhaps from my maturing intuition gifted to me as one of the Chosen Vampire Hunters. My knowledge and perception continued expounding after each vampire I had slain, but it had limitations. Even if I killed a thousand master vampires I'd never become omniscient and omnipotent. I was still a mortal and mortals, even the Chosen Hunters, could be killed. What I gained was knowledge and sensitivity, what most people called 'gut feelings,' but mine were much stronger. Most vampires possessed a survival insight warning them of approaching enemies, allowing them to prepare themselves for such encounters or giving them adequate time to escape. I possessed this, too, but stronger than ordinary mortals.

"We have a problem," I said.

Jacques glanced toward me. "What exactly? A vampire?"

"I'm not certain what it is but I sense its power."

The high squeals and shrills swarmed in the darkness and with the odd chorus came a smell of decaying refuse. Jacques lifted the lantern. We stood back to back. Hundreds of eyes gleamed white off the lantern's glow. Rats swarmed out from each path and spilled from holes in the walls. All of them trained their attention and headed toward us.

"What do you make of this?" Jacques asked.

"I don't know. Some master vampires control different animals."

Jacques smirked. "Yeah, don't remind me."

The bevy of vermin blocked our path, preventing us from returning to the place where we had descended from the street. From our left side the ground was carpeted with layers of black and brown rats. With their great numbers they could easily have swarmed us and ripped the flesh off our bodies, but they didn't. They stood on their hind legs and left a path for us to follow where the boys had disappeared. I was certain if we attempted to go any other direction, they would attack.

"Not leaving us any alternate route," I said, pointing.

"They're not."

I slid my hand into my pocket and withdrew a stake. "I guess we see where the path leads."

He nodded and held the lantern before us. He held the silver cane like a club and not an aid for walking. Like me, he was on alert. For a moment I wondered what might happen if he chose to strike the cane against the medallion around his neck. How would the blinding light affect the rat masses? Would they attack or could we use their blindness to our advantage and escape? He never produced the radiate light, so I imagined that his curiosity was as great as my own.

With each step we took, the rat swarm closed in behind us. None attempted to bite or even acted hostile, but they were insistent we follow the path outlined ahead of us. They regarded us with intent curiosity.

The boys had taken this path, but without the rat masses insistence or guidance. No light other than our lantern glowed in this long narrow tunnel. The old rail tracks weren't shiny from recent use but were coated with thick dust and cobwebs. The sound from the other tunnels where the rumbling trains moved grew fainter. This tunnel had been abandoned long ago.

Where the tracks ended the path narrowed and stopped at an open door. A set of crude steps led downward. I turned sideways and hunched to fit through the doorframe. After we started down the stone steps, light flickered along each of the walls. Flames danced from iron sconces, three on each wall. Water dripped from the ceiling, occasionally causing a hissing sound as the fire evaporated the moisture. Near the back of this room a small fire pit blazed. A large stone chair shaped like a throne was the only object in the center of the room, other than the pit. From behind the chair the five boys stepped from hiding.

Jacques looked at me. I shrugged.

At least the rats had not entered the room. None poked a head through the door, either.

"So you two are the ones harassing these young boys?" the male voice asked.

The flickering flames in the fire pit hardly presented this man's outline. He was well hidden on the shadowed throne.

"Harassing?" I said, partly in anger. "Is that what they told you? One of them tried to steal my box. What kind of man defends little thieves or perhaps you're the one who has trained them?"

"Man indeed. Approach." His voice was harsh and menacing and a bit too demanding for my taste. I immediately disliked everything about him.

My hand tightened around the stake. It didn't matter if he wasn't a vampire. Stakes killed people, too, if his threatening tone arose to physical violence and it became such that I needed to defend myself.

After Jacques and I stepped past the fire pit, the lantern revealed that the man in the chair wasn't a vampire, but a shape-shifter. He wasn't a werewolf like Jacques. He was a were-rat and so were the five boys. The boys' eyes glowed red and their gnarled teeth became more pronounced. Their fingernails lengthened like thin razor-edged blades. They looked even more threatening than the elder were-rat.

"Who are you?" I asked.

"Lord Albert," he replied, bridging his long boney fingers and resting his narrow chin atop them. "And if you'll indulge me the same?"

"I'm Forrest, and this is my cousin, Jacques."

"England is not your homeland. Where are you from?"

"Romania," I replied.

"What brings you into my tunnels?" His green eyes reflected in the fire's glow.

"A woman was murdered last night, and we believe he might have used these tunnels to escape. We also suspect that he's a vampire and might have set up residence down here."

"A vampire?" He sounded amused.

"Yes."

He eyed my box and then looked into my eyes. "You're a Hunter?"

I nodded.

"And you?" He glanced at Jacques with a sly grin. "You're a werewolf."

"I am."

"The man you seek came this direction last night," Albert replied.

"Is he a vampire or human or worse?" I asked.

The were-rat shrugged. "He's a vampire, but it's highly doubtful he'll ever pass through here again."

"Why's that?"

The were-rat grinned, revealing his pointy teeth. "Certain death will befall him."

"You don't fear him?" I asked.

"Not as much as he fears me."

"So the rats in the tunnels are controlled by you and not he?"

Albert sneered. "What do you think? They led you to me, didn't they?"

I nodded. "So you wished to meet us?"

"I don't like intruders, Forrest. A man of my . . . nature needs a place of privacy. I won't tolerate trespassers."

"Why don't you blend in with the others on the surface?" I asked. "Like these boys?"

"I cannot transform. I'm cursed to remain in this form, which isn't all that bad once you've adjusted. I'm far more powerful in this form than I ever could be as a mere human. I never was one fashioned for society."

"But you're a lord?" I asked.

Albert laughed. "Titles are of little importance, unless you're an actual king or queen. Folks are naïve to believe a title holds more prominence than the commoners. Without common folks, there'd be no rank of hierarchy. Being a lord has done nothing for me."

"And yet you boast it nonetheless," I replied.

The five were-rat boys gnashed their twisted teeth. Their eyes narrowed, and they glanced eagerly toward Albert, perhaps hoping for him to command them to attack Jacques and I. Should they charge, things would get bloody and messy fast. While I was certain Jacques could survive such an attack, I didn't know what my fate might be. Death or possibly contaminated to become a were-rat, too?

"Guests should be cautious of the tone they take with me," Albert said. "One bite or a severe slash from our claws would allow you to view a different type of existence, Forrest. Of course, such wouldn't affect Jacques any."

Well, that answered one of my questions.

The were-rat noticed the apprehension in my eyes. He smiled. "I've never known a Hunter that was also a were-creature. You might consider the possibilities of how your strength could increase, Forrest."

I shook my head. "I'll pass."

Albert shrugged. "If you ever reconsider—"

"No."

He sighed. "I use *lord* because there is not another higher in authority than myself in these tunnels. I could use king since none oppose me, but it's too lofty. I'm the reason the railroad company abandoned this tunnel."

"So others know you're here?"

He shook his head. "No. They know about the rats and that some-thing much larger lurks here. They've seen my shadow but never actually seen me, which is probably more frightening than the true reality. Either way, it's safer for them to stay away."

"You'd kill them?"

"Whenever necessary. Again, I don't take kindly to intruders."

Jacques rested his hands atop his cane. "Did you recognize the vampire when he came into the tunnels?"

"He's wealthy."

"I gathered that much myself."

Albert's eyes narrowed. "You encountered him on the surface?"

Jacques nodded. "A few moments after he had killed a woman."

"I see. And you simply let him slip away?"

"No less than you did, I suppose."

Albert hissed. "You two have such pompous attitudes. Such disrespect—"

"No disrespect intended," Jacques said. "But you leveled a direct accusation at me."

Albert waved his boney hand and nodded. "Fair enough. But to elaborate upon the information about this vampire . . . he's not a Londoner. He has no lair down here. He might not even have one in all of London."

I frowned. "You think he's a vagabond?"

He shrugged. "My guess is he's an emigrant from Romania, Hungary, or Russia. Within the flooding great horde of refugees comes the darker, more dangerous fiends who wish only to cause death and destruction. Vampires are new to the West, but steadily rising in the number of neophytes. There are a few masters in London, but none who dare make themselves obvious to the general population. The olden countries are where their populations are the thickest."

"I know," I said, lowering my Hunter box to the earthen floor.

"And yet, you're here, in London? What made you flee your homeland? The population of vampires was too much for you?"

I shook my head. "No. I needed time to heal."

His eyes regarded me with keen interest. "Heal from what exactly? You appear strong and foreboding."

I took a deep breath.

Jacques spoke before I could reply. "His mother was killed by a vampire. He, in turn, killed the vampire."

The five were-rat boys lowered their gazes to the floor. Their threatening appearances diminished drastically. Sorrow filled their eyes and their shoulders slumped.

"My condolences," Albert said softly. His hand went to the golden cross on his necklace. "We understand such losses here."

"I do plan to return to my homeland after we find and kill this murderer," I said. "I would dishonor my calling if I chose otherwise."

Jacques eyed Albert. "For what it's worth, last night's vampire wasn't trying to turn his victim. She was dead before he fed upon her."

"I see," Albert said with narrowed eyes. "On this side of Whitechapel there are thousands of potential victims. Murder is not uncommon amongst the impoverished."

Jacques and I nodded.

"My boys and I will do whatever we can to help you."

"Are you religious?" I asked, staring at his cross.

"We're all religious in one way or another," he replied. "You have crosses on the outside of your box. I imagine you possess others on your person as well."

I nodded. "I do, but I didn't craft the box. It was gifted to me."

"If you had made it, you wouldn't have placed the crosses upon it?"

I sighed. It always seemed to come down to religion, but I had seen the hatred between two warring religious factions that wished to take over Bucharest in their progression to control the world governments. "It's doubtful I would have."

"You're not a believer in the cross?" He looked stunned and somewhat mortified.

I explained the culture of my people and the turmoil that had torn our country apart. A great number of people controlled by conflicting religions had been killed simply because neither side agreed with the other's view of God, his prophets, and eternity. "I have my beliefs, and for me, they are sacred. What I believe requires no man dictating my faith."

"I can understand how war can make one bitter—"

"It is not bitterness I follow."

"If you're not a believer in the cross and its power, you're a fool to fight against these vile undead creatures of the night," he said sternly.

"Not if they believe." I smiled.

"What do you mean?" His eyes narrowed.

"Their fear in the sacred cross eradicates them, sending them to whatever Hell they believe exists."

"You don't believe in a Hell?"

"Life is Hell. Perhaps after I endure the torment I face in this life, I can be blessed with the everlasting peace in whatever afterlife there might be. And if there isn't one? It's peace all the same. Right?"

Albert regarded that for a few moments. He smiled. "I never thought of it in *quite* that manner, but your point is a valid one. Deceptions are everywhere, even in places you least expect, like the cathedrals."

"So, what about this vampire?" I asked. "Where did he go after you confronted him?"

"He fled west."

"May we have permission to search the tunnels?"

Albert acquiesced a nod. "Of course. And should we discover any pertinent clues, one of my boys will contact you on the surface."

I wondered if these five lads were his actual offspring or whether he had turned them after adopting them. They could have been orphans that had wandered the streets before they found him. I didn't pry because it wasn't a relevant point. At least they had acceptance and considered one another as family, which was the greatest asset one could have when one was dirt poor and questioned daily whether they'd have enough food to sustain them another day.

"Boys," Albert said. "Escort them to the tunnel where we saw last night's intruder."

They nodded and eagerly led the way up the stairs to the tunnel where the rat infestation had cornered us. When we crossed the threshold, the rats were gone. I marveled at how such a substantial number of rodents could become essentially nonexistent in less than a few minutes.

CHAPTER 7

*J*acques and I spent the better part of the day exploring the tunnels without finding any evidence of the vampire. Not that we expected to find clues that led us directly to him. He was more intelligent than that. But we learned more about the tunnels and how to navigate should we need to pursue him underground.

"We should head to the surface and find your father," Jacques said.

I closed my eyes and winced. In his struggle to remain sober, I had foolishly abandoned him when he needed me the most. Fearing the worst, I hurried to find a ladder that led to the street above. With the number of people wandering the streets, the great many pubs, and other shops, finding Father wasn't likely. At least not quickly.

On the corner of the street, I rose on tiptoes, trying to look over the mass of people and hoping to capture a glimpse of him, which I didn't. Frantic, I pushed my way through the crowd, peering in storefronts, pub doors, and at each face in the crowd.

"Calm down, Forrest. What's your hurry?"

"He swore he'd never drink again. But, in our absence I worry that the temptation to resist might have been more than he could withstand."

"He's a grown man. He can take care of himself. Such decisions are his. Not yours."

I shrugged. "Perhaps, but some temptations are difficult for a person to solitarily confront and resist."

"So is the struggle of mankind. If he fails in his resistance, he can try again."

"He shouldn't need to try again. He's been lost to me ever since Momma died. I can't risk losing him to drunkenness now."

"I understand your concern, Forrest." He clasped my shoulder. "But there are too many places to look, and we were under the streets for several hours."

I nodded. "I know. That's why I'm concerned. We left him alone for too long. His mind tends to ramble back to the painful memories he cannot cope with."

The scent of charred hickory wood drifted with the slight breeze. With the smoky scent was that of something being cooked. Steam and smoke rose near the center of the next street. We came closer. Above a large smoldering log was a heavy black, cast-iron pot. A man with a long wooden oar stirred the bubbling contents. Poor folks stood in several lines with bowls, waiting to be served.

"Forrest!"

I looked to the right of the boiling pot. Father stood with a broad grin and lifted his bowl upward. I nodded toward him and smiled.

"Come see," he said. "See who I found."

Ignoring the food line, Jacques and I walked to where he stood. The woman beside him turned.

Matilda.

"You remember Matilda?" he asked with no hint of alcohol on his breath.

"Of course," I replied.

Jacques glanced toward her, tipping his top hat, and when their eyes met, he froze.

They eyed one another and simultaneously said, "You!"

She broke her gaze from Jacques and glared toward me. "When I said that I detected the scent of a werewolf on you last night, I never knew it belonged to this dog."

Jacques' eyes became fierce, wolf-like. His jaw tightened. "Dog? Have you been away so long as not to recognize me?"

"I recognized you now, which is *why* I called you a dog, though you're unworthy of such status. You deserve far worse!"

"Why you little wi—"

I grabbed his shoulder and turned him. With a harsh glare worthy only of an enemy, I admonished my cousin with a stern whisper. "Don't say it! Not here in public, or she's dead. They'll kill her."

"The world wouldn't grieve if such a blessing occurred," Jacques said, gritting his teeth.

"How dare you!" she snarled and lunged toward him.

I stepped between them, still frowning at him. "You don't mean that. Tell me what's the tension between you two?"

"It's a long story," Jacques replied, "And not one we can discuss in public."

"Agreed," Matilda said, seething.

Father looked at both of them and laughed. "Looks like a lover's spat."

Both Jacques and Matilda turned their anger toward him.

"It would appear that you called it correctly, Father. Come on, you two. We need to find a place that's not out in the open so you can sort this out."

"There's nothing to sort out," Jacques said.

"Apparently there is," I replied. "Your anger toward one another is too passionate for your hostilities to not be something more personal and deeper."

"This isn't an issue that concerns you, Forrest, especially since you have no experience in such matters."

"It does if we plan to stop the murderer."

"Our situation has nothing to do with that," he replied.

"Anything that deviates us from our focused goal places me and my father's safety into jeopardy. Distractions can be deadly. That's advice you and Dominus both have given me. Remember? So let's find a place to stay for the night. I'm tired of lugging this heavy box around. Besides, it seems to draw people's attention to me, and right now, that's an extra aggravation we don't need."

The soured angry expression didn't fade from his face, but he followed me without so much as giving Matilda the slightest side-glance or acknowledgment.

Father suggested that we find a place to lodge near the dining house where we had eaten earlier in the day. I agreed. The rates would be higher, but our accommodations would be worth the extra money. The downside was having a longer distance to travel through the dark streets.

After we found a decent room, we all entered.

Matilda seated herself at a small window that overlooked the street. She folded her hands on her lap. Her fierce anger had subsided. Sadness tugged at the edge of her eyes, and she refused to look in our direction.

Jacques placed his top hat on the small desk, crossed his arms, and stared toward a corner. I half expected wallpaper to peel from the walls. The tension between them was thick. Chill bumps rose on my arms as their emotions flared at one another without any spoken words. I had never felt the battle of intense energy lashing between two individuals before. Sure, energy had been flung toward me many times, but I had never been caught in the center of a conduit like this, between two people that had once been lovers and were now enemies.

Father sat on the edge of a bed and sighed. He and Momma had been at odds several times. I supposed all couples eventually came to crossroads of indifference, at which time they had a decision to make. Either mend the division and continue down the same path in life, or part ways, which sometimes weighted each with regret and resentment.

The look on Father's face detailed memories of such times he and Momma had struggled similarly, and from the hurt in his eyes, I sensed that he missed it.

"Well?" I asked, gazing at the back of Jacques' head. "You two going to come to terms or what?"

He didn't reply, nor did he turn to face me. He simply shook his head. His insistence to come to London had been for different reasons.

At least, that was what he had *told* Father and I. But now, I wondered if he had secretly hoped to happen across Matilda to correct past wrongs.

Still eight years of age, I acted the diplomat. "Look, it's obvious to me and Father that the two of you have a past with each other. What happened to cause this rift between you?"

Jacques released a long sigh. A moment later, he slid his hands into his jacket pockets. "It's because of what we are."

"You're a werewolf and she's a witch. What more am I missing?"

"I'm a werewolf, too," Matilda said. Tears trailed down her face.

"Shouldn't that be a good thing?" I asked. "Kindred spirits?"

"I wasn't one until *after* I met him," she replied.

"I see. What happened Jacques? Did you not tell her beforehand?" I asked.

"She knew," Jacques said softly. "And I was aware that she's a witch. That's what brought us together in the first place. She promised that she could remove my curse, but instead, she became cursed."

"Because you bit me!"

Jacques jaw tightened. "I insisted that you chain me while you performed the incantation. You refused. I changed before you were able to finish the spell, and you didn't plan an escape route ahead of time. I didn't have control over my beast then and charged after you."

"So you weren't lovers?" Father asked.

"Not after that night," Matilda said with anger in her voice.

Jacques sighed, looked into her angered eyes, and softened to his remorse. "It wasn't entirely my fault, but I do regret that you became what I am. I'd never wish this curse upon anyone."

She turned. Her brow furrowed. "I regret that we parted ways. The first few months were difficult . . . adjustments."

"I offered to stay. To help you during the transformations. But you insisted that I leave."

Matilda approached and stood toe-to-toe with him. "Do you still wear it?"

Jacques took the chain around his neck and tugged it upward, revealing his silver-colored medallion. "I do."

She revealed hers.

"You both have one?" I asked.

Jacques nodded. "She made them."

I glanced at Father. "I thought an alchemist made it for him?"

"That's what Jacques had told me."

Jacques grinned. "It's a less complicated tale."

I gave him a curious stare. "I suppose it is. Matilda, how is it that you could craft a medallion to restrain your beasts but you failed to remove the curse before he attacked you?"

"The spell given to me was inaccurate. It didn't work, but we risked the ritual because there isn't a known spell to purge the beast that rages inside. It is exactly as described: a curse."

"Nothing can eliminate it?" I asked.

Tears welled in her eyes. "No. Believe me, if there was, I'd have used it on myself before now. My failure to drive his beast out caused him to hold bitterness toward me ever since. That's more painful to me than my early transformations into wolf form."

I glanced toward Jacques with harsh disappointment in my gaze. I didn't have to voice my opinion. He read it in my gestures.

"I didn't leave you due to bitterness," he said. "I left because of my guilt for biting you. For cursing you when you had tried to heal me."

"I've missed you. Our talks," she said, reaching a hand toward his.

Jacques smiled, took her hand, and gently pulled her closer, kissing her forehead. A tear spilled and ran down her cheek. He wiped it away with his thumb.

"I thought when you left that you were gone forever," Matilda said.

"I'm here now. I've thought about you, us, for many years. And after Forrest's—" He choked back tears. "After a dear friend died, I knew I needed to make things right between us while we were both alive. I gambled by coming back to London since the banishment had come into law, but I didn't think I'd find you. I'm surprised you're remained in this city."

"It hasn't been easy staying," she replied. "I have few friends, simply because of what I am. In the eyes of the law, I'm twice cursed being a witch and a werewolf."

"When I leave," Jacques said, embracing her. "You shall come with me. We'll find a safer place to reside."

She pressed the side of her face against his chest. The radiant smile on her face increased her beauty, erasing the drab appearance she had displayed in the pub. "I'd like that very much."

I waited until what I thought was the proper moment. "Now, should we return to the streets to see if we can find this vampire?"

Father stood and winked at me. "Son, I think it's best that we give them some . . . time alone. They need to catch up. One day, you'll understand."

I set my box onto the desk, opened it, and grabbed a bottle of holy water, a cross, and a vial of crushed garlic. Keeping these in my coat was much easier than toting the heavy box. I walked to the door with Father and turned to regard them.

Matilda took Jacques hand and faced me. "We'll meet you at the pub where you first saw me."

I nodded. "Very well."

Jacques smiled. "We can plot our route for the night then."

Father walked through the door. I followed and pulled it closed.

"Come on, boy. No loitering around the door. I don't care how big you are. You're still a child to me. Let's go."

I chuckled, but held my peace and followed. I was young, yes, but due to my evolving mind, I had a slight idea what type of catching up they needed to do.

Love was indeed strange and complicated.

CHAPTER 8

*N*ightfall came.

Our patrols along the streets proved fruitless. We found no evidence of the murderous stalker hiding in the shadows. The worst part was not seeing the hidden women on the streets, but being aware of their presence in the darkness. They hid in the shadows, awaiting the arrival of shipmen and half drunken men in hopes of obtaining money for favorable pleasures. Occasionally, one called out to me in my passing, but at Father's prior stern warning, he insisted I not engage in conversation with any of them.

Perhaps they had not read the daily post and realized the brutal murder from the night before? Perhaps they knew and didn't care. Some people were willing to face death in times of desperation, hoping to gain enough money to satiate their thirst for alcohol or somewhere to stay the night off the street.

Unlike the night before, the thick layers of dense fog that had concealed the evil reaper were absent. The air was cold for a summer's night, which might have been enough deterrent for most people to stay indoors. I imagined a lot of folks were more worried about encountering the murderer than anything else and were too reluctant to stay inside the pubs late into the night. Regardless of their reasons, we encountered few people and returned to our room a few hours before sunrise.

Jacques and Matilda seemed inseparable. In the short amount of time I'd known my cousin, I'd never seen him maintain a broad smile. His eyes were brighter, and he was jovial and at ease. He laughed heartily when she told him about the bizarre things that had occurred in London soon after he had left. Things, which to Father and I, weren't humorous at all. She, in turn, did the same whenever he spoke. I glanced toward my father and all he offered was an odd grin. So, I supposed acting slightly ridiculous was part of love. Needless to say, I found a corner in the room and wrapped a blanket over myself and slept until midmorning. Father finally aroused me.

"Let's go get coffee," he said, eagerly with a broad smile. His eyes weren't bloodshot like the days before. They were bright, full of life and vigor.

I rubbed my eyes, shook my head, and sat up on the hardwood floor. My back was slightly sore, but I returned his smile because I realized he had gone a full day without drinking. Looking around, Jacques and Matilda were already gone.

After putting on my heavy boots, I grabbed my hat and overcoat. The question in my gaze seemed obvious.

"Those two lovebirds have already departed. Said for us to meet them for coffee," Father said.

I remained silent as we left the room and locked the door. For some odd reason I found myself thinking about Rose and ached inside. As hard as I might try, I couldn't deny that what I felt inside for her was love. But I feared what came with such commitment. The dangers I placed her life in. Our future, if any, and if we had children, the worry I'd forever have in keeping them safe from the vampires. After all, as a Chosen Hunter, called by some bearer of Holy Light, I had the ability to find the dark undead demons of the night, the vampires. They in turn could sense my presence and if they chose, they could come after me. Or worse, they'd target those I loved the most. What better way to inflict torment on a Hunter?

I grieved inside. That's why I cannot give myself to you, Rose. As much as I long to, I cannot.

Father glanced at me with a furrowed brow. "What is it, son?"

I shook my head. "Nothing."

"Rose?"

I swallowed hard. "How'd you know?"

He grinned. "One cannot hide the feeling of true love."

"At this point, Father, I cannot say that it's true love."

"It's been months, and she's not faded from your heart and mind. No other terms define that kind of binding power."

"Perhaps," I said. "But I cannot risk that kind of pain."

"Love hurts. I know. I've lived with it, and I grieve now due to its absence. But Forrest, there's no greater power on this Earth. No better feeling inside than being near the person who holds your heart."

For some odd reason, I pictured Rose dying at the hands of a vampire. Her heart being ripped from her chest. I cringed. "While that may be, the risk it imposes isn't for me, but her for what I am and because of those I have been called to kill."

"Your calling doesn't mean you have to spend your life alone."

I sighed and headed down the stairs to the lobby. "I'm not alone. I have you."

He chuckled. "It's not the same thing, and it probably won't be long before you tire of wandering the mountains and cities hunting for the undead with your old man. In fact, you'll grow to despise it."

"Today with you is already much better than the days before. How are you feeling?"

"Much better, but I still have that demon to wrestle. Probably on a nightly basis."

"I'll help you," I replied.

"I appreciate that. But son, you're not changing the subject so easily. You could live a thousand years killing vampires, but if you've not opened your heart to the love of a good woman, your whole life would have been in vain. And children. The love for a child. It's different than for a spouse, but genuine and pure. Seeing them discover the things of nature with excitement in their eyes and broad smiles. You'll—"

"Age wise I am still a child, Father. I'm not ready for such responsibilities. I'm barely sorting through what being a Hunter is all about."

"I realize all of those things. I'm not asking you to plan for all this within the next few years. All I'm suggesting is that you don't shut out the dearest things life has to offer."

I nodded. "I promise that I'll keep this in mind. I do anyway."

"From the contorted expressions on your face, I'd say that you're attempting to sear the thoughts away, more than consider them."

"I'll admit that I'm torn. But, I'm still young. In time, if the time's ever right, I'll make those decisions, but never before I'm comfortable in what I'm doing as a Hunter and know beyond any doubt that I'm able to protect my family from the undead."

Father clasped my shoulder and squeezed.

The dining room was empty. "Where are they?"

"Jacques wanted us to meet them where we eat yesterday. He's hoping that Constable Shields will be there."

"Why?"

"To get to the heart of the murder, if we can."

"You think the constable will offer information so readily?"

Father shrugged. "How can we know unless we ask?"

"I suppose that's true."

At the receptionist's desk, I paid for another night so we didn't need to deal with it later in the day. Near the sign-in pad was the morning's post. The headlines didn't report another murder overnight. At least none had been discovered. I was partly relieved and partially stressed, wondering where this killer had gone. The biggest reason for my underlying fear was that an active vampire needed to feed. Nightly. Had he become more secretive? Polly's murder had been bold and out in the open, as though he made certain her body was found. Perhaps it could have been sheer carelessness on his part, or his hunger was too great for him to contain, but I wondered if it were more?

Of course, all of this was speculation on my part, as I was still a novice, but since the ports of London brought in shipments from its worldwide colonies, it stood possible that this vampire had arrived aboard a ship. Polly might have been his first victim upon his arrival.

But someone else must have died overnight, and if so, where had he hidden the body?

Father and I arrived at the dining house. We hung our hats and coats near the door and a waiter seated us with Jacques and Matilda. Before we had joined them, I studied them momentarily. They were enthralled with one another, encapsulated in each other's gaze. They completely ignored their food. A part of me hated to intrude, but we did have a greater issue at hand.

A waiter came for our orders and departed with perfect, proper posture.

"How's the food?" I teased.

They stared down at their untouched plates and both blushed.

"I take it not as good as the conversation?" I smiled broadly.

"One day you'll understand," Jacques said evenly.

"I keep hearing that response. I'll await the actual enlightenment."

The waiter brought my father and I cups of coffee on small saucers, setting them before us. I causally sipped mine and playfully allowed my eyes to glance back and forth between them, much to their annoyance and like the eight-year-old inside insisted for me to do.

Jacques leaned toward me and harshly whispered. "Forrest, how any higher power would usher a child into the Chosen few is beyond me, but now is not the time to act like the youth you are."

I frowned. "Oh?"

The door opened, ringing the bell attached it. I turned to see Constable Shields entering. I nodded. "My apologies, cousin. It's just that I've never seen a grown man blush before."

"Believe me, you'll have plenty of blushing moments yourself," he replied.

I shook a cloth napkin open and placed it on my lap. "I have no doubts."

Jacques raised his hand, getting Shields' attention, and motioned him to join us. Shields gave a broad smile and nodded. Seconds later, he stood at our table.

CHAPTER 9

*C*onstable Shields was hospitable and gracious. He nodded toward Matilda, "Milady."

She smiled.

Then Shields acknowledge each of us with a slight nod. Regardless of Shields' kind smile, his eyes always held a modest glint of suspicion toward Jacques. "Gentlemen."

We nodded in return before he pulled out his chair and seated himself. A waiter brought a small tea kettle and teacup for Shields. He graciously smiled and poured hot tea into his cup.

"Did you find anything useful last night?" he asked, pressing his glasses against the bridge of his nose.

Jacques shook his head. "All was quiet."

"We discovered the same. Of course we posted more officers, which might have kept him at bay. But we might simply be dealing with a one-time murderer, and if so, it doesn't make any sense."

"Why not?" I asked.

He volunteered information somewhat eagerly. "We really don't have anything conclusive about Polly's death. There wasn't any obvious motive."

Jacques and I exchanged glances. Although Shields was offering additional information, he didn't understand *why* she was dead. For us, her death wasn't a mystery since we understood the reason behind her death.

Of course, explaining that a vampire was actually responsible for her murder was a quick way to be fitted for a straitjacket in an asylum, and in many ways, that outcome was far worse than a prison sentence.

"Does there need to be a motive?" I asked.

"No. But you, for whatever reason, seemed to believe this person would kill again. Without a clear motive, it does make your theory more plausible. If intentional, it narrows down the reasoning, but no one had any true purpose, so it's a random murder. Based upon one reporter's notion some of the other detectives want to link her death to two previous murders. Two detectives wish to purport the murders to a gang."

"Why a gang?" Jacques asked.

Shields shrugged and blew steam off his tea. "All speculation right now."

"So what can you tell us about Polly?" I asked.

Shields sighed, sipped his tea, and stared at the tablecloth while he spoke. "She didn't have money, was barely scraping by, and had worked in various workhouses over the years. But she had a problem with overindulging in the spirits, losing a few jobs because of her drinking habits. Lately, she had been seen working as a prostitute. Her roommate even told us she had seen her about an hour before Polly's body had been discovered. She said that Polly absolutely *reeked* of alcohol. Apparently she had made enough money on the streets to pay for her bed in their lodging house three times over, but instead of heading to the house, she chose to buy several drinks. I suppose she was trying to get more money for boarding after her roommate walked away. It's difficult for most to pry themselves free of alcohol's hold."

"It is," Father said softly.

"She was a prostitute?" Jacques said, looking at Shields. "Isn't that against the law?"

The constable nodded and held a glum expression on his face. "It is, but due to a humiliating court case last year dealing with a woman of prominence that was accused of soliciting, we were ordered to . . . look the other way unless a direct complaint had been filed. So, even though we know it's going on, we have our orders to ignore it. Might as well, I suppose."

"Why's that?" Jacques asked.

"Lack of jobs. Women have children to feed. They need places to sleep at night. Of course, us ignoring it might have caused problems of its own."

"How's that?" I asked.

"Such a profession is frowned upon by the Church. Some parishioners might actually view murder as a lesser evil," Shields replied.

"Seriously?"

He nodded.

Some religious people actually thought killing an unwanted element in society was justifiable. Unbelievable. My anger got the best of me. "Aren't they playing God?"

"I didn't say people have done that."

"Yet."

Shields' brow rose, he cocked his head to the side, and then nodded. "Should it happen and the person is arrested, he will be put to death for the murder. But with so many women on the streets soliciting, it's only a matter of time before someone takes it upon himself to make an example out of one of them. In no way is it justifiable."

I sipped my coffee and set the cup down. "Mind if I ask you a question?"

Shields shrugged.

"Have you had any ship captains report murders of crew members after they reached port?"

He frowned. "None have been reported to me. Why?"

"I've been wondering if the man who killed Polly might have recently arrived by ship."

"And if he did, you seem to believe that he has killed others. Is there something you're not telling me?" Shields asked.

"It's just a feeling that I have," I replied.

"Me, too," Jacques said.

Shields sat in silence for several moments. "The ports are outside of my jurisdiction, but I will send a messenger to that precinct and see what information I can retrieve."

"From what you said earlier. How might this be tied to gangs?"

"The East End of London has numerous problems, Forrest. With the influx of emigrants there's been local groups that have organized to fight against nationalities they loathe. In return, those new to the area have formed their own factions to defend themselves. So they've formed little gangs to protect territories, but after the population inflates too much, one has no choice but to infringe upon the other, which leads to hostile scuffles. Usually, a few get battered pretty badly, but sometimes these fights have led to murder of a rival person or group. And other times, an innocent bystander happens to be in the wrong place and gets killed."

"I see."

Shields wiped his mouth with his napkin, folded the cloth, and placed it on the table. "So I need to warn you. In your scouting the streets in the night, if you happen upon groups of people that appear to be guarding an alley or building, don't approach them. They will take your advancement as a threat and will react in kind."

He stood.

"We'll be careful," I said.

"If I discover anything from the ships, I will inform you. I hope you'll share any information you discover with me."

Jacques stood. "We will. Thanks for sharing the table. Your tab is on us today."

"Thank you," he said. He placed his hat on his head and walked to the door.

"By all means, gentlemen, be vigilant."

After Shields left, the waiter brought me a plate of scrambled eggs saturated with garlic, as I had requested. The strong smell of garlic lofted above my plate.

Jacques waved his hand back and forth, wincing. "How can you stand to eat those?"

"A lot easier than the vampire who approaches me tonight."

He coughed. "I suppose a whiff of garlic that strong would be a deterrent to any vampire."

"Or any woman who sought to kiss him," Matilda said, covering her nose.

I grinned. "So I'm safe on all accounts?"

"Maybe," Jacques said. "But I don't plan to walk downwind of you. Or beside you, for that matter."

Shrugging, I grabbed the pepper and sprinkled a heavy layer atop the eggs. "I know nothing was reported in the paper, but I can't help but wonder where the vampire fed last night."

"You think he did?" Jacques asked.

"Don't you? That's why I asked the constable about the ships. You're the only one of us who ever got close to him. What's your perception? How strong do you think he is? How active?"

Jacques thought for several long seconds. His eyes shifted as memories jostled inside his mind. "As fast as he moved, he wasn't a vampire that had been dormant for a long period of time."

"That's my feeling, too," I said.

Father sipped his coffee and read the post. If he were listening to us, it wasn't obvious by his facial expressions.

"Of course, he had just fed," Jacques said.

"Did you ever touch his flesh?"

Jacques shook his head. "Only his clothes."

"He fed somewhere. Albert never really indicated the vitality of this vampire except that he seemed to fear the were-rats. Do you really think Albert and his sons could defeat a vampire and destroy him?"

Jacques shrugged. "It's possible. Depends on what weapons he has."

"Like a cross or stake?"

"Those are the most beneficial weapons, but not necessary. You saw the rat masses. They could tear a vampire to shreds. Vampires heal quickly, but it's unlikely he could mend faster than they could rip away his flesh. And if Albert has a cross or holy water or anything that can weaken a vampire, he could prevent the vampire from fleeing. Those rats could overpower him long enough for one of the were-rats to stake or decapitate him."

"That's interesting," I replied. "Can I ask you something?"

"Sure."

"Why is it that when you were controlled by Dracula's grandson that you and the rest of the pack didn't overpower and kill him?"

The question made Jacques visibly uncomfortable. His eyes moistened. A flood of various emotions rushed through him.

I placed my hand on his forearm. "I'm sorry. I didn't mean to upset—"

I caught my father's intense glare. His hand tightened into a fist.

Jacques waved a hand toward my father. "It's okay. I'm fine. It's a fair question. Who knows what Forrest might face in the years to come?"

"While that may be true," Father said, "he needs to be more sensitive in regard to how he phrases things."

"My apologies, Jacques," I said.

Jacques sighed. "Forrest, even if the entire pack had wanted to attack our … Master, he is a direct descendent of Count Dracula with the purest of bloodlines. His power is unmatched. These masters you've killed, like the baron, they pale in comparison. I can never return to his castle. Ever."

My eyes met his. Fear hollowed them. "He'll kill you?"

Jacques shook his head slowly. "He'll enslave me. I will never know my human form again. He'd see to it."

Chill bumps rose on my arms and rushed down my back. I had never realized the depth of his captor's power. I supposed there was a reason why some of Dracula's grandchildren were still alive. Well, walking undead.

"Forrest," Jacques said softly. "You've fought some tough battles, but nothing like him. His lineage is vast. One day you will, whether intentionally or not, encounter Dracula's children or grandchildren. When you do, my advice is to flee, especially at this early stage in your life. In fifty years, provided you've survived that long, you might actually have the knowledge and strength capable to combat them. But for now, the four of us at this table have no hope to defeat one of Dracula's direct descendants."

Matilda placed her hand upon his. "He still holds power over you?"

Jacques nodded.

"My dear," she whispered. Her gaze held pity and grave concern.

"I'm fine, provided I never return to his domain or he happens upon me. But unlike his grandfather, he's not one for traveling."

"Again, cousin—"

"No, Forrest, it's vital information that I should already have told you. It's difficult for me to discuss because it proves my own vulnerability. It's the male ego. No man wishes to proclaim his weakest point. Now, let's finish our meals, scout the streets again, and get better prepared for tonight. I think we might have a good chance of encountering this vampire after the sun sets. Perhaps, if we're fortunate, Albert has news that he will share through one of his sons."

CHAPTER 10

Seeing the terror in Jacques' eyes when he had mentioned the power Dracula's grandson still held over him unnerved me. I had witnessed my cousin's power when we had fought a few strong vampires. His lack of fear and the incredible strength he possessed whenever he allowed his inner beast to take full control had almost led me to believe he was invincible. And yet, at the mention of Dracula's name, his composure imploded. He dreaded becoming enslaved by that vampire again. He still called him his Master out of fear and respect, which also troubled me.

In Romania, the whisper of Dracula's name struck terror into the hearts of most people, ordinary people, and that was easy to understand. Mere humans weren't a match against the mind control a vampire like Dracula and his offspring possessed.

Fierce compulsion like Jacques described I had never seen or experienced. I hoped that I never encountered it. Dominus had warned me that the worst thing for the Hunter population was for one of us to become undead or controlled by a master vampire. Baron Randolph had attempted to charm me, to lure me, but he had failed. The baron had been powerful, which made it nearly impossible for me to comprehend the level of Dracula's strength.

I knew the history of Dracula the Impaler, his armies, and his thirst to torture and drain people's blood. He had been a ruthless ruler. He had killed thousands and controlled thousands more. The rumors were that he was a spawn released from the pits of Hell. His charisma was beyond hypnotic, but these powers had passed down through the generations. I had yet to encounter his kind. Destiny ensured that eventually I would.

Once darkness shrouded the lightless streets, PCs blew their whistles and cleared the walkways insisting that everyone find a safe place to retreat for the night. They, like us, expected horrible things to occur during the night. Even though Constable Shields had granted us permission to aid in the investigation, his approval had not been made official to the other constables and detectives.

We were subjected to arrest should we disregard the curfew orders to head indoors. So while the PCs enacted this night's curfew, Jacques, my father, Matilda, and myself, hid in the corners of the dark alleyways until most of the constables made their early rounds.

My father and I were at a great disadvantage in the pitch-black streets. Neither of us was blessed with night vision like Matilda and Jacques. She stayed close to my father to be his eyes of warning. Jacques stood beside me, even though I insisted they both protect my father.

Jacques still treated me like a child in need of safeguard, and I understood why. But I detested it as any youth might because I had proven myself in the heat of battle. I had killed vampires and a dozen or more ghouls by myself.

After the whistles faded farther down the streets as the constables did their final sweep to send everyone home or to housing lodges, red eyes peered from the alleyways. My hand wrapped tightly around a stake and I stood in a defensive pose.

"It's the were-rat youths," Jacques whispered.

I released my breath, not realizing I was holding it in. Complete darkness had a strange way of making bravery quake since it was where the monsters played. The number of hiding places increased whenever light vacated.

It was good to know we had more allies, even though they were children. We had not encountered any of the rat boys during the daylight, like we had hoped. Albert had promised to send them with information if they discovered anything useful. Seeing them appear possibly indicated they sensed a sinister force.

No fog shrouded us, but it wouldn't have made the night any darker.

Farther down the cobblestone street footsteps echoed. Dark energy pricked the back of my head. The hairs on my neck stiffened. He was there, headed in our direction. His power undulated like tiny expanding ripples on a lake reached for the shore. The way his power unfolded was similar to the baron's and other vampires I had faced. This wasn't a mortal. I held no doubt that he was a vampire.

"He's here," I whispered.

"I know," Jacques replied.

I withdrew a stake in each hand from my side coat pockets.

"Don't be hasty," Jacques said. "That's how he got an advantage over me the other night."

I nodded.

The were-rats eyes lowered. I supposed they had crouched down, preparing themselves. Father and Matilda were across the street but not visible to me.

With the approaching footsteps reverberated a slight tapping sound. A cane?

Perhaps. Or he might carry some other type of weapon.

"Can you see him?" I asked.

"Yes. He's still about a block away. He might be out to feed, but he's determined to confront us. He wants a challenge."

"What makes you believe that?"

"He's not slowing his pace, and the pompous bastard is staring right at us. The eagerness in his eyes suggests he craves violence and bloodshed. Tonight, I wipe that smirk off his face." The boldness in Jacques' voice resounded with heavy bitterness. He wasn't proud of how their first meeting had ended. He intended to inflict damage and drain blood before we killed this vampire.

"Can you describe him?"

"He's over six foot tall. Like I said to the constable, he's dressed eloquently."

Most master vampires did. They held the power to impress and influence those they encountered. The first thing most people recognized when approached by a stranger was how the person was dressed. Folks judged others by what's on the exterior. Wealth and prominence has often granted unwarranted notoriety in many circles. Add to that a vampire's glamour and the victims were nothing less than puppets controlled by mental strings—tiny threads relaying impulse and desire and obedience.

Jacques continued, "He carries a cane, wears a top hat and cape, and though he might not be from London, he is venerated elsewhere."

"You can tell that from his clothes?"

"No. He exhibits such in the way he walks and how he carries himself."

"This is the one you fought the other night."

"The same."

"Let's kill him," I said sternly.

I took a step forward, and Jacques placed a firm hand against my chest.

"Wait."

"Why?"

"His interest is directed at you. He wants you to attack first."

"So?"

Jacques whispered at such a low tone it was difficult for me to hear standing beside him. "Must I spell it out for you? He senses you're a Hunter. I'm not certain if he's able to discern how old you are, but if he knows you're a novice, he will rip your throat out, ending you first."

My jaw tightened.

"Don't get angered by the truth," Jacques said. "The darkness *is* his domain. He has the advantage over you. Now, Matilda and I on the other hand are one with the night like he is."

The chain around Jacques neck snapped. He shoved the medallion into his pocket. After that, he rushed ahead into the darkness. A ball of light appeared on the other side of the street. Matilda held the light in her hands and flung it toward the vampire. The light followed Jacques and grew even brighter the closer it came to the vampire.

The vampire shrieked, lifting his cape to shield his face from the blinding light. Jacques struck the vampire dead center with both fists and flung the vampire backwards.

The radiant ball of light domed over the vampire, preventing him from uncovering his face. A second later, Jacques reared back his head and howled.

He was transforming, snarling and gnashing his teeth. Almost on cue, Matilda began changing into her wolf form, too. The vampire hissed and growled beneath his black cape. His body writhed.

The were-rats crept along the edge of the wall, wary of approaching him from the center of the street.

The bright orb lit up the street almost a block in both directions. Its intense glare equated a direct glance into the sun, and for a few moments it seemed like it held this vampire captive. I wondered if this light burned a vampire's flesh in the same way sunlight did.

While Matilda and Jacques underwent their transformation, something moved outside the light's radius. It grew and expanded. Rolling fog swirled out of nothing, building again into a wall like the night before last. Glancing the other direction, I noticed another wall rising behind us.

The vampire flung open his cape, shattering the orb of light. He was on his feet in an instant, grabbed Jacques by the collar, and hurled him ten feet away.

The were-rats' growls rumbled as they ran through the sudden darkness toward the vampire. A sharp gasp of pain rose and died in an instant. The odd sound was a cross between human and rat. A slickening splatter on the cobblestone turned my stomach. At least one of the boys had been eviscerated.

Matilda produced another ball of light. The vampire was hunched over the were-rat's open chest. Blood dripped from his hands. His face was sinewy, strange, and revealed his true beastly nature. He was an animal, holding what could only be a heart. The other four were-rats backed away, lowered on all fours, seemingly debating another attack.

Jacques sprinted at him, bringing his cane overhead and slashing downward. He struck the vampire in the back. The vampire snarled in pain, rolled, and grabbed the silver cane. Due to the quick roll and Jacques holding the cane tightly, the vampire swung Jacques over him, slamming Jacques against the brick wall.

Father limped along the walkway with a stake in hand. Matilda held the ball of light. The vampire stared down at Jacques limp form with a victorious grin on his face. He turned toward the two were-rats nearest him. Lunging partway toward them, his hard-soled shoes clacked. The rat boys sprang back with timidity. The vampire bellowed a deep laugh.

The four boys stared at their torn bloody brother. His mouth was open in the shape of his last cry of terrified pain. His wide eyes revealed his unexpected death. His long serpentine tail twitched back and forth like a dying snake.

The vampire pulled a long sharp knife from the end of his cane. It looked like a butcher's knife. He turned toward Jacques again. Without thought or hesitation, I ran with both stakes in hand. He must have heard my approach, expected it, or he was baiting my attack because he was gone before I could plunge a stake into his back.

"Behind you, Forrest!" my father shouted.

At this point, getting a stake through the heart wasn't necessarily the easiest strike. He was faster than any vampire I had ever fought. With our numbers, we might have to inflict numerous wounds to weaken him because he was too fast to corner. Hunting vampires during the day was safer and easier, provided one knew where the vampire's lair was. With this vampire new to the area, I doubted he stayed at the same place each night. I had no proof but it was my best assumption. Since we didn't know, the only way we even had a chance to kill him was when he was prowling the streets searching for his next victim.

I turned. His long sharp blade sliced through the air, slashing into the arm of my thick overcoat. The cloth of my sleeve peeled away. A line of heated pain on my biceps dripped blood. Before he drew back the blade a second time, I hammered my thick fist into his mouth. Teeth cracked, as did bone in his nose.

He might be fast, but I was twice his size and succeeded in landing a powerful punch. He winced and the blow staggered him. In his attempt to prevent falling, he lowered the knife to his side.

Two of the were-rats lunged toward the vampire's legs. They sank their gnarled sharp teeth into his thighs. He growled like a mad animal, grabbed them both by the back of the neck, and yanked them into the air. Blood dripped from their mouths. The vampire's blood. He stared momentarily at them. Pure hatred loomed in his eyes. In a fluid like movement, he smashed their heads together, dropping them onto the street.

Matilda hurled the ball of light at him. He dodged to one side and my father plunged a stake into the vampire's shoulder. He backhanded Father with such force, my father was lifted into the air and crashed onto a stack of wooden crates tradesmen used during the day. The other two were-rats snarled. Their long claws lengthened.

The vampire reached for the stake driven into his shoulder, noticed my approach, and the two stakes in my hands. He turned slightly, to keep an eye on me while watching the other two were-rats stalking toward him.

Blood trickled from his mouth and nose. Huge bite marks on his thighs leaked blood as well. He tipped his hat toward me and grinned before darting into the congealing wall of fog.

I kept a stake in each hand, watching the fog wall, and waiting to see if he reemerged.

Matilda hurried to Jacques.

"Is he okay?" I asked.

She nodded. "He's breathing. His eyes are opening."

The two unconscious were-rats awakened and pulled themselves to all fours. The other two helped them up.

I backed my way toward Father without shifting my gaze from the fog. He groaned and reached for me. I grabbed his hand and hefted him to his feet.

Jacques pushed himself up and stood. Anger flared his nostrils and burned in his eyes. "He's gone?"

I nodded.

"Damn," he said, gritting his teeth. He took a step toward the fog. I pressed my hand against his hairy chest and Matilda wrapped her arms around his waist. They both stood in werewolf form.

Whistles blew and echoed from the other wall of fog. "You two best hide until you return to human form. The constables are on their way. I don't know how to explain all this."

Jacques panted through his mouth, glancing around. "What exactly?"

"The dead were-ra—" The four boys and their dead brother were gone. The pool of blood, however, remained.

"Perhaps we all should hide," Jacques suggested, grabbing his clothes while Matilda gathered hers.

The two walls of fog slowly moved toward one another. Soon they'd merge and swallow the entire street.

"Good idea," I said.

Matilda shone the ball of light toward the narrow alley. We found a metal door at the edge of the street, yanked it up, and descended underground. Once we pulled the door into place, Matilda extinguished the light.

CHAPTER 11

Using the underground passageways, we emerged near the inn where we were to lodge for the night. Inside our room, we inspected our injuries. None of us was seriously wounded. The cut across my biceps was superficial and had not bled much.

Jacques fumed with anger. No coaxing from Matilda lessened it. He sought immediate vengeance. Being bested twice by the same vampire wrought his fury and determination to find and kill it.

I worried about how Albert would take the death of his son. I was certain his anger outweighed Jacques. I wondered why Albert hadn't come to the surface to aid us in the battle. He had implied that this vampire feared him, but the vampire had ripped one of the boy's insides out of his body without hesitation or any fear of possible retaliation.

"We had him," Jacques said, slamming his palm on the top of the desk. His hands formed tight fists, and he glanced at me. "I warned you not to get sloppy, but I didn't even heed my own advice. Twice he's rendered me unconscious."

"We'll find him," I said.

"But there were nine of us, Forrest," Jacques said, gritting his teeth. "Nine! And he still slipped away."

"With some injuries," I added.

"What injuries?"

"Father stabbed a stake deep into its shoulder," I replied.

"I tried for the heart, son. He was too damn fast, and I'm no longer agile."

I nodded. "I know. I cracked some of his teeth and shattered his nose. Two of the rat boys tore hunks out of his thighs with their teeth."

"Phht," Jacques said, waving us off. "Superficial wounds at best. He'll heal and kill again."

"He's leery of us now."

"You really think so, Forrest? A couple of you managed to draw some blood and you believe he's worried about us?"

"I do. He fled. Two of the boys were coming up behind him. I had two stakes and was ready to attack. He read my intent. That's why he fled."

Jacques frowned and shook his head. "Is this a game to you?"

"It seems to be a game to him," I replied. "You said so before you attacked him."

Father frowned and stared at Jacques. "You told Forrest that?"

Jacques shrugged. "The vampire boasted great arrogance and wanted us to challenge him. He particularly wanted to fight Forrest."

I grinned. "And he ran away from me."

"Be careful," Jacques said. "That might be his ploy. To make you think he's afraid of you. You let down your guard, and he's going to kill you. Make no mistake about that. You saw what he did to me?"

I nodded.

"I've fought a lot of vampires but I've never dealt with one like this before. He's faster than I am. That's his greatest strength."

"He brought back the fog," I said.

"Vampires have some control over weather elements," Matilda said.

"I thought the glowing orb was a good spell."

She smiled at me. "Thank you. But he dissolved it, which means he's an older vampire and quite strong. A young vampire would have become too vulnerable to escape from the light. Regardless of his age, had my blinding light touched his flesh, he'd have experienced the same pain as being caught outside in the sunlight."

"Is he a master?" I asked Jacques.

"Possibly," he replied. "He might even be an ancient. But his lesser vampires are not with him."

"You're certain?"

He nodded. "If they were, he'd have them fighting for him."

"It makes no sense why he'd travel to London without them. Does it?" I asked, sitting on the edge of the bed.

"It's rare but not unheard of," Jacques replied.

"What might prompt a master to make such a decision?"

"War."

"War?"

Jacques nodded. "Most master vampires have their lairs hidden deep inside fortresses or castles. Should the place be destroyed, they scour the countries until they find a new residence. But, they also look for a place where no other masters reside since they are territorial. There's also the possibility that all his children have been killed, and he's been forced into hiding or government officials think he died with his offspring."

Someone knocked at the door. Hard. We exchanged concerned glances.

Father opened the door. Constable Shields stepped across the threshold and removed his hat and adjusted his glasses. He promptly closed the door with a solid thud. In his hand he held Jacques' silver cane. Jacques cursed under his breath and shook his head, angry with himself.

Shields narrowed his skeptical eyes, strode across the room, and handed the cane to Jacques. "Strange how this cane keeps turning up in the most unusual places. This was found at another crime scene tonight. If we can even call it a crime scene, being as all we've found so far are blood splotches and a pool of blood. We can gather more information after sunrise. I know the lot of you have offered your services in this investigation, but right now, Jacques, you're close to becoming my chief suspect! You mind telling me what happened there?"

Jacques sat on the edge of the bed beside me. "We encountered him again."

Shields' eyes flicked toward mine. I nodded. He noticed my sliced open shirtsleeve and the dried blood on my laceration. "He did that?"

"Yes, sir."

"You actually saw him this time in the dark?"

"We had a . . . lantern," I replied.

"Good. So you can describe this man?" Shields asked.

Jacques gave him a thorough description. Shields jotted it down on a pad of paper.

"Did you get a hint of his accent?" Shields asked. "So we can narrow down where he's from?"

"He never spoke," I replied.

"Not a word?"

We shook our heads. Shields stared at Matilda with surprise. "You were with them, dear lady?"

"I was," she replied.

Shields shook his head and opened his mouth to say something more to her but quickly refrained. He returned his attention to Jacques. "So if he never spoke, what makes you so certain he's the one we're after?"

"Look at my arm," I said. "He had a long sharp knife. One like a butcher uses. It sliced through my thick overcoat."

"He attacked all of you?"

"That's one way to describe it," Jacques said. "He was out for blood."

Shields nodded. "Yes. There's a large puddle of blood, but no body. Whose blood is it? His?"

"No," I replied.

"Other than a few abrasions on the lot of you, you're no worse for wear. I know that blood isn't any of yours. Now, fess up."

"To be honest, sir," I said, "we don't know whose blood it is."

"I see. Yes. Hmm. No body. Lots of blood. And how did he get away?"

"He ran into the fog," Matilda said. "That's how we lost him. Even a lantern is useless when the fog's that thick."

"Indeed. It was quite thick, wasn't it? Seemed to have come out of nowhere, from what the one detective told me. Are any of you in need of a doctor?"

We shook our heads.

"I suspected such, but I needed to ask anyway," Shields said. He glanced at Jacques. "It's best you keep better hold on that cane. I can't keep finding it for you."

Jacques gave a wry smile. "Thanks for returning it, again."

"The good news is that we now have a better description of the man we're looking for. The bad news is that he's still out there somewhere stalking his next victim. Since he blatantly attacked all of you, I tend to believe your theory is correct. He will kill again. So, should you keep searching for him, and I honestly don't suggest that you do, please be careful."

He reached for the doorknob and hesitated. Looking at Matilda, he said, "Miss, what ever persuaded you to take up with this gentlemen?"

She smiled. "Jacques and I are old friends."

Shields' brow rose. He glanced toward Jacques. "I see. I understand why you'd venture back to London. She's worth the trip."

Jacques nodded.

"Have you heard from the docks on whether any ship captains have reported lost crewmembers?" I asked.

He shook his head. "Nothing yet. After tonight, I want to know that information as well. I might take a train later today and find out first-hand. Be safe."

Shields put his hat on and opened the door. Without another word, he walked out and pulled the door closed. A few minutes after he had left, another knock, softer, rapped at the door.

I opened it. One of the rat boys stood before me in his human form. His eyes were red from tears. His lower lip trembled.

"What is it?" I asked.

"Albert has requested your presence. All of you. He said that it's urgent."

CHAPTER 12

With the constables and detectives combing the streets while trying to figure out the mysterious pool of blood, it took us several hours to travel through the labyrinth of underground tunnels to find the route that led to Lord Albert's throne room.

His room was lit with rows of fire pits. He was clearly visible sitting on his stone throne. His chin rested upon his fist. Anger stirred in his eyes. I expected to see the dead were-rat on the floor, but the young rat boy sat with his back at Albert's feet with his eyes closed. He appeared to be weak and meditating.

"How?" I whispered to Jacques.

"It's difficult to kill a were-creature."

That explained why the vampire didn't act concerned about gutting the boy. He knew the boy could heal. I couldn't imagine the pain the boy had undergone when his entrails were ripped from his body, but I wondered how painful his healing process had been, too. Surely, it was painful when nerve endings reconnected and the body began mending. I shuddered.

"Where did this vampire go?" Albert asked. His gruff voice echoed through the room.

"We don't know. He disappeared into the fog," I replied.

"We hunt for him. He dies for hurting one of my own."

"When I saw your children," I said, "I thought you would have emerged with them."

Albert stood. His narrow green eyes turned crimson with bright white pupils. "When you visited before I mentioned that I never expose myself on the surface. I cannot risk it."

"I remember."

"There's no end to where I shall go now to tear this vampire apart. He will suffer incredible pain before he turns to dust."

"We wish to help."

Albert smiled. "From what my children told me, it might take all of us and more. He's dangerous. What have you learned about him?"

"He's quick and has incredible strength," Jacques said.

"Name?"

He shook his head. "None of us know. Not even the constables."

"I see. A nameless vampire. My guess is he's foreign. Until he entered my tunnels, I had never felt his presence before."

"We need to find where he sleeps during the day," Jacques said.

Albert nodded. "Come morning, we'll scout our tunnels, after my confrontation with him the night before, it's doubtful he'd dare reside on this side of Whitechapel."

"But he favors hunting on the East End," I said.

"That doesn't mean he hides here. Vampires aren't known to do what's expected. You might have better results if you examine the areas near the docks."

"We were thinking the same," I replied. "Even the constable plans to inspect the port dockets and ask questions."

Albert smiled. "You'd have better success than he."

"Why's that?"

"Some ship captains deliver contraband and don't want officials nosing into their affairs. It really depends on what country the captain is native to, and more importantly, if this vampire came ashore by ship. He might have arrived by train or even horseback. That's the worst part about having an enemy you know absolutely nothing about."

"I agree," Jacques said.

"Keep alert," Albert said to Jacques. "You're like me and have the ability to sense the evil that saturates this undead beast, so you'll detect when he's close."

Jacques nodded, but I often received similar sensations whenever a vampire was nearby.

"What's the quickest underground route to the port?" I asked. "Before we begin hunting this vampire during the day, it's probably best to see if we can discover how he got to London."

Albert pointed at two of the rat boys and motioned them toward him.

"Follow Clyde and George. They can show you a platform where you can get aboard a train without paying a fare or being seen. It's how I get from one side of London to the other without anyone seeing what I am."

"We have money," Father said.

"I'm not implying that you don't. But I'm certain you don't want this vampire to see you take passage if he's aboard the same train, do you?"

Father shook his head.

Albert folded his long bony hands into a prayerful manner. "We must assume great ignorance in order to outmaneuver this vampire. Not only is he an incredible adversary, he has superb knowledge. The best way to deceive a haughty mind is to let him believe he holds all of the advantages."

That was the best advice I had heard in quite some time. I thought about the look in the vampire's eyes when he had tipped his hat and vanished into the fog. He was daring me to enter after him, and had I, most likely I'd be dead or severely injured. Like I had mentioned to Jacques, I believed this vampire was playing a game. Hunter versus Vampire, or as he probably accessed it: Vampire versus Prey.

Albert looked at me. "While you search the port, my boys and I will scour the tunnels, caves, and other recesses on this end of Whitechapel. Please return to me this evening and we'll exchange information."

I nodded.

Clyde and George walked past me and through the narrow door. The rest of us followed. The path we took was dark and cold. In the back of my mind, I thought about the similarities this environment had to that of our newfound soulless enemy's mentality. Death-dealers possessed no soul or conscious for a reason.

Murder was calculated. Often without a second thought. With vampires, part of their savagery came from their need to feed and increase their clan numbers, but this particular vampire had not acted like the others. He was more vicious, using a weapon to exhibit his brutality, to inflict pain. Most vampires used compulsion, fed, and disappeared without killing the victim.

The two rat boys led us to a dark platform at the edge of train rails. An old steam engine train waited. They led us to the rear of the train, crawled under the car, and pushed up a small square door. They pointed and insisted we climb inside and close the door.

We did.

The small room was filled with tools and barely large enough for us to fit inside. We were pressed together uncomfortably for over an hour before we arrived at the other platform across the city. I was thankful I had not taken my box. We'd never have all fit in the cramped space. After a lot of careful acrobatic maneuvering, we opened the door and lowered ourselves onto the track.

While it had been easy to board the train unseen, joining the exiting passengers at the platform to climb to the surface was more difficult. A man stood ready to check bags and ticket stubs. I was certain we'd be held until constables arrived, but Matilda cloaked us, allowing us to blend into the crowd and hurry to the cobblestone street.

Now, we all needed to do was get to the port.

CHAPTER 13

"We'll have better luck searching the pubs for the ship captains," Jacques said.

"Why?" I asked.

"If a ship has a short crew, the pubs are the best places to find new recruits. You've seen it when we were in Bucharest."

We walked along the wooden sidewalk, our boots thudding heavy hollow sounds on the boards. Several pubs bustled with crewmen lined outside the door. Most had not shaved or bathed in weeks. Some were hardened men with scarred faces and arms. They talked brash with one another, scuffling and shoving each other.

Father and Matilda decided to sit at a small table while Jacques and I walked along the dock. My father's legs had stiffened and caused him severe pain, probably from being confined in the small train car.

At the edge of a dock near a ship sat a man with a captain's hat. His face was pale; his eyes hopeless. He whittled a small piece of wood with his knife. Occasionally he glanced toward the pubs but didn't seem eager to fight through the crowds, even though he probably wanted a strong drink to erase his mind of his troubles. I had seen the expression on my father's face so many times that it was easy to read on other faces.

Jacques stopped in front of the man and watched the sharp knife peel long strips of wood from his sculpture and fall to the ground.

The man paused his carving and cocked a brow, glaring at Jacques. "Help you, mate?"

"Your ship?" Jacques asked, nodding toward the flagship tied to the dock.

"Aye." He rubbed his sparse beard. "For what good luck I've had."

"Are you hiring crew hands?"

He shook his head. His eyes were haunted. "No. I arrived three days ago, but I've not been looking to hire anyone yet. Thinking about selling the ship actually, especially after this last voyage."

"How long have you had it?"

"A few years."

"Why sell it?"

"I fear it might be cursed or haunted. Late in the night, footsteps can be heard coming into different sleeping quarters, but no one has ever seen anyone else. At least that's what some of my crew told me days before they died in their bunks."

"What happened?" I asked.

"Don't rightly know, lad. Lost half my crew before we were halfway into our trip."

Jacques and I both frowned.

"How?" Jacques asked.

"Disease. Plague, I suppose. But it was the oddest thing I'd ever seen."

"In what way?" Jacques asked.

"Big rat bite marks, on the necks of the ones that died while they slept. They were strange bites with only two puncture holes. But all of them looked the same. The dead men's skin was gray. Their flesh was cold like marble. That's what was strange. Rats randomly bite a person anywhere, but normally one won't die from a single bite. That's why I think it was the plague. But the plague doesn't normally kill that quickly."

"What did you do with the bodies?" I asked.

He shrugged. "Threw 'em overboard. It was too dangerous to keep them aboard. As fast as it passed to all the others."

85

"Other than this . . . disease, did any of your crew happen to disappear?" I asked.

He frowned while thinking. After a few moments, he shook his head and his eyes widened. He scratched at his beard. "Actually, yes. One. In all the chaos, I seemed to have forgotten about him. But he was never one of my crew. He was a wealthy chap and paid me handsomely to allow him to board. Odd that I had forgotten him. I never saw him get off the ship when we docked."

"Do you recall his name?" Jacques asked.

"No. I don't. It escapes me."

"Do you remember where he boarded?"

"Not offhand. My guess was along the Yangtze River. Why?"

"Perhaps he's still aboard your ship?" I said.

"Not in any of the sleeping cabins, he's not. I've checked."

"Below deck?"

"Doubtful," he replied.

I stared at the ship for several moments. "You mind if we searched?"

He rose to his feet and his hand tightened around his knife. Madness swirled in his eyes. "Actually, I do. My new cargo has yet to be loaded, and besides, what happened aboard my ship is none of your concern. The diseased dead bodies were thrown overboard far from London's port, so there's no threat to anyone here. Now go!"

We didn't argue. We walked away.

"Hungry or diseased rats don't leave a singular bite," Jacques said. "They bite and gnaw. Those people were bitten by a vampire."

"I agree, but was it the same one?"

Jacques shrugged. "The timeline is accurate."

"I was thinking the same thing. He used some kind of mind control over the captain to make him forget."

Jacques nodded.

"I wonder if he's using the ship for his lair."

"Interesting but unlikely," Jacques replied.

"Why?"

"Too many risks. They had to unload the cargo and now the captain says that it will be loaded again, even if he sells it."

"The captain could be a human servant. You saw his reaction when I asked to search the ship."

Jacques smiled and then laughed softly. "If he has illegal supplies aboard, he's not going to want *anyone* to attempt a thorough inspection."

"What could be so illegal?"

"Poppy seeds, for one, but there's other goods from the Orient that people smuggle in simply to avoid outrageous taxes."

"Do you think the crew tossed over dead bodies or the vampire's neophytes?"

"There's no way to know since we didn't see the bodies. If all they had were bite marks on their necks, he was probably siring."

I stared back at the ship. The captain walked up the ramp. "It wasn't a wasted journey coming here, but we're still no closer to knowing this vampire's identity or where he came from. A part of me is still eager to search the lower levels."

Jacques shook his head. "I still don't think he's aboard the ship. Perhaps somewhere along the docks or in a warehouse. Those abandoned tunnels and caverns probably would be the best places to search. But the greatest probability is where we encountered him last night. That's twice I've crossed paths with him there."

"You have far more experience than I. Let's get Father and Matilda and catch a train back."

CHAPTER 14

A week passed and the unnamed vampire had not killed again. At least the constables or the newspapers had reported nothing. I regretted not searching the ship at the dock. I was almost convinced that this vampire had boarded another ship or a train and left London for good.

Albert and his were-rat children had scoured the abandoned tunnels, the caves, and some of the active tracks, finding no trace of this undead intruder. His trail was cold.

Jacques and I had even spent one night in a large cemetery. The only activity was an occasional bat and a bored owl. No vampires, ghouls, or zombies. A good night altogether.

Father and I were ready to head back to Romania, as I needed to eliminate more of the vampire population in my homeland. Jacques and Matilda had rekindled their love and affection for one another. Both wanted to travel to America. Watching their interactions had renewed my internal struggle of my feelings for Rose.

Our plans were to part ways the next morning, so we decided not to roam the alleyways during the night.

. . .

September 9th, 1888

THE FOLLOWING MORNING a harsh desperate rapping rattled our inn door. I bolted from my pallet on the floor with a stake clenched tightly in my hand. Instinct, even though a vampire wouldn't waste time pounding on a door, especially not after the sun had risen. I slid the stake under my father's pillow and hurried to the door.

I pulled the door open slightly and peered out. "Constable Shields?"

His face was pale and haggard. He looked sick. His eyes were tormented with shock and repulsion. He removed his hat with a shaking hand. "May I come in, Forrest?"

"Certainly." I pulled the door open, allowing him to step inside.

Shields took a deep breath and leaned against the wall to hold himself upright. His legs were shaky. I pulled the chair from the desk. "Here, have a seat, constable."

"Th-thank you."

"What's troubling you?" I asked.

Matilda slipped a housecoat over her gown while Jacques sat up on the edge of the bed. He ran a hand through his wavy hair.

"Did you by chance patrol last night?" he asked.

I shook my head. "No. In fact, we were getting ready to leave London."

"Leaving? Why?"

"It's been a week since the murder, and we've not encountered any suspicious folks on the streets. Nothing's been reported in the post, either."

Shields wiped sweat from his brow with a handkerchief. "He struck again. He murdered another woman last night."

"Near the same place?"

"No, he killed this one on Hanbury Street. Annie Chapman. Her name. Gruesome murder. Much worse than the last one." He placed the handkerchief over his mouth and gagged for a few moments. "Only a devil could do something so dreadful. Like Polly, Annie's throat was slashed, but her stomach was also cut open. Part of her . . . her entrails were strewn over her shoulder. Her womb had been cut completely out with almost surgical precision."

A long five minutes of absolute silence hung in the room. None of us even made eye contact with one another. Even if we had patrolled during the night, it would have been where we had last encountered this vampire and not on a different street. Certainly *not* where this woman had been killed.

During my vampire hunts, I had seen some gruesome things, but none done to other mortals with the exception of my mother. Fighting and killing zombies, ghouls, and vampires, a Hunter witnessed a lot of dismemberment, usually in the process of killing these undead creatures. But, this particular murderer was different—sadistic—and not characteristic of a routine vampire.

After his nausea subsided, Shields lowered his handkerchief and braved looking me in the eyes. "You honestly weren't out on the streets last night?"

"We weren't. We stayed inside," I replied.

He took a deep breath and looked to the floor. His eyes darted back and forth as his mind raced. He released a long sigh and shook his head. "It's a bit early in the morning for drinking, but after seeing that poor woman . . . I'd down a whole bottle of scotch if I thought it would erase that gruesome scene from my memory."

I honestly didn't know what to tell him. What advice could one give? With him being a constable, I was certain he had seen some vicious murders before. But this one horribly shook him.

"I need to ask you something," Shields said, looking at Jacques.

Jacques shrugged and gave a nod.

"I know the last time we talked I was more accusatory toward you than what I should have been."

Jacques smiled. "You were simply doing your job. Finding my cane at two different bloody scenes gave you every right to be suspicious."

Shield sighed. "But, it wasn't really that."

"Then what?"

"I sense something different about you. Well, all of you, except Forrest's father. An energy of some sort that I don't understand and can't explain. There's a reason you all have been concerned about this murderer and why you've shown keen interest in helping us hunt him down. Can you please tell me what you're not telling me?"

I glanced toward Jacques and he toward Matilda. Matilda shook her head slightly. She appeared apprehensive.

Shields spoke with a pleading tone. "This is serious. Otherwise I'd never pry. You were certain this man would kill again. He has. You held no doubts. I know you have a deeper reasoning for believing that. But this murder was much worse than the last one. He will kill again, won't he?"

I nodded. "He will."

"Then can't you see why I need your help?"

"In a way, you already answered your own question," I said.

"What? When?"

"You said that only a devil could do that to a person."

"He's a demon?" Shields looked bewildered.

"Not in that sense."

"I don't understand."

"I need you to swear something to me," I said.

"Like what, exactly?"

"What I tell you cannot leave this room, and you must promise exemption from any charges that might lead to arrest."

Shields frowned. "What crimes have you committed?"

"No crime, but perhaps a violation of your city's statutes."

"You need to be more forthcoming than that."

"In return for us helping you find this man, we ask that you pardon us from any—"

"Forrest!" Father said, shaking his head. "Don't."

I gave my father a harsh stare. "No, he needs our services, our aid, or this thing will keep killing."

"Thing?"

I nodded.

"What exactly is he, and why do you insist that your party can find and kill him?"

I stood, grabbed my Hunter box, and set it on the bed.

"Forrest, no!" Father said.

Matilda shook her head. "I agree with your father on this."

I ignored them. "We have fought this kind of creature in Romania and other countries. We're good at finding and killing them. And I have been chosen to exterminate such beasts."

Shields stared at my box. "Is he a werewolf?"

I shook my head. "No. He's a vampire. An undead, and has ties to the cursed things of darkness. That's why he's never going to attack during the daytime and why he performs his slaughters late in the night. He's not a demon, but he opposes everything mortals deem holy."

I opened the box. Shields rose and inspected the contents. "These creatures actually exist?"

"Just like werewolves. And from what I've been told, any werewolf in London is to be put to death."

He nodded. "But we had no choice in enacting that. Not after the major massacre."

"Which is possibly why this vampire has chosen to live in London," I said.

"Why?"

"Werewolves are their primary enemies. Since you've essentially banned them from being in London, you've opened the door for the vampires to begin taking up residency. You've provided them shelter and a plentiful population to feed upon."

Shields leaned over the contents of my Hunter box. "Interesting. You really hunt vampires?"

"We been hired to eradicate them in various cities."

"I've read the legends of vampires," Shields said, "but that's all I thought they were. Legends."

"They are very much real."

"But don't they bite to feed off human blood?"

Jacques nodded. "That is the typical means. When he killed Polly, he was drinking her blood from her gashed throat. That's when I had come upon him and why I attacked him. But he's faster and stronger than I had expected him to be."

Father stood and winced, taking a few steps toward the bed. "The reason my legs are in such bad shape is due to a vampire beating me to near death with his cane. He shattered my legs, but they didn't heal properly. I'm a vampire hunter but not like Forrest."

Shields eyed me with curiosity. "And what makes you different?"

"I'm one of the Chosen."

"Chosen?"

Jacques nodded. "Every so often a child is born with such a calling on his life, and he's destined to eliminate these cursed undead. They have a blessing upon them. They bring balance to our world."

"From God?" Shields asked.

"From a higher power," I replied.

"When did you discover you were one of the Chosen?"

"At eight years of age."

He frowned. "So you've been fighting them for how long now? Ten years? Fifteen?"

I smiled. "Almost a year now. I'm still eight years old. Soon to turn nine."

Shields frowned from his skepticism. "That's not possible. You can't be eight years old."

"I really am."

Jacques and my father both nodded.

"I sort of stood out in school, but not in a good way. Most of the children and my teachers didn't understand my size and intelligence either. I was an outcast from the lot of them."

"That's incredible," he said. "But you all have my sworn word. What we discuss won't leave this room."

"Good," Jacques said. "Because there's more that we need to tell you."

Matilda paled. She swallowed hard.

"Like what?" Shields asked.

CHAPTER 15

"Werewolves?" Shields said uneasily. "You and she? Werewolves?"

Jacques nodded. He lifted a finger while making his point. "I'm not certain what caused the massacre, which has banned our kind in London, but rest assured, constable, the majority of werewolves are rather docile. We don't wreak havoc upon society. It is not our true nature."

"Those did about fifty years ago. They rampaged through the London population, not killing people, mind you, but deliberately infecting others into becoming like them."

Jacques shook his head. "You see, that's unethical. Most of us despise our inner beast. We know it's a curse. We wouldn't wish it upon others, not even an enemy. We certainly don't attempt to inflict our disease upon the world."

"They did," Shields said. "But they were a sordid lot. They were bands of Gypsies seeking refuge who eventually became rebels against the Crown. I think their minds were twisted before they had become werewolves themselves."

"That's possible," Jacques said. "Once a mentally unstable individual becomes cursed as a werewolf or a vampire, his worst traits are magnified. So a deranged person, a lunatic, inflicts as much carnage upon society as possible. Such people have no remorse for the pain and suffering they cause. Sort of like the vampire we're hunting now."

"You think he was a lunatic prior to being turned into a vampire?" Shields asked.

"Don't you, constable? I have no doubts about it," Jacques said. "He's not trying to turn these female victims into more vampires. The fact that he's gutting and butchering them indicates he enjoys their suffering more than anything else. A sane vampire, if such a creature exists, maintains a low profile. They don't want to draw attention to themselves. This one strives to strike fear into the hearts of society by his gruesomeness."

Shields took a sharp breath and nodded. "He's definitely done that. Our detectives and constables refuse to travel after darkness unless they walk in small groups. But how did this vampire get here?"

"We think he came ashore on a cargo ship," I said.

"Odd. You mentioned that before, and I went to investigate, but I could find no evidence."

Jacques smiled. "That may be due to you being a constable."

"You found which ship he was on then?"

"We think we did, but the captain refused to let us inspect his ship."

"What led you to believe he was on this ship?" Shields asked.

"From what the captain described happening during their journey to London. He thought some of his crewmembers had died from the plague. He thought rats had bitten them, but the bite marks he described were what a vampire bite looks like. They threw the bodies overboard, thinking they were dead and hoping no one else became infected."

Shields frowned. "You think this vampire is staying on the ship?"

"Not anymore," Jacques replied. "He'd be too vulnerable. He's moved somewhere into the city where he can hide during the day."

"I see. Any ideas?"

"Underground," I said. "You have a lot of tunnels and caves."

Shields returned to the chair and sat down. "I don't know how we're going to handle this situation. I mean, how do we go about finding him?"

"The way London is set up, with all the docks, warehouses, underground tunnels, it will be a tedious process," Jacques said.

"And when we find him, then what? I can't tell my fellow constables that we're looking for a vampire. If I do, my credibility is ruined as is my career. They'd send me to the asylum. A certain death sentence."

"They believe in werewolves, but not vampires?" I asked.

"Forrest, we have written accounts of the werewolves and documented reports by officers and royal family members. But no one has ever reported vampires in London. It's doubtful there are any others outside of this one."

"You'd be surprised," Jacques said.

Shields glanced at him with wide eyes. "You think so?"

Jacques nodded. "Like I said, most vampires maintain a low profile. They don't want others to know they exist. The most frightening aspect is that some of the wealthiest and most influential people in the world are vampires. They have the ability to charm others. With such influence they often achieve high social status."

Shields rubbed his eyes. "This day continues to get even more bizarre."

"It's early yet," I said.

"Your secrets are safe with me," Shields said. "But how can you guarantee that our citizens are safe by having werewolves reside here?"

Jacques tapped the chained medallion on his chest. "This amulet is blessed to keep my inner beast at bay."

Shields studied it and then glanced to Matilda. "And you?"

She pulled hers from her nightgown and revealed it.

"I see. You both have them?"

Jacques nodded. "Yes."

"And they work?"

"Like a charm." Jacques grinned. "The only chance of you seeing us become werewolves is when we confront this vampire. In human form, neither of us are a match for him. In both encounters, he's proven to me that I cannot overpower him in my human form. But as werewolves, we can do him severe harm, provided we can find him again."

Shields sighed. "Parliament should reconsider this werewolf death decree, but any person proposing such would find himself shackled and beaten."

"Why do they oppose our kind so fiercely?" Jacques asked.

"One of the victims was the infant grandson of the Prince. It's hard to forgive such a brutal attack directed at the Crown."

Matilda said, "You might be surprised to know how many were-wolves still reside here. Banishment laws won't prevent them from living here. They just become more cautious and secretive."

"People tend to view anyone that's different with extreme prejudice," I said. "Judging them without even knowing the truth. It's part of nature and engrained into our minds before we ever learn to speak. All it takes is for one ruthless member of a culture to tarnish its entire reputation before the world."

"Sadly, that's true," Shields said.

"What did you discover at the scene before this one? When you found Jacques' cane the second time?" I asked.

"If a murder took place, no body was ever found," Shields replied. He stood. "So, I can rely upon you to stay and help us find this . . . vampire?"

We nodded.

"Even with all of us," I said. "We're going to have a difficult time finding him. There are too many hiding places within his hunting grounds, and no way we can be everywhere at the same time."

"That's true," Shields replied. "But what can my officers do to better protect themselves?"

"They have silver bullets?" I asked.

He nodded.

"Silver won't kill a vampire, but it hurts them. It slows them down."

"Then should I suggest that they be armed to kill werewolves?" he asked. "That could put the two of you into danger."

Jacques nodded. "If we get shot, it will kill us. But we'll be aware of our surroundings."

"Insist that they carry garlic," I said. "Or eat a lot of it."

"Garlic? I don't know that I can be *that* persuasive. I can try." He walked over to my Hunter box. "What are all these things?"

I pointed from item to item. "That's a vial of holy water. The yellowish liquid is garlic juice. Of course, a silver cross. Several stakes. Mallet. A bottle of blessed salt."

"Should I carry a cross?" Shields asked.

"It wouldn't hurt," Jacques said.

Shields walked to the door. "This visit has been quite . . . educational. As much as I dread it, I must return to the crime scene and the autopsy. At least I have a better idea of what we're looking for."

"Yes, but finding him might be nearly impossible," Jacques said. "There's another issue that you need to know."

"What's that?"

"Active vampires feed daily. He killed the first woman, fed from her, and nothing else happened for over a week."

"Correct."

Jacques shook his head. "No. He's still feeding elsewhere. He's simply not killing them."

"People actually allow that?"

"They won't remember because a vampire can compel a person and make him or her forget. My assumption is he's still choosing people in the slums because the constables notice them less. If he's feeding, they'll have bite marks on their necks. That's what we need to be looking for during the daylight. His living victims. How far apart were the two murdered victims?"

"Several streets from one another. Why?"

"Then we start scouring the streets in between the two murder scenes. We find his victims, and we might be able to pinpoint his location or narrow down where he might attack next."

"That's a good idea," Shields said.

"And if we don't find these victims, we have an even bigger problem," Jacques said.

"Why?"

"It means he's siring new vampires, which allows him to feed while propagating his undead children."

"You think he is doing that?" Shields asked.

I nodded. "We think that's what he was doing on the ship. Those bodies thrown overboard might not have been completely dead. They might have been his offspring waiting for the next sunset to rise."

Shields' mouth dropped open.

Jacques nodded. "And London thought werewolves were a threat? You've not seen true horror until you've witnessed what a master vampire can unleash on an unprotected population. Our home country knows the ruthlessness of such bloodthirsty leaders. Werewolves take a month to undergo their first transformation at the first full moon. Vampires within two days. Young ones can become feral and go on vast killing sprees due to their bloodlust, unless the master vampire properly guides them."

"Do you think this one will?" Shields asked.

"Depends upon his ultimate motive. As vicious as he's killing these women, he might only produce spawns to unleash as much carnage as possible," Jacques said. "The best we can hope is that we find the master before he creates his own undead army."

I grabbed the white oak stake from beneath my father's pillow and handed it to the constable. He took it and studied it for a few seconds.

"What do I do with this?" he asked.

"Through the heart. That's one way to kill a vampire," I said. "As I was told, 'not near the heart, but through it.'"

Shields' face paled again. He swallowed hard. "The more I'm learning, the less I like the situation we're facing."

"It's better than not knowing at all," I replied.

CHAPTER 16

While in many ways we dressed and looked similar to a lot of the slum population, they readily recognized that we were not. They regarded us with the same skepticism Shields had done when he first encountered us. We were unwelcome outsiders and were treated as such. But it didn't inhibit our visual search for possible vampire victims.

Several hours passed and even though we looked for folks with bite marks on their necks or abnormally pale complexions with dark circles under their eyes, we never found anyone the vampire had fed upon.

The most worrisome part was the long week in between the murders. With as much agility, strength, and speed as this vampire possessed, he needed to feed every night. If no victims were above ground, that meant only one thing. He was building an undead legion.

"This doesn't make sense," I said to Jacques.

"What?"

"We've spent the night at the one cemetery and no new vampires rose from any of the graves."

"Yes, but that graveyard was for the wealthier people. Look at the thousands of people that live in the most impoverished section of the city. If any go missing, not many will even notice. So this vampire might lure unfortunates into an underground tunnel, kill and bury them, and then wait for them to awaken in their undead form. Nothing dictates they must be buried in a cemetery, and it would be far less likely he'd allow them to be buried in sacred ground, which is what a church cemetery would be considered."

"Then we're wasting our time looking above ground, aren't we?" I asked.

"Quite possibly. But there are dozens of cemeteries."

"So instead of hunting and killing the one vampire, we might be up against a dozen or more of them?"

Jacques nodded. "If he's fathered more children, yes. They will be distractions or obstacles trying to prevent us from stopping him for some time to come."

"After we find Father and Matilda, we should visit Albert and inform him."

"They've thoroughly inspected all the tunnels within his territory."

"I know. But he might point us in a different direction where we could look."

"Definitely having no luck up here."

"There's too much territory for us to cover," I replied.

"Agreed."

Two blocks later, we found my father and Matilda seated at an outside table, drinking tea. I worried about my father because he was having a harder time walking. His legs stiffened quicker, decreasing the distance he could walk before his nagging pain forced him to sit down. Even he had said that he was thankful he was able to walk, but the agony in his eyes indicated he was almost ready to stop walking altogether. The pain was too great.

A year hadn't passed since he suffered the baron's attack, but Father seemed shorter, smaller, like an elderly person slowly drew up. He looked twenty years older around his eyes. His body had grown more frail and withered.

"Did you find anyone with obvious bite marks?" I asked.

Father shook his head. "No, son."

I glanced toward Matilda. She shook her head.

"When you're finished with the tea, we're heading underground to talk to Albert."

"Whatever for?" Father asked.

I explained what Jacques and I had discussed.

"Does that acquire my attendance?" he asked. "I'm exhausted. My lower back and legs ache."

I smiled. "You can stay here and rest, if that's what you wish."

"I'd appreciate it, son."

"Matilda?" I said.

"I can go with you and Jacques."

Father looked hurt and pouted like a child. He liked being in Matilda's company. I think her female companionship helped lessen the pain of Momma's absence.

"We shouldn't be gone long," I said.

Father shrugged with a soured expression on his face. "Take your time."

"We need to find where his lair."

He huffed and crossed his arms. "I'll be fine. Don't worry yourself about me."

I sighed. "I'm sorry that you hurt, Father. Truly I am. But I cannot deny my duty."

"Sorry I'm holding you back."

"You're not, Father. That's not my point. But where we can do the legwork, we will. That doesn't make you less important. You have a host of knowledge that will always be essential to me. You've made a lot of sacrifices over the years, like any good parent or spouse would. Now it's my turn to reduce your workload."

"Do me no favors," he replied, refusing to make eye contact. He half reminded me of an agitated momma hen that puffed up when disturbed. He'd sulk long after we returned from visiting Albert.

I nodded toward Matilda and Jacques, and we walked away.

My father had always been a complex man, but he was steadily becoming more moody after his injuries and Momma's death. At times, like now, he was bitterer than wormwood. I supposed his lashing out was more toward himself than us, but it was hard to determine. He had been helpless to save my mother, and with his nearly useless legs, his lack of mobility made him feel insufficient. But he was far from it. No amount of coaxing from me would ever allow him to understand that. Stubborn men cannot be convinced of anything they don't already perceive to be the truth. Arguments were futile.

The three of us crossed a street and headed down a narrow alley, but not without notice. Two men followed us. They were big men with thick black beards, Jewish hats, and heavy overcoats. Their eyes set colder than ice and hatred chiseled their hardened faces. There was no denying that they were brothers. Not twins but remarkably close in resemblance.

"This is our side of the street," the one said in a thick accent. "You're trespassing."

"We're passing through," Jacques said. "Not looking for any problems."

"You've already found plenty of problems," the other one said, revealing a long blade. "You're not one of us. You're intruders."

Jacques and I turned. He took Matilda by the arm and pulled her behind us.

"You can pay with money or blood," the man said.

I eyed the long blade. He grinned.

"Interesting," I said, grinning back.

"What?" he replied. He was surprised by my lack of fear.

"That looks like the type of blade used to butcher that woman. I imagine the PCs would be interested in talking to you."

"I didn't kill her."

"You're threatening us, so that doesn't help your argument, does it?"

"I have the right to protect what is ours."

"An alley? This is a passageway where people walk. We've not infringed upon anything that belongs to you. If you think intimidating strangers for money will work, you have no idea who you're threaten-ing." I reached into my pocket and gripped a stake.

His eyes glanced toward my pocket. He became more apprehensive when I didn't pull out a weapon but kept my hand hidden inside my pocket. Since I was a bit larger in height and weight than they were, that increased my counter threat.

Anger stirred in Jacques' eyes. Whenever he was threatened his eyes darkened. It was noticeable to anyone that happened to be watching him at that particular moment. It was like looking into the eyes of a wolf.

Uncertainty arose in the one man's gaze, as if he couldn't believe what he had seen. He turned his frightened gaze toward me. His voice became softer and less threatening. "We've had an impostor plague us recently. Some of our people have gone missing."

"Do you know what this person looks like?" I asked.

They shook their heads.

"He comes in the dead of night. Only his shadow and glowing eyes are visible. He's a monster. He steals people. Our people."

I smiled evenly. "Then we are allies, not enemies. We are looking for the same man. Rest assured, when we find him, we will kill him."

The two men studied us for several long seconds before sliding their knives from view. They nodded, turned slowly, and walked back to the crowded street.

Jacques found a metal door, lifted it, and we hurried underground. He struck a match across a wooden beam and used the small flame until he found a lantern. It was good that some shop owners left lanterns beneath the door. "I never took you to be one for scuffling."

I shrugged. "I'm not. But it's better to be aggressive than passive with people who draw weapons without waiting for reasoning."

"That's true. But they had knives. What do you have? A stake?"

I nodded.

He shook his head. "That'd leave a nasty scar."

"I imagine it would hurt for quite some time first."

Jacques laughed softly. "It would indeed. But even though they were hostile in their approach, they're like us. They want answers. They want to find this murderer. He's caused a panic."

I nodded. "I know and I understand that. But, frightened desperate people are often more dangerous."

"They can be."

"Do you smell that?" Matilda asked.

"It's a rancid odor," Jacques replied, placing a hand over his nose and mouth.

I scrunched my nose and covered it. "Reeks of death."

We walked for several yards until we noticed small objects scattered along the rocky floor. Jacques brought his lantern closer. Dead rats. A few dozen of them. Their little bodies had been twisted in quick harsh manners. Their mouths were opened with dead painful snarls. They looked like they had been crushed and thrashed on the ground.

"Are these rats Albert's?" I asked.

"Possibly," Jacques said softly.

Matilda knelt in the midst of the rats and waved a slow hand over one rat's corpse in what I assumed was her attempting to feel their lingering energy. "Not necessarily his rats. We're well outside of Albert's lair and his tunnels. While he has control over a large rat population, he doesn't over all of them. No were-creature has that range of power."

One larger rat twitched near her foot.

"They've not been dead long," Jacques said.

She grabbed one rat's long tail and lifted it off the floor. Its body hung limp. No stiffness. "Recently killed."

"Then whatever killed them isn't far away," I said. I reached into my pocket and pulled out a stake.

"These rats aren't what smell of decay," Jacques said. "They've not been dead long enough."

"What I smell is too large to be the rats," I replied. "Walking death."

"Zombie?" Jacques asked.

"Not sure. But a zombie would have tried to eat those rats."

"You're correct."

It was a time when I wished we had more light. The glow from a singular lantern didn't brighten a large enough radius, especially not for three people. The underground tunnel narrowed ahead of us. The brick walls dripped water, forming small pools. Cool air wafted, bringing with it the decaying smell. This pungent odor increased as we neared the door. With the light outlining the doorframe but nothing beyond, we stopped and listened. The constant pings of dripping water resounded around us. No sounds, other than our shallow breathing, were audible. But if a master vampire were beyond our line of sight, it would be nearly impossible for us to detect him due to his faint heart-beat and extremely shallow, almost nonexistent, breathing.

Pinpointing the closeness of a vampire was the most particularly dangerous part of being a Vampire Hunter, based upon sound detection. A vampire hidden on the other side of this dark door already knew our presence and proximity since they possessed heightened, acute senses. Not to mention, we were possibly standing inside his territory.

I glanced with uncertainty at Jacques. "Do you sense anything beyond that door?"

He narrowed his eyes and sniffed the air. "Nothing out of the ordinary. You?"

I shook my head. Instead of retreating, I pulled another stake from my other pocket and headed toward the open door. Perhaps I should have allowed the werewolf to enter first since he had better sight and hearing than I did, but I was a perpetually overzealous youth who thought myself as virtually indestructible. At least this time good fortune favored me. However, added unexpected mysteries would puzzle us even more.

CHAPTER 17

*A*cross the threshold nothing supernaturally undead or living awaited us. We did find a few corpses. One was a medium sized pig drained of its blood, which emitted a powerfully rotten smell. The slick sound of maggots and worms writhing beneath the pig's skin, its eyes and other orifices was unnerving. It was another aspect of after death that disturbed most humans.

We could only assume the pig had been drained due several punctured bite marks along its thick neck. But wiggling maggots spilled from those holes as well. Not far away from this pig were two dead humans, also with vampire bites in their necks, but thankfully, no maggots, yet.

"He's fathered at least a few children," Jacques said. He held the lantern over the pig carcass and counted three different bite marks.

"Why a pig?" I asked.

"More blood. Easier to feed a larger group at once," Jacques replied.

"Where would they get a pig here?" Jewish refugees wouldn't have them.

"There's a butcher shop a few streets over," Matilda said.

Jacques continued examining the human corpses. "The two dead females were probably drained due to the uncontrollable hunger of the younger vampires. These two young women would have been vampires as well, but I'm guessing the master is having a difficult time weaning his children's desires to tone down their cravings. These two were killed before he could instruct them properly. Vampires undergo a euphoric sensation when they feed and young ones gorge themselves beyond their own self-restraint."

I stared at the two young women. Their skin was bright alabaster and their facial expressions were frozen in their last few moments of sheer terror. They had not been compelled and suffered immense pain. I felt remorse for them and wondered who in their families missed them. "How do you know that?"

The tone of his voice lowered. "I witnessed such things near Dracula's castle. A newly sired vampire has a rampaging hunger, a heated temper, and is almost beyond control. Without the master standing by to coax and demonstrate, half a village could be slaughtered before sunrise."

"How'd these young women get down here?"

"Probably lured here by the vampires. Most likely by family members who are now vampires."

I thought about that for a several minutes. I couldn't think of a more horrible betrayal than for a new vampire to seek out family or friends and lure them back to a lair to turn them or simply to drain them to death. Not all family members were loyal to one another in the first place. Some secretly despised siblings or parents to the point of wishing them dead. As a vampire, they held the power and influence to actually carry it out. The poor victims who might have been looking for the safe return of an absent family member must have been overjoyed to see the estranged one finally return. He or she would never hesitate to follow the undead sibling underground when told, "Come see what I have found. This is why I've been gone." Curiosity outweighed rationality at times.

Matilda grabbed Jacques by the arm to lower the lantern. "We're not alone."

And we weren't.

A shirtless young man stood before us. His pallid skin almost glowed in the dim lighting. Dark bite marks were prominent on his neck. But all over his body were other bite marks. The dead rats had made these. They must have tried to swarm and overtake him.

The young man stood with a blank expression on his face. His sunken eyes appeared lost and disoriented. He didn't seem to notice us. I tightened my grip on the stakes and readied myself.

"He's not a vampire," Jacques said.

"You're certain?" I asked.

"Yes. If you kill him, he most likely will turn. The others have been feeding from him. He's human livestock. He's been compelled and even if we get him out of here, he will return. This essentially is his home now. He remembers nothing outside of this tunnel," Jacques said.

"We just leave him?" I asked.

"For now."

Matilda stepped closer to the young man and placed her hand against his chest. He didn't react to her touch. He looked through her as if she wasn't there. "He's cold like a corpse."

"He has a pulse?"

She slid her hand over his heart. "Yes, his heartbeat is strong, but he's so cold."

"Come on," Jacques said. "We need to move farther into the tunnel."

"There's nothing we can do for him?" I asked.

"Not until we kill the vampire that holds control over him."

Jacques stepped around the young man. Matilda followed, although her eyes were troubled.

"How'd he get here?" I wondered aloud.

"Not sure. He might have escaped his holding pen and is wandering the tunnels, looking for the master. Unless the master seeks him, the young man might keep searching until he dies. Then he'll awaken as a vampire."

"From the others feeding off him?"

"Most likely, he has fed off the master. It sustains his health, especially since he's being fed upon by the new vampires."

I kept my stake in hand while we followed the tunnel. "Then that means we might find more like him or we're about to find where the young vampires hide during the day."

"That wouldn't be a bad discovery."

"Listen," Matilda said softly.

We stopped walking. Jacques lowered the lantern and craned his neck. The narrow tunnel was wetter the deeper underground we had walked. Water stood. In some places, the path was completely underwater, almost ankle deep. Ahead, in the darkness, beyond our sightline, the water splashed in a consecutive rhythm, growing fainter with each passing second. Someone or something was running away from us.

Jacques handed me the lantern. "You need this more than we will."

I frowned, tucking one stake into my coat pocket.

He and Matilda sprinted ahead, leaving me with the only light source in the tunnel. Of course, they didn't need light to see. I ran to catch them, but they were too fast. I lost them.

Although I was one of the Chosen Vampire Hunters and a man by my outward appearance, I discovered that the frightened eight-year-old part of my mind occasionally surfaced. This was one of those moments, being alone in a dark tunnel where undead creatures hid. The lantern only offered a small radius of light. The slightest shift of the lantern created moving shadows at the edge of the light's path, which sometimes looked like a person's shadow retreating.

I took a deep breath and held it. Why did the mind play such horrid tricks in the darkness? Sounds were louder, creepier, and more mysterious. I felt watched by unseen eyes.

I shunted fear from my mind, gripped the stake in my right hand, and ran after Jacques and Matilda.

CHAPTER 18

The long dark tunnel seemed endless. Several times it narrowed to the point where I had to turn sideways and squeeze through the fallen stones and bricks. A good fifteen minutes passed, and I still had not found Jacques and Matilda. Other than my heavy breathing and cumbersome thudding footsteps, no outlandish sounds caught my attention. The tunnel had never branched, so they had not taken a side path.

Leaning against the damp wall, I closed my eyes and held my breath. My heart pounded in my ears as I attempted to distinguish noises. Water dripped from the ceiling with irregular rhythm. I exhaled slowly, quietly, through my mouth. A sudden echoing shriek caused me to bolt upright. The sound sent shivers down my spine.

I tore into a sprint, racing toward the cry, which was even farther down the dark tunnel. Thinking the scream had come from Matilda, I didn't slow my pace until a more disturbing sound caught my attention. Vicious growls rumbled. I hoped these were from Jacques and Matilda. If not, I was running into a battle I might not be equipped to survive.

The tunnel widened into a large rectangular room. Light filtered through a few holes overhead, illuminating enough to allow me to set the lantern on a large carved stone and focus my attention on the three vampires Jacques and Matilda had cornered in what looked like the cellar of an abandoned workhouse.

Another female vampire lay on the floor. Her throat was gashed open, leaking black blood, but she wasn't dead. I supposed the loud shrill had come from her right before Matilda or Jacques had slashed their sharp claws through her neck. She pressed a loose ribbon of her flesh against her throat while pulling herself on hand and knees, trying to sneak closer to Matilda. The vampire gnashed her teeth. Her fangs protruded abnormally longer.

Matilda's attention was on the three male vampires that she and Jacques were advancing toward. Matilda was oblivious of how close the injured vampire was to reaching her.

I rushed toward the female vampire, grabbed her shoulder, and flung her over onto her back. Her eyes widened, and she hissed at me. She lunged upward, trying to bite me, anywhere it seemed because she wasn't near my throat. I hammered her forehead hard with a closed fist, snapping her head back against the stone floor. Before she could react, I placed my left hand firmly around her bloody throat and pinned her.

She clawed at my arm but my thick coat spared me injury. While pinning her, I rammed the stake through her heart, watching her eyes fully blacken and her body grow limp before she dissolved into a pile of ash beneath me.

One of the male vampires screamed in anger. I glanced up. This vampire leapt high into the air and far outside of Jacques' reach, landing on the floor in front of me. I pushed myself up and backwards but not fast enough. He flailed his sharp nails across my face. The burning pain was instant. Warm blood dripped down my left cheek. I winced and turned with his momentum, following his swing through.

For a young vampire he was fast. Had he been older, I'd have suffered far worse an injury from his attack than simply getting raked across the face. Due to how hard he had swung, he continued moving forward. I grabbed his elbow and continued with him, slamming him face first into the wall. Upon impact, I pressed my thick hand against the back of his neck and held him a foot off the floor.

His legs dangled. He kicked and snarled, trying to break free of my fierce grip, but from the angle I held him, he found no leverage. He was thin, light, and absent of any humanity. He managed to turn his head back enough to see me. He frothed at the mouth like a wild animal. His eyes revealed his hatred for humanity and how much he wanted to kill me, but unless I let him go, he remained harmless.

From behind him, I positioned the stake over his heart and thrust it through his back. He stiffened for a moment before dissolving into ash.

Jacques rushed one vampire, and Matilda attacked the other one. They used their werewolf claws and slashed the vampires' necks back and forth until they decapitated them.

I scanned the room thoroughly before dropping the stake back into my coat pocket. I wiped bright blood from my cheek. I took a cloth from my pocket and pressed it against the lacerations.

Slowly, Jacques and Matilda reverted into their human forms. They sat on thick rock slabs that had once served as overhead beams before part of the ceiling had collapsed. Leaning against one another, they took deep breaths. Sweat covered them. Their eyes revealed how exhausted they were. They needed long naps to recuperate, but we couldn't stay here. This place was still too dangerous.

"Four less vampires," I said, squatting beside them.

Jacques nodded.

"Do you think there are more?"

He gasped for air. "If there are, they're elsewhere."

Matilda pulled my hand away from the side of my face. "Are you okay?"

I nodded. "It'll heal."

She smiled and took a small vial from her pocket. She rubbed the ointment across the cuts. It smelled like mint but burned when she spread it on my bloody cheek. "This will help."

I smiled my appreciation. "We need to get the two of you to the surface before you fall asleep. If the master vampire finds you, he's certain to kill you in retaliation for his children."

Jacques pointed. "There's an old set of stairs. It should lead above ground, provided they're still intact, but I have no idea where we will emerge."

"Even as far into the tunnel as we have traveled," I said, "I don't think we're even close to Albert's lair."

Matilda shook her head. "We're probably nowhere near."

I stood over them. Matilda readjusted and buttoned her blouse to cover herself. I extended my hands and helped them both to their feet.

At the top of the stairs I pushed open a rusted door that opened into an overgrown garden with moss-covered birdbaths, weedy flowerbeds, and tarnished cherub statues. Jacques and Matilda walked to the wide tree trunk of a giant weeping willow and sat down. They fell asleep in one another's arms within minutes, which meant I had to keep watch over them for at least three hours while they recuperated from undergoing such quick transformations and expending their energy to fight.

Normally, Jacques could alter back to human without sleep, but never after he exerted himself to complete exhaustion fighting.

I had told Father that we weren't going to be gone too long. Initially, it had not been a lie. But now, it would be a few hours before we returned to find him. He'd be even more agitated than when I had left him. But Jacques and Matilda were too vulnerable to leave unattended. I was certain he'd understand that. He might never admit it, but he'd understand.

I sat on a granite bench half-covered with ivy where I could keep an eye on them and the door we had exited. By the time she and Jacques awakened, darkness would surround us. Should the master discover four of his children were dead, I held no doubt he'd emerge after sundown, seeking us. From how Jacques had described his fights with this master, I didn't expect to survive a one-on-one battle against him.

A bat fluttered out the cellar door with a harsh shrill, catching my attention. I turned to see the green eyes of a large hairy creature watching me from the shadows on the other side of the shadowed door. My hand went into my pocket. I waited, but I didn't need to wait long.

CHAPTER 19

*A*fter a few seconds, the creature left the door and walked out where I could see him. It was Albert.

He walked through the dry weeds and grass, which made gentle crunching sounds beneath his feet. His long tail trailed behind him like a large winding snake. Fresh blood was on his sinewy hands and smeared across the front of his robe. His nose scrunched and his whiskers twitched as he sniffed the air. His eyes widened like a child full of new discovery while he examined the trees, the birds, and his surroundings.

He took a deep breath, sighed, and sat on the bench beside me. "It's been ages since I've been outdoors before the sunset."

I eased my hand out of my pocket. "What brings you out this evening?"

"I needed to finish a task that you and your party failed to carry out."

I stared at the blood on his hands. "And exactly what did we fail to do?"

"You left one of the vampire's human herd alive."

"You killed him?"

Albert nodded. "You should have."

"He was harmless."

115

He shook his head. "Far from harmless, Forrest. He was marked. While he might have appeared fragile and unaware, the vampire controlled him. He could use his eyes to see. Because he controlled this feedbag of blood, he could have used the boy to kill or be a decoy to draw others underground. He might have already."

"I wasn't aware."

Albert shrugged. He glanced toward Matilda and Jacques. "Fine time to take a nap."

I explained what had happened.

He nodded in the direction of the sleeping couple. "That's the down-side of having to transform. It takes so much out of the human side that one succumbs to sleep so quickly. Since I never undergo any type of metamorphic change, I don't suffer in that regard. Like I mentioned to you before, perhaps you should consider becoming a were-creature. It has its added benefits."

I shook my head. "I'm having a hard enough time to adjusting to my Hunter senses and discerning their whispered insight."

Albert smiled and pointed toward the grass at our feet. "Four young vampires were under the ground where we sit?"

I nodded.

"So a marked human near four vampires. The master's not far away then."

"That'd be my guess."

Albert grinned. His beady rat eyes studied me. "Since it is only you and I at the moment, perhaps we can talk?"

"Sure."

"Something about your nature betrays you."

"What do you mean?" I scratched at my thickening beard.

"You're a giant of a young man but seem overly naïve at times. For me, it seems that you should have far greater knowledge about the world of the undead. But, for some reason you have far more questions than answers. I don't mean any offense by these statements."

I shrugged. "None taken."

"How long have you been a Hunter?"

"Not even a year."

"I see." His eyes searched mine.

For a were-rat that lacked ever becoming human again, his manners were impeccable and proper. Except for appearing as a giant rat, he could sit at the Queen's table unnoticed, acting like the best of royalty and nobility. He had been brought up in a wealthy home. I wondered what had happened to alter his life in such a drastic way.

"How old are you, Forrest?"

"Eight."

He smiled and a deep chuckle rolled in his throat. "You're a rarity of sorts. It explains so much."

"Like what?"

"Your childlike innocence. It also explains why you didn't kill the human feedbag in the underground tunnel."

"I could not justify killing him since he wasn't an actual vampire."

"You've never killed anything other than vampires?"

"Ghouls."

Albert reared his head back and winced. "Oh, how I hate those wretched beasts. Damn near impossible to kill."

"They are. I've killed zombies, too."

"Who hasn't?" he asked with a sly grin. My questioning stare caused him to laugh. He turned on the bench and faced me. "At some point, Forrest, you're going to face humans that are controlled by darker forces, whether it be demons, vampires, or witches. Evil shuns no form. Remember that. You will have to kill something that's still human. The justification for doing so will be there. On that day, trust me it will come, a part of you will die, too. You'll feel it. You'll grieve over its absence, but once it occurs, you'll never have it again. Ever."

My mind returned to the day of my mother's death, and Baron Randolph's human servant who had killed her. Jacques had spared me from committing the murder, even though it would have been justified. In retrospect, had the opportunity come for me to kill the servant, I'd have done it without hesitation. After all, he had killed my mother.

"I've met few Hunters, Forrest," Albert said softly. "But in all honesty, none are better suited for the task than you."

"Why do you say that?"

He took a deep breath and sighed. "You've mentioned your lack of faith—"

I shook my head. "No. I have faith but not in what these fancy cathedrals or temples around the world mandate."

Albert raised his hand and shook his head. "Patience. Let me explain. I have met holy men, spiritual women, and those who work miracles. I've deliberately sought some of them out. Simply because a person professes he or she is this or that doesn't make it so."

"That's my point."

"Ah, but when you encounter a person who has been touched by a higher spiritual power, no one has to tell you. It doesn't need to be proclaimed. It's evident the moment you come in contact with them. You feel the power oozing off them. That is something I sense with you."

I frowned.

"Not holy or evil power. I sense that you're one of the Chosen Hunters. Mysticism gushes through you. You have more power than what you're even aware of. In time you'll have better understanding of your gifts."

"Each day brings something new."

Albert stood and adjusted his robe. He glanced toward Jacques and Matilda.

"How long do you need to keep watch over them?"

"I'm not sure."

"It will be dark soon. Where's your father?"

"We left him near the coffee house." I shook my head. "I told him that we weren't planning to be gone long. He'll be angry."

"Not to worry, Forrest," Albert said. "I shall send my boys to find him and let him know of your delay."

"I appreciate that. Please relay a message?"

"Certainly."

"Have him wait at the inn for us."

Albert acquiesced a nod. He took in another deep breath while turning in a circle, admiring the area. "Oh, how I do miss the outdoors. This place is splendid solitude. I shall visit here again. After we have killed that fiendish vampire, that is."

He took slow strides to the door but never looked back.

After Albert was gone, I studied the vacant building beyond the overgrown garden where I sat. The building was three stories high with shattered windows, part of the roof had collapsed, and slender trees forked up the walls, trying to encapsulate it or to delay its inevitable fall. It was a menacing place from afar, but I imagined even worse after the night came. I wasn't familiar with this area. Strangely no vagrants loitered, almost as though the land was cursed, and perhaps it was since the only others here had been the four vampires right beneath us.

The building wasn't an old church. It looked like the workhouses in other areas of the city. From my vantage point I didn't see any entrances except the door that led to the tunnels below. For all I knew, I was probably at the rear of the building where the owner once had this fine botanical garden so he could relax. But for whatever reason, the place was more dismal than the confined streets of Whitechapel. No one had maintained the building or grounds for years. I wondered why and what had happened to cause the city to disregard what had once been a thriving industry.

I didn't wish to get my hopes up, but since we had found and killed four young vampires near this building, I suspected we were close to finding the vampire. The biggest obstacle facing us was not knowing our actual locale, but it made sense that this abandoned building might be where the vampire had chosen to reside. We had found one of the humans he was using to feed from and the two brothers had reported family members disappearing. All of this had occurred within a narrow vicinity. The vampire was most likely easier to find near this building than by tracking the murder victims he was leaving on the streets. Those bodies were nothing more than a distraction to strike fear into the hearts of the residents and keep everyone's attention away from the actual reality.

Unless we hunted down this vampire and killed him soon, he was about to unleash a new infestation of vampires to London. One destined to disrupt its infrastructure to the core. While it might help to know this vampire's origin, it wasn't essential information, not if we figured out his stalking pattern.

The vastly overpopulated streets made it impossible to predict where he'd strike next. I wondered if we inspected the lower floors of the workhouse, would we find him? Before the darkness settled, it was possible, but I couldn't leave Jacques and Matilda defenseless. In the ornery games Fate often played, the moment I left my cousin and his rekindled love to explore the building, the vampire would kill both of them. Never tempt Fate. It was never in one's favor to attempt to outsmart the dealer who shuffled the cards of life. Experts set the deck when the stakes were at their highest, so the odds were always set against the competitor. All I could do was watch the building, as the sky grew dimmer and wait.

Wind rustled through the weeds and shook the leaves on the vines and trees. Fog billowed from the far side of the building. I eased from the bench and studied the rising mists. They churned in an isolated spot, like a dust devil spun sand and silt upwards, forming a small harmless whirlwind. This mist rose only at that corner of the building and not elsewhere. I didn't know if it were possible or not, but I hurried to Jacques and Matilda, hoping to awaken them.

I shook Jacques' shoulder firmly. His eyes opened, narrowed, and he snarled. If I hadn't known he was a werewolf, his reaction might have been more laughable. It took several seconds to register in his mind that I wasn't his enemy before he finally relaxed and examined his surroundings.

"What is it?"

"I think I've found him."

"The vampire?"

I nodded.

Jacques stood quickly and followed me to the edge of the overgrown garden. I pointed toward the rising fog at the corner of the building. He watched for several minutes. Daylight fled. Night approached.

"What is it?" Matilda asked, standing beside me.

I stiffened. I had never heard her advance.

"He thinks it's where the vampire has been hiding," Jacques said softly. "He may be right."

She watched for several moments and nodded. "Something not human is definitely there. I sense evil pulsing from him."

"He has awakened," Jacques whispered.

Dozens of birds billowed toward the side of the roof. At first glance they appeared to be bats. Their piercing shrills brought chills down my back. The swarm swirled around the rooftop almost blackening what little light remained overhead. Thousands of them cried and flittered, eating whatever mosquitoes and flies they happened upon. They carried on for about fifteen more minutes. With calculated accuracy, they flew upward and descended, flying down inside the old chimney and into the top floor of the building to roost. Their wild chirps and shrills slowly settled.

After their sound died down, a thunderous explosion of flapping wings broke the silence behind us. We turned to see hundreds of large brown bats exiting through the slightly open door that led to the cellar and underground tunnel. It was a massive cloud of sharp teeth and leathery wings heading directly at us. We dove near a low tree branch.

Although bats never attacked humans, it was dangerous to stand in their flight path when they left the roost. They moved so rapidly and in such vast numbers, one could never avoid the claws or sharp teeth if they stood in their way. Once the bats lofted into the night sky, we looked toward the building. The misty fog was gone. I immediately wondered where our enemy had gone and where he might suddenly reappear.

CHAPTER 20

"Since it's dark, we should find a way out of here besides the underground tunnel," I said.

Jacques returned his attention to the side of the building. "He's gone, isn't he?"

"I think so. And for all we know, he might already be in the cellar where we killed his children, if he entered through another passageway."

"There was only one door that led in," Jacques replied.

I nodded. "Yes, but the light from up here shone through several large holes. Those are probably somewhere in this garden where part of the ground fell through, so we need to take caution where we step as we leave."

Jacques sighed and stared at the cellar door. He shook his head. "It's quicker if we go back the way we came."

"Also more deadly. You two need more time to recuperate."

"I feel fine," Jacques said. He glanced at Matilda. "How about you?"

She shrugged but her eyes drooped heavily.

"She's not alert enough, Jacques. You're an older werewolf, so you recover quicker than she does."

"Maybe so, but where are we? How do we get out of this place? I will wager the place has a fence around it. Once we get over that, which direction do we head?"

I shook my head. "I don't know but we'll figure it out."

Jacques studied the perimeter. "Your father's probably quite sore at us right now."

"Maybe not," I replied.

"He stays that way anymore, Forrest."

"But he's kept his promise to stop drinking, which might be in part to his abstinence."

Jacques nodded. "Abstinence does increase one's temper and hostility when his mind and body yearns for a drink."

"Depending upon his anger, he might start to spite me and visit a pub."

"Maybe we can find him before he allows such temptation."

"Albert was here while you slept."

"Really?" Jacques said.

"Yes. He promised to send his were-rat sons to tell Father of our delay."

"That's good, I suppose, but why was he here?"

"To tell me that he killed the wandering young man in the tunnel," I replied.

Matilda gasped. "Why'd he do that?"

"He said that we should have killed him."

"Oh?" Jacques narrowed his gaze. "Why?"

"He insists that the man was marked and being controlled by the vampire. He not only feeds from him, but he can see through his eyes."

"I never sensed that about him, but considering how close he was to the four vampires we killed, that's probably true," Jacques replied. "And if that old building is the vampire's lair—"

I placed a hand on his shoulder. "Look. Since we're standing over the room where the vampires were, we need to get out of here. I don't believe you're ready to confront this angered vampire yet."

Jacques frowned at me. "I'm tired but . . ."

"Cousin, I'm not trying to undermine your abilities or add insult to injury, but twice you've faced him *without* fatigue and it has not been to your advantage."

His jaw tightened, but instead of ensuing into a heated argument, he nodded. "You're right."

"Which way should we go?" I asked.

"Well, Forrest, due to the thick trees on this side of the garden, there's no reaching a fence in that direction. The same holds to the area on the other side of the cellar door. So either we walk in the direction of the building, which leads us farther away from our destination, or we go to the right and hope for the best."

"There's really no alternative."

We walked several hundred yards past the gardens, narrowly missing two drop-offs where the ground had collapsed. The fall probably wouldn't have killed Matilda or Jacques, since they healed quickly. But I never would have survived it. These holes were probably why the master vampire had left his children in the crumbling cellar. Should a human or any large beast fall through, their bodies would be broken and bleeding, offering the young vampires food without having to hunt.

While we made our way across the field, I thought about Albert's suggestion for me to become a were-creature. I couldn't imagine living a life like he was. I didn't want to be a rat, nor did I think I'd want to be a werewolf. Regardless of the advantages, I liked the less complications of remaining a human. Sorting through the intuitive voices that often spoke inside my mind was challenge enough. I didn't need to worry about turning into another creature in the wrong place at the wrong time. I didn't understand how Jacques had accepted his radical life-altering evolution as calmly as he had.

It was obvious that Matilda had not. But she didn't flaunt her resentment toward him any longer. Perhaps it was because he had returned to help her.

We reached the edge of the property line where a row of jagged uncut privet hedges presented a great deterrent to keep people out. In our case, they protested our departure.

Jacques glanced toward me. "Facing the vampire appears to be a better strategy to me."

I touched one of the sharp branches and released it. The thick hedges didn't look normal. Knives had not sharpened the tips nor had nature caused the abnormality. The privet towered twenty feet, forming a tight fence that lined this side of the perimeter. The tall, spindled branches wrapped around one another and prevented any space in between the lower trunks. None of us could even wedge a foot into the privet to attempt to find a path.

Matilda waved her hands in counter-opposite circular motions while whispering a chant. She stopped a few seconds later. "A magical barrier has been placed here."

"What?" I asked.

She nodded.

"Can you get past it?" Jacques asked.

"I can try," she replied. "But working an incantation might take a few minutes."

"We might not have that much time," I replied.

"Why?" they both asked, staring at me.

I pointed.

In between the building and the overgrown garden stood the silhouette of a man wearing a top hat. His cape ruffled in the breeze as he walked in our direction.

The vampire had seen us, and he was coming. Fast.

CHAPTER 21

atilda closed her eyes tightly, held her hands toward the privet, and chanted in a language I didn't recognize.

Jacques and I stood with our backs to her, watching the well-dressed vampire take swift, unfaltering steps down the hill toward us. The gracefulness of his approach made him appear to be walking on air. The half moon was mid-sky, providing enough light to reveal his determined shadow. He carried a sword at his right side.

I pulled stakes from my pockets.

Jacques hand went to his medallion. He gripped it, ready to yank it from his neck. If the situation became necessary for him to change, I feared what the vampire would do to him. Jacques was too weak to hold his own. Transforming to a werewolf at this point would weaken him even more. While the vampire had spared Jacques twice before, it didn't guarantee he would a third time, especially not after we had killed his offspring.

From the way the vampire dressed and how he carried himself, he wished to establish his superiority over others through fear and by flaunting his strength. To effortlessly render a werewolf unconscious twice and not kill the wolf was meant as jeering his dominance while insinuating how weak his werewolf opponent was. Such continuous downplay ignited fury from the underdog, goading him into future attacks, only to stoke the vampire's pompous ego more and more each time the vampire was the victor.

The vampire continued toward us. He flung his left arm forward. His eyes glowed red. He leaped toward me with his mental power, trying to coax and caress my mind, but the tendrils failed to take hold and slipped away. His next wave of energy was filled with rage at my refusal to yield. His intent was to break and maim, but again I resisted.

"Are you making any progress?" Jacques asked.

"Yes," she whispered.

The vampire stopped. He was less than twenty yards away. If he chose, he could cross that distance before I snapped my fingers. He was that old and held such ability. But yet, he lingered from the distance. He was sizing us up.

I lowered the stake in my right hand, dropping it into my pocket. I reached into my pocket and brought out my silver cross. My ears tingled. Invisible feathery wisps glided around my neck and face. Again, he reached subtly but not unnoticed. My jaws tightened, and I thrust at his approaching grasp. Before he withdrew his reach, I placed the silver cross against my right ear. His fingerlike projections recoiled from around my head and retreated. Instead of fleeing into the night like I had hoped, he continued walking toward us.

"Hurry," Matilda said.

Jacques turned, saw the narrow opening that had appeared in the hedge wall, and dove through. Once he was on the other side, I followed, but I was a bit slower due to my size.

"You should have taken my measurements beforehand," I said, staring at Matilda. I grinned. "I'm stuck."

"Sorry," she said.

She grabbed my left arm while Jacques reached around my chest from behind. I pressed my elbows against his arms to brace his hold. He tugged. The vampire sprinted toward us.

"Why can't you weigh what a normal eight-year-old weighs?" Jacques said, straining and pulling. He had me midway through the privet row. Sharp-tipped branches forked all around me, and remarkably they didn't snag my pants or overcoat. Where my body was no longer inside the hedgerow, the branches lengthen and began resealing the gap Matilda had opened.

"The vampire is getting closer," I said.

"I see that." Jacques groaned and pulled.

The vampire rushed to the edge of the closing hole and reached to grab my boots. He howled in pain, yanking back his hands. The sharp tips of the hedges hurled toward him, stabbing into his flesh, drawing blood.

Jacques yanked once more and my feet hit the ground. He eased me down and gulped deep breaths. I rose to my feet with my cross and stake ready. But we faced no battle tonight. The long winding privet branches coiled and struck like snakes, jabbing their pointy dagger tips at the vampire. If he attempted to squeeze through, these branches would stake him to death or distract him with enough significant injuries that we could properly stake or decapitate him.

His attention was on the hedges and not us. It wasn't going to let him pass, and because of its precarious mass of stabbing branches, we weren't able to cross toward him, either. Not that we wanted to. But for added measure, I reached into my inside pocket and retrieved a vial of holy water. I hurled it through the winding privet limbs. The bottle struck one branch and shattered. A showering mist of holy water coated the vampire's face. He growled and wiped his skin with his satin gloves. While he tried to remove the water from his peeling flesh, several sharp hedge tips struck him, forcing him to flee back uphill.

Jacques rested his hands on his knees, trying to catch his breath.

I patted his shoulder. "You still think you could have fought him tonight?"

Jacques shook his head. "Do you carry rocks in your pockets?"

I laughed.

"You've packed on incredible weight. You're padded with thick muscle. It's no wonder you eat like you do."

I shrugged and walked to where Matilda stood examining the privet. Since the vampire had run away, the privet limbs had grown still. "What had appeared to be an impenetrable obstacle turned out to be our ally."

She smiled and nodded.

"Any idea who enchanted it?" I asked.

"No," she replied. "Another witch cast the magical shield on the hedgerow. Apparently someone knows the vampire is there."

"And that witch lives on this side of the fence, trying to ensure the vampire doesn't seek victims in this direction," I said. "We could use another ally."

"Careful," Matilda said. "You need to remember witches prefer solitude and privacy. They won't risk public attention due to the prejudices and the brutal trials of yesteryears. You stand a greater chance of gaining a curse than cooperation."

I nodded.

"Silent allies are often better," Jacques said. "They can aid you without your knowledge. Since vampires can occasionally invade the mind, they can discover your strengths and weaknesses. And while we often believe our friends and allies are our strengths, they can become our greatest weaknesses. You know why."

"Yes. Those closest to us are the ones our enemies seek to destroy first. Striking loss and sorrow devastates and drops our guard," I replied.

"Exactly. Which is why your mentor, Dominus, walks an isolated path."

"That's a hard destiny to maintain." Without wording it, I knew my walk would probably be similar to Dominus'. A part of me had come to accept that. Walking alone as a hunter, I didn't put other people's lives in danger. Just my own.

"It is," Jacques said. He glanced toward Matilda. "And it's another reason why I thought you were safer without me."

Sadness filled Matilda's eyes.

"But I was wrong."

"Before you two get lost in each other's arms again, let's meet with my father. Regardless of Albert sending him a message, he's going to have a fit when we get there."

Jacques sighed. "He will."

I took a few more moments studying the privet. I slid my silver dagger from its sheath on my belt and sliced off a long slender limb. The width of the wood was thicker than my thumb. I tried to bend it but the sturdiness held like steel. Odd. When the hedge was attacking the vampire, branches thicker than this one were as pliable as dough.

I tucked the cut branch inside my coat pocket and joined the others on the dark cobblestone alleyway. We walked past a block of old rundown buildings. Other than the curiosity of rats and a few startled night birds, nothing stirred. But in the distance we heard faint melodies and music. Once we entered the next street, things were a bit different. The music was louder. People stood around burning fires, laughing and sharing stories. Others danced and clapped their hands in time to the music. A man stood on a wooden crate playing a fiddle, differently than I had ever heard before. Women and children smiled and laughed in celebration. It had been the only laughter I had heard in quite a few days.

Unlike the dark streets of Whitechapel, wherever we were now, these people seemed less threatened by the stalking murderer. There was happiness here, even though they were poor like the folks in Whitechapel, but you couldn't see it on their faces or in their actions. In spite of their living conditions, radiance blazed through them greater than any star twinkled on the darkest night. The joyous mood was infectious, lifting heavy hearts, soothing hungry bellies, and drying the tears of the hopelessly downtrodden. The sound was spiritual and almost hypnotic, capturing the listener like a seductive siren.

I found myself drawn in, smiling. With a slight breeze a prickling sensation touched the base of my skull, causing me to stiffen and pulled my attention away from the street festivities. I felt the presence of magic, similar to Matilda's, but dangerously deceptive. I wondered if she sensed it as well. Probably, since she was a witch.

But for fear of drawing the attention of strangers, I didn't dare ask.

Witches often were capable of identifying one another without drawing attention to themselves. As a Hunter, my acute senses alerted me to practitioners, and the more vampires I slayed, the clearer this recognition became. But the worrisome part for what I had just felt was

I had not detected it sooner, before we had gotten this deep into an unknown section of the city.

From the corner of my eye, I watched Matilda, wondering when or if she'd feel what I had. We took a few more steps, and she gasped slightly with an almost muffled sound. She tugged Jacques' arm.

"What is it?" he asked, looking to her.

"We need to leave this area now."

The music, singing, and dancing suddenly stopped, as if the pan's magical flute had broken. All eyes gazed toward us. The cheerfulness faded and was replaced by their disdain. We were intruders.

When we turned to change direction, six men with tattooed faces lined the alley behind us. More men stood behind them with torches. Where they had come from, I had no idea. But with the harshness in their gazes and the crude weapons in their hands, we weren't about to walk or talk our way past them.

CHAPTER 22

*J*acques stood, leaning slightly forward, which I had learned to be his charge stance. Even in human form he was swift and faster than most men. As a werewolf, none of them would ever see him move. That is, if he weren't already exhausted from his earlier fight.

I pulled my dagger since it was the best weapon I had against humans.

"What do you want?"

"That's a question reserved for you to answer," the tanned skin man replied.

He gripped a piece of heavy metal. The top end had been flattened and sharpened. It had a longer reach than my dagger.

"We're heading to Whitechapel," I replied.

The man shook his head. "I don't think so."

I tipped my hat back slightly and frowned. "And why not?"

"Because you reek of blood and magic," a woman said from behind us.

I turned slightly so I could see her while keeping an eye on the human roadblock. She was an older woman with golden rings on most of her fingers. She wore gold bracelets. Her silver hair was bunted and covered with a black cloth pinned by a gold pendant. Her skin was dark and her accent thick. She was what Father, Jacques, and I were continually called. A Gypsy.

"Blood has been shed this evening. It drifts on the night air. It permeates from you," she said, pointing at me.

"I have killed no one," I replied.

She frowned, studying me. Her eyes softened but her face contorted with confusion. "You tell the truth, but why does the smell of blood linger on you?"

I thought about Albert and his blood-covered hands. It was possible that he might have inadvertently touched me. But I couldn't reveal that without exposing Albert. Residing underground was bad enough without the added interruptions of curious people that might seek to find him.

"I don't know," I replied. "But if you wish, you're welcome to search me for blood?"

Two of the men with weapons stepped forward but she sternly shook her head. "No. A respectable man should be taken at his word."

I nodded slightly. "I'm sorry for our intrusion. We were passing through and stopped to enjoy your street celebration."

She smiled and motioned toward the musicians. "My apologies for disrupting your music. Please continue and entertain our new guests."

The man with the violin grinned and returned to playing. The men with the torches and crude weapons disbanded and went separate directions. The older woman descended the steps to stand with us. Energy pulsed off her. She looked at us. A slight smile curled her lips. "You explained the blood, but you've yet to divulge the magic that flows around you. You came from the derelict workhouse. Without magic you could never have passed to this side of our streets."

I crossed my arms and looked into her dark eyes. "You know of the animated hedgerow?"

Her brow rose. She became uneasy. "Animated?"

I nodded.

She took a step back and pulled a gold cross from her skirt pocket. We all stared at her cross for a moment. She expected more of a reaction from us apparently. I slid my cross out for her to see. Her apprehension lessened.

"Since we are armed against the same foes, may we talk in private?" I asked.

Her eyes flicked to each of ours. She lowered the cross and nodded. "This way."

She walked up the steps, slid a wooden door aside, and extended a hand to usher us inside. A small round table covered with a purple silk cloth stood in one corner. Like Rose, she had a crystal ball resting upon a black pillow. An oil lantern, set at low flame, offered the only light. Long chains of garlic hung all around the room. So much that it almost quashed the scent of her incense.

She pointed to several empty chairs. "Please, sit down."

Jacques and Matilda found seats, but I remained standing. Her chairs didn't look sturdy enough to support me.

"My name is Esmeralda," she said softly in her thick accent. "The spell on the hedges is one of mine. If they became animated, a vampire must have been nearby."

"He came after us," I replied.

"It is as I feared." Her eyes widened.

"What is?" Jacques asked.

"The vampire. He came from our old country." She sat at her table and placed nervous hands atop her Tarot cards.

I stepped closer. "Romania?"

Esmeralda nodded.

I pointed at Jacques and back to myself. "We are from Bucharest."

She offered a kind smile. "I had hoped we had lost him when we had fled, but his pursuit has been . . . merciless."

"He's after you?" Matilda asked.

"All of us. My family. Our people."

"Why?"

Esmeralda folded her veiny hands in a prayer-like manner and rested her forehead against them, staring at the table. "He was a charming man, pleasant and kind. You never wanted to look away from his beautiful blue eyes, which were a brilliant sky-blue. His voice, smooth as the finest silk, was a rich baritone. He made you want to be around him, just to hear him talk. His gentle whisper weakened a woman. Often the women, myself included, found ourselves desiring to be his. We fought for his attention and affections, but he didn't desire any of us, except one. He had chosen my brother's daughter, Fifika, to become his bride. Not knowing what he was, we gave our blessing without question. None of us could have denied him if we had wanted, in spite of our secret jealousies."

I frowned. "He gave you no reason to be suspicious of him?"

"No. After all, he was a wealthy man and could offer her prosperous life. Something no Roma male could ever give her."

Matilda straightened in her chair. "Did Fifika seem excited about marrying him?"

Esmeralda sat silently for a few moments. "Eager? Not really. Calm and obedient, more so than the jubilance most young girls have for marriage."

I glanced toward Jacques. "Compelled?"

He shrugged. "Possibly."

"When did you discover he was not what you thought?" I asked.

"Months later, when Fifika returned to visit us one night. She looked different. Very pale. Dark circles under her eyes. We worried that she wasn't taking proper care of herself. We were eating supper, but she'd have nothing. She refused to eat, which became a bitter argument between her, her father, and her mother. Before she married, they had never argued. Always got along. But the fierceness of her words was more than her mother could take. In tears, her mother stormed from the table. Angered, my father stood and scolded Fifika. That's when we discovered Fifika had become something else. She was a bloodthirsty demon of darkness. Forever cursed. She attacked my father, trying to bite his throat. Two of her teeth had lengthened like a wolf's. Frightened, my brother and I pulled her off. She tried to bite me but her face pressed against my cross."

"It hurt her, didn't it?" I asked.

She nodded. "Burnt into her flesh. She screamed. My brother noticed and grabbed our crucifix off the wall. He walked her into a corner where she dropped. Balled up on the floor, covering her face with her arms, she begged and pleaded for him to let her leave. She sounded pathetic, like a crying child. Several times he lowered the crucifix with agony in his eyes. She was his daughter. He loved her. He wanted to hold and comfort her. But each time he lowered the crucifix, her face contorted like an enraged trapped animal, and she snarled at us."

"Did you ever release her?" I asked.

Esmeralda shook her head. Her prayer-cupped hands trembled. "No. We held crosses toward her. Father kept his rifle aimed at her. Other family members joined us, holding their crosses and bibles. We had never seen anything like her. We didn't know what she had become. Since she feared the crucifixes, we had hoped the crosses could excise the demon inside her, but we were wrong. Despite her pleading, we kept her pinned against the wall until morning, planning to take her to the priest. Using the crosses we forced her outside. When she stepped into the sunlight, she burst into flames and turned to dust."

"And what of her husband?" Jacques asked.

She lowered her hands and gazed at us. "We fled. We did not wait around for him. A passerby had seen her burst into flames and told us what she had become. He said that these vampires come during the night and cannot set foot in the sunlight. He said that he hunted vampires and explained to us the different ways to kill them. But if the vampire learned we had killed her, even accidentally, we knew he'd kill us without prosecution. He held too much influence in the area to fear any punishment for killing us. We packed our caravan and left our temporary cottage behind, never looking back. We didn't stop for three days and nights, trying to put as much distance between us and him as possible."

"What prompted you to seek a priest?" I asked. "Before she burst into flames? Are you a Christian? Most Gypsies don't accept organized religions."

Esmeralda gazed into my eyes. Her tone became solemn. "Christian? No. You mentioned that you're from Bucharest, then you know the dilemma. You must choose a side, Christian or Muslim, if you wish to survive."

I nodded. What she said was true. Swear allegiance to one side or the other; otherwise both sides labeled the person an infidel and sought to kill him or her.

"The religious war continues," she said. "But, understand, I've never abandoned my old traditions or my use of magic and charms. None of my family ever has. If the cross had not burned Fifika, I'd have never known to use one. I would have tried numerous spells to try to heal her."

"And died during the process," I said.

She nodded. "You're right. I knew no magic that could have killed a vampire."

"You do now?" Matilda asked.

A prideful smile brightened Esmeralda's face. "Yes. You saw the hedge?"

Matilda smiled.

"If ever the branches gripped and pulled him into the hedges, they'd eventually stake him through his heart, but he'd suffer severe painful cuts first. He needs to bleed for the harm he's caused others. For the murders of our children."

"What is his name?" I asked.

"Duke Raginwulf."

Jacques and I exchanged glances and shrugged.

"His name is not known in these parts," Esmeralda said. "Except for all of those celebrating outside. We know and fear him."

"Even with your magic?"

She nodded. "Even with it."

"What he did to your niece," I said, "he's doing to others in Whitechapel. We killed four vampires near the old workhouse. He's building an army and plans to shed a lot of blood in London. Tell me something."

"If I can. What is it you need to know?"

"How'd you know to enchant that particular line of hedges?"

"That's not the only place I've enchanted. Where we sit is dead center of our community. I've placed protection spells at all four corners to repel him. We are safe as long as we stay within those barriers or no one destroys them." She glanced at Matilda and smiled. "But you broke through the barrier. You're a witch, aren't you?"

Matilda nervously looked toward Jacques and I before nodding.

"There's more to you than just magic. I sense it, but I do not understand what it is. Something dark, but not evil."

Jacques tensed.

"And you, too," Esmeralda said, pointing toward him. "The blood. It's on both of you."

"The vampires we killed," I said.

Esmeralda glanced toward me. "You killed four vampires?"

"The three of us did together," I replied.

"I see. But it's something else." Her eyes fastened upon their medallions.

"Magical amulets?"

Matilda reluctantly nodded.

"Your magic?"

"Yes."

"For what purpose?"

Matilda was at a loss to speak, so I interrupted the conversation. "What do you know of this duke, other than what you've told us? Why would he pursue you across so many countries? You even expected that he would. There has to be a reason. A duke would not abandon his prominence under ordinary circumstances. It'd be a waste of his resources and his time. What have you not told us?"

Esmeralda shook her head.

"We've been hunting this vampire for over a week," I said. "We plan to kill him when we find him. But he's quite elusive. It might be weeks more before we're able to track him down. He's siring more vampires, and if he's determined to kill all of you, he'll have the numbers to do so. We can help you, but only if you tell us what more you know."

Tears brimmed in her eyes. "I'm sorry, but there's nothing more I can say."

I nodded toward Jacques. "Then cousin, it's time we move on."

"Agreed," he said.

I tipped my hat to Esmeralda. "Blessings to you and yours. Until we meet again."

Fear mixed with sadness claimed her facial features. She looked like she might request us to stay longer so she could reveal what she held secret, but she didn't. So we left her alone and headed into the darkening night.

CHAPTER 23

We left the Gypsy community and returned to our room. Father was already in the room. I had expected him to be angry and withdrawn. Instead I found him drunk and disoriented.

"Tish good, you found your ways back," he said with a strange grin. He squinted, trying to see us. "Any luck?"

I took a deep breath and sighed. My heart ached from the disappointment of seeing him drunk again. I placed a gentle hand on his shoulder. "Father, you should get some sleep."

"Hands off me, boy!" He turned toward me with his hand held high. "Don't think you're too big! I'm still your Father."

"John," Jacques said.

"Not you, too! You're all grand now, having yourself a woman. Why I has lost me own." He staggered and hiccupped. "If there be God-s-s-s, none bless me. I've been cursed."

"You know that's not true," I said.

"Forrest, let him be," Jacques whispered, shaking his head.

"You, boy!" Father said, pointing a stern finger into my chest and pressing hard. "Think you're a man, do you? Trying to outdo your old man at every turn. Out kill my number of vampires, eh, makes you superior over me? Oh, you be such big Hunter! One of the Chosen."

"And you're a foolish old drunk," I replied.

His eyes widened. "What did you say?"

"You heard me, Father. Drinking hasn't made you deaf, but it sure has made your tongue bigger and spouting stupid things and hurling nonsense insults. That's what good drunkenness is, Father. You know why? Because you're a coward."

His face flushed red and snapped his anger. "What?"

"A coward. You're not man enough to face your fears and your heartache, so you drown yourself in liquor, like a sniffling little coward."

"Forrest," Jacques said, walking toward me.

"No," Father said, stepping back and pointing at Jacques. "Let the boy talk, cause he's going to see how hard this old man can strike him in the mouth."

"Do you realize how disappointed Momma would be to see you like this? Your weakness? How do you think she'd feel about it?"

"Boy, I'm about to—"

"What? Hit me? Do you think that would make Momma proud? If you think it would make you feel better, then go ahead. But on your soberest day, you're no match for me. Not anymore. You need to remember that."

Father's face flushed crimson. His jaw tightened, and he ground his teeth. His chest expanded and his hands formed tight fists. He eyed me up and down but wisely kept his distance. "You should respect your father more than this."

"You should respect yourself enough to keep your promise to me. You said you'd stop drinking. That was a promise. I had thought you meant it. How well are you honoring Momma by getting drunk?"

He turned away and sat on the edge of the bed. His anger subsided into tears. He placed his hands over his face and sobbed.

In a lot of ways I hated myself for saying those things but if the truth didn't get his attention, nothing else would. I grabbed several stakes out of my box and headed to the door.

"Forrest," Jacques said. "Now is not a time to be on the streets alone."

I nodded with my eyes toward my father. "It's better than being in here."

"Wait—"

I yanked the door open, stepped out, and pulled it firmly shut. Jacques scolded my father, but Father never offered any rebuttal. I hurried to the door that led out to the street.

The night air was crisp when I stepped outside the inn. It was difficult to drive Father's angry face and voice out of my head, but I forced myself to think about the vampire. A duke. Vampires were able use their glamour to bewitch people under their influence and take prominent roles in society. It was quite frightening really. I questioned the number of rulers in the world that might be vampires, capable of controlling entire populations, and convincing their citizens to obey their every command.

A vampire czar never needed to fear a blood shortage. A ruler of this nature controlled armies to protect him or her. He had no need to travel. He certainly didn't have any reason to pursue an escaped enemy himself. He'd send mercenaries to carry out the assassination.

That's what puzzled me about this duke. Why had he journeyed so far? Doing so had exposed him. He probably had never expected a group of Hunters to seek him out. He had come for Esmeralda's people or possibly only her. But why?

She knew, but she had refused to tell us. She knew the secret to this mystery and apparently was willing to die to keep it hidden.

I kept walking. I did my best thinking while walking or seated in a wagon or aboard a train. I supposed moving released nervous energy because I never maintained steady concentration whenever I was seated at a table or desk.

Ahead, a man stood beneath a street light about half a block away. He leaned nonchalantly against the metal pole, smoking a pipe. He wore a nice brown suit and hat and fancy shoes, but held no cane, nor did he wear a cape as the vampire had earlier in the night.

His eyes regarded me in passing, but he offered no words. No greeting at all. I walked another few feet before casually glancing back over my shoulder.

He was gone.

Like that. In the time of a few heartbeats, he had vanished.

I stopped and circled in place, searching for him within the faint circle of light. His hard-soled shoes had never made a sound. I could tiptoe in my boots and still make loud steps on the cobblestone.

I gripped a stake and headed toward the light where he had stood.

Had my eyes deceived me? Was he a ghost? I found no trace of him.

My mind thought back to the hedgerow and its vicious attack on the vampire. Those narrow sharpened branch tips had inflicted some damage. Nothing fatal for a vampire, but enough that he needed to heal. And with the damage I had caused with the vial of holy water, he'd seek fresh blood to replenish him. Healing drained his energy.

The more I thought about that, the less I believed I'd encounter him tonight, so who was this stranger? Perhaps I was wrong. The duke might not be acting alone or other vampires had emerged because the duke had infringed on their territory. That was another thing I had learned about vampires in my short time as a Hunter. Vampires were territorial.

This, too, backed my theory concerning the duke's pursuit of Esmeralda.

Something was amiss.

If I could discover what she was hiding, we could draw him into a trap and slay him.

I stood beneath the streetlamp for a couple of minutes longer. Frustrated, I glanced toward the next lamp a block or so away. The man with the pipe leaned against that pole, watching me. No mortal moved so silently into the shadows and reappeared without making some sort of sound.

He raised his head with a taunting grin. A puff of smoke drifted from the side of his mouth. He held no weapon, but his eyes made his threat. He offered a challenge, if nothing less than the meeting of our minds.

With stake in hand, I headed in his direction. My boots thudded heavily against the cobblestone and determination tightened my jaw. The street seemed empty except for he and I, but that wasn't a guarantee that we were alone. My steady march toward him turned into a sudden sprint. I wanted to reach him before he decided to bolt again. But with my handicap of being awkward and clumsy, I had yet to develop accurate speed for my height and weight. I was getting better at running, but I'd never possess the agility and gracefulness that Jacques had whenever he ran.

His smile widened as I approached. I was about ten feet from the lamppost when he disappeared again. A growl of frustration escaped my mouth. I skidded to a stop, using the lamppost for leverage to keep from toppling forward. I glanced around, and he stood in the center of the street.

"You're a Hunter?" he asked, staring at the stake in my hand.

"I am."

"The vampire you seek isn't me."

"I'm not partial when it comes to slaying vampires," I replied.

He frowned, taking the pipe from his mouth. He tapped it against the bottom of his shoe before tucking it inside his vest pocket. "You regard me as your enemy? Even though *he's* the intruder murdering innocent people in our streets?"

"You are undead, which makes you an enemy to all mankind. You are what I was chosen to eliminate from this world."

"So we cannot work together to kill this intruder?" he asked.

I shook my head. "I'll deal with him afterwards."

He laughed.

"I'm glad to see you can have humor minutes before your final death."

"So regardless of my contributions to rid this community of their stalker, you'd ignore that simply because I'm undead?" he asked.

I shrugged. "It doesn't make you any less undead, does it?"

His eyes looked at my stake and then flicked to my cold hard gaze. "That makes you a monster, too."

"With the tasks I have been burdened to fulfill, becoming a monster is inevitable."

"Everything is black and white with you?"

"There is no gray area when it comes to protecting humanity."

"Humanity is filled with as many evil people as good. Perhaps even more."

"Perhaps, but it isn't my duty to eradicate them. I am not their judge, but I am your executioner."

Frustration set in his gaze. "I've performed no grievances against you, Hunter. Becoming what I am was not my choosing. I didn't seek this. So, why must I be slain?"

His energy crept slowly toward me. Even though it was invisible, I sensed its movement like thin tendrils meandering in my direction, reaching, trying to seek any weakness I had.

"Why? Because of your power and what you're attempting right now. While your glamour and control won't work on me, you're capable of seducing weaker people into becoming what you are. It's an urge you cannot control. No vampire can. Left unchecked you'll do to others what has been done to you. That's why you must be removed."

"I've never killed a Hunter before," he said. His fangs suddenly became visible. His eyes turned black. "But I understand the thrill of the fight is greater than the fulfilled bloodlust of feasting on the blood of virgins."

"Few vampires have ever experienced killing a Hunter."

He hissed. "Arrogance and misjudgment have allowed the deaths of many Hunters, fool. Yours shall be a painfully slow one."

I had been foolish, considering how swift he could move. I didn't know how old he was, but I suspected he was strong.

He moved, as I feared, without me noticing that he had. The palm of his hand struck the center of my chest with such force I was lofted into the air. I crashed on the other side of the lamppost, flattening a thorny bush. Sharp thorns dug into my thick overcoat but luckily didn't penetrate through the material. But the broken branches still stabbed at my flesh.

I rolled, tightening my hand around the stake, and pushed myself to my feet. I turned slightly, glancing in each direction, hoping to find him. I didn't see him.

"Come now, Hunter. I expected a greater challenge than this."

I glanced in the direction of the voice but was struck across my back from behind. The impact jarred me, knocking the air from my lungs, and I toppled face first, catching myself inches above the cobblestone. My stake bounced across the street.

"And to think you believe you have the necessary skill and strength to kill the intruding vampire? I'm at least a hundred years younger than he, and you can't hold your ground against me."

He stood a few feet in front of me, barely outside my reach. I prepared to push myself forward to grab his leg, but he stepped to the side and spun. His hard shoe caught my jaw and slung my head to the side. Had I been a smaller man, he'd have snapped my neck. I rolled onto my back and groaned.

Pain radiated through my head. When I opened my eyes and looked around, everything spun and blurred. He peered down at me with a condescending smile. For a few seconds, it was a rotating set of smiles.

"You disappoint me, Hunter. I truly expected more of a challenge." He grabbed the lapels of my overcoat, yanked, and held me overtop his head. With little effort he tossed me toward the thorny shrub again.

I landed on my back with a hard thud. My entire body pulsed with pain. It hurt too badly to even attempt to get up. An instant later he stood over me. I groaned and shook my head.

He leaned down and struck my face with his fist. Blood leaked from my nose. He hit me again. He noticed the blood running down the side of my face, ran his finger through it, and sucked the blood off his finger. His eyes closed, and he took a deep breath as his body shuddered. "Ah, a Hunter's blood. Yes. There is definitely a difference. The rumors were truth, not old wives' tales. I need more."

After running his fingers across the trail of blood, he quickly stuck them into his mouth. His eyes darkened.

I reached into my coat pocket until my fingers touched a stake. I slid it from my pockets. "Didn't anyone ever tell you not to play with your food?"

He craned his neck, looking at me with curiosity. I drove the stake through his left foot. A high-pitched wail escaped his mouth. In his attempt to yank out the stake, he toppled to the side, placing his weight on his right foot. I shoved him, knocking him off balance. He fell to the cobblestone.

Despite my pain, I pushed myself to my hands and knees. His attention remained focused on the stake. It was causing him more pain than it should have, and it was then when I realized that one of my bottles of garlic juice had broken in my pocket and coated the stake.

I slowly rose to my feet and reached into my pocket. While the stake might not kill him, I didn't expect he'd have the speed he had had earlier. A large hole through the foot should slow anyone down, mortal or vampire.

"What was that you said about being overconfident?" I asked, taking a bottle of holy water from my pocket and uncorking it.

He snarled and yanked the stake from his foot. Before he could stand I flung the holy water into his face. Steam rose from his skin. The water melted his flesh like acid. He bolted at me, striking my face with left and right hooks, so fast I was unable to block them. He struck again and again. I was losing consciousness and knew if I did, he'd drain my blood. Feasting on me would be the quickest way for him to heal.

I brought up my arms and crossed them in front of my face, preventing him from getting any more headshots. But his pain had turned into heated aggression. He intended to keep his promise about making me suffer before he killed me.

My face, especially around my eyes, swelled. Seeing became difficult. He punched my gut hard, expelling the air from my lungs. I dropped and rolled to my side, trying to breathe, and trying to avoid further pain.

"It's time you die," he hissed. He grabbed my coat and yanked. Instead of pulling me up, he ripped my pocket open.

My silver cross clanged on the cobblestone and bounced. He stepped back. I wanted to grab the cross, but I was too weak and too slow to reach it. My eyes barely had slits wide enough to see through. Next to the cross were two stakes and a couple of vials. But in my battered condition, I didn't have any hope of retrieving them.

The vampire touched his blistered face and winced. "It's a shame you never took my offer, Hunter. You would have made a great distraction for the other vampire, making it easier for me to kill him. You didn't need to die today. Perhaps you'd have fared better by aligning yourself with me, instead of classifying me as your enemy."

I laughed and tasted blood. "To the contrary, you're every bit as evil as any other vampire. My injuries testify to that."

"That was to *your* choosing." He took a step closer, avoiding the cross.

I tried to widen my eyes to see. A watery film coated my vision and blurred the images around me. I reached toward the stakes, but even stretched all the way out, they were too far away. He laughed softly, taking another step. One of the stakes quivered on the ground.

He glanced down, noticing the movement at the same time I had. The stake pivoted back and forth, building momentum.

"Is this your doing, Hunter?" he asked.

I shook my head slightly and gritted my teeth. "No."

His curiosity drew him closer to the quivering stake. Like a magnet drawn to steel, the stake hurled itself through the air and struck the vampire directly through the heart. His eyes widened, glancing toward me. "How?"

Before I could reply, he collapsed to the street in a pile of ash. I stared in disbelief. I lowered my head, panting. My head ached. So did my chest and face. He had battered me quite severely. I crawled until I reached the cross and slid it inside my massive hand. I rested my head against the cold wet cobblestones and closed my eyes. Blood leaked from my nose and mouth, forming a small pool. Even though I lay still, the world seemed to be spinning. The coolness of the cobblestone felt good against my cheek. I hurt too much to even open my eyes. But I couldn't stay exposed on the street. If the duke happened upon me, I stood no hope of seeing the morning.

I forced myself to crawl. I got my vials and the stake that had spilled from my ripped pocket. As I crawled to the vampire ash, I wondered who had come to my aid, firing the stake into the vampire's heart. A witch?

I pulled the stake from the ash and realized it wasn't one of my stakes. It was the cutting I had taken from the enchanted hedge. Even separated from the hedgerow, the branch sought to kill any vampire that came close enough to it.

That was indeed a powerful spell.

I examined the pointy branch beneath the streetlamp. The first thing that came to my mind was Dominus and his crossbow. I thought about how essential a quiver of arrows carved from those enchanted limbs could be for a Hunter. No greater accuracy could ever be achieved, especially since the cutting had turned itself into a projectile and killed a vampire that would have certainly killed me. I had not willed it. It had acted upon the spell cast upon it.

Wincing, I pushed myself into a seated position. Pain pulsed throughout my body. I slowly stood and staggered to a bench. I sat down with an exhausted sigh. I wiped blood from my face. My lips were cut and swollen.

I stared at the vampire's pile of ash and felt cheated. While I was thankful he was dead, he had inflicted an incredible beating on me. I had done little damage in return. He had vigorously set out to keep his promise of hurting me before he killed me. The stake had intervened, and had it not I'd be dead. The stake had won the battle. The vampire had lost, but in a way, so had I, at least physically. I fully understood Jacques' resentment toward the duke now.

I couldn't believe the vampire's impudence in asking my help to kill the duke. I could never see myself becoming the ally of a vampire, regardless of the stakes, no pun intended. The duke was a master, much stronger than the unknown vampire that had just died. Not knowing his name troubled me. I didn't know his history, other than the few tidbits he had offered, nor did I know his true status and what vampires he was in league with.

Although he had incredible speed and strength, I didn't believe he was a master. But I did fear that he might not be alone. That troubled me because I wasn't in any condition to fight. I was halfway certain that he was alone since no other vampire had emerged, but I wasn't taking any further risks. I needed to get back to the room while I could still partially see.

I rose to my feet. I was only a couple of blocks from the inn.

Breathing was difficult. I took a cloth from my inside pocket and blew my nose. Thick blood clots filled the cloth, undamming loose blood behind them. My nose was bleeding again. I held the cloth to my nose while I staggered down the center of the street. I walked faster. My blood was certain to attract any vampire within the vicinity.

Every few steps I glanced over my shoulder. Even though my vision was limited, I was relieved that no one was following me. I reached the inn, walked to the side hall door, and pulled it open. In less than a minute I'd be at our door.

CHAPTER 24

I knocked at the door.

Jacques peered out and then opened it wide. He reached for me with both hands. "Forrest? What happened?"

Matilda hurried to the door and covered her mouth.

Jacques gripped my elbow and helped me to the side of the bed. I plopped down and the bedsprings creaked. "Who did this? The duke? Did you encounter him?"

I shook my head slightly, immediately regretting it. "No."

I lowered the cloth from my nose. The bleeding had at least stopped. My pains had not.

"Who did it?"

"Another vampire," I replied.

"You took a severe beating," Jacques said.

"I'm quite aware of that."

He looked disappointed in me. "You need to hit back."

"He was too fast. There was no blur. I never saw him move."

"Did you slay him?"

"He's dead."

Matilda brought a small pouch with different salves and teas.

Jacques touched my bruised face, which was hot and swelling. "Is he one of the duke's offspring?"

"No. In fact he offered his assistance to kill the duke."

"Doesn't seem you two could work out an agreement?"

"Should we have?" I asked.

Jacques hesitated in replying. "He made a proposal?"

"Not a good one. He's dead. Those were my terms, so I suppose it worked out."

Jacques shook his head. "You're fortunate to be alive, Forrest."

"I realize that. I refuse to join forces with a vampire even if we have a common enemy. How would you view such a coalition?"

"I agree, but you're still not experienced enough as a Hunter to try to kill them all. Not by yourself."

"He was stronger than I credited him to be."

"The undead cannot be judged by their appearance. Some wield incredible strength even when they have small thin statures. Never underestimate them."

I nodded.

"Your face is bruised pretty badly. I'd say in the morning you won't be able to open your eyes. Maybe not even for a few days."

"Where's Father?"

"Asleep. I had quite a few choice words for him and his behavior. I'm sorry that you had to find him that way when we got back."

"It's not your fault. It's his own."

"While that may be, I know he loves you," Jacques said, softly. He helped me out of the overcoat. I unbuttoned my shirt. "Damn."

"What?" I asked, looking down but not seeing anything clearly.

He placed his hand against my ribcage. I winced.

"You're solid muscle, Forrest, which is probably why you survived this fight. Your overall strength is greater than even you acknowledge. Being a Hunter, you have great agility and speed capable of thwarting attacks like you just endured. You're not invincible, but you could have prevented most of this damage. Don't think because you're huge that you are slow. You aren't. Never hold back or limit yourself."

He pressed slightly beneath my muscled chest. I grunted.

"You're bruised deeply, Forrest. A few of your ribs might be broken. He really wanted to hurt you."

"I believe he succeeded in doing that."

"What prompted such rage in him?"

"I told you. He was offended that I viewed him as a monster and for not seeing him for something different."

"Like what?"

"How good he was inside." My bloody cracked lips formed a crude grin.

Jacques laughed. "That's a common argument you'll hear vampires use. We're supposed to ignore their murders and feedings because they have contributed other charities to the city or township, but their evil outweighs any kindnesses they could ever bestow. But as badly as he assaulted you, how did you ever manage a killing blow?"

"I didn't."

His eyes narrowed from his curiosity. "Who did?"

I slid the wooden limb from my pocket. "This. I cut this from the hedgerow. It somehow flung itself off the ground and struck the vampire dead center in the heart, killing him."

Jacques held the branch in his hand and studied it. "So even though it's no longer connected to the hedge, her spell remains?"

I nodded. "It saved my life."

"Incredible. Who was the vampire it killed?"

"I never got a name."

"Interesting," Jacques replied.

"What?"

"Usually a vampire will boast his name well before he attacks. It's part of their conceit."

I squinted, trying to see more than a blurry image of Jacques. Viscous hot tears leaked down my cheeks. "He has nothing left to boast of now."

"The fact that he asked you to help him kill the duke is important information," Jacques said.

"Why?"

"Well, for one, it means that the duke is not from this region, as we had theorized. And the duke must have been a powerful foe for this vampire to seek assistance."

I frowned but still couldn't see. "Why's that?"

"Judging by the injuries you've sustained from the vampire, he viewed the duke as a bigger threat than himself, which means no more roaming the streets alone. The duke is more powerful than the one that the enchanted branch killed. He was fast enough to hit me before I have a chance to defend myself."

"He's been toying with you," I replied.

Jacques' jaw tightened. "It's only made me madder, but I'm not a match for him alone. We had nine together the other night, trying to overpower him, and he still got away."

"How many will it take?"

Jacques shook his head. "I don't know, Forrest. It took quite a few of us to destroy Baron Randolph, but we had him cornered."

"And Bodi betrayed him."

Jacques smiled. "His friendship with you was stronger than the promises the baron had made to him."

My head throbbed relentlessly. Even though my eyes were closed the room spun, causing my stomach to twist with nausea. "Help me lie back. I don't feel so well."

Jacques wrapped his hand around the side of my biceps, placed his other hand at the center of my back, and lowered me onto the bed. I sank into the feathered mattress and the bedsprings creaked beneath my full weight.

Matilda stepped beside the bed and explained what herbal remedies she thought could be help me recover, but her voice seemed so far away. I fought sleep but felt like I was endlessly falling. Their voices vanished. The bed didn't exist. All my pains disappeared as darkness surrounded and engulfed me.

CHAPTER 25

When I awakened and first opened my eyes, everything was blurred. I blinked hard several times, forcing thick tears from my eyes. Things became less blurry. I reached up and touched the sides of my face, wincing slightly.

The swelling was gone but my skin remained tender to touch. Turning slightly I noticed Jacques and Matilda were asleep on the other bed. His arms were wrapped around her. Both slept with smiles on their faces.

From the faint brightness spilling through the window, it was first light. Roosters crowed in the distance. Sparrows sang from the vents of eaves and the rooftops.

I pushed myself up and hung my feet over the side of the bed. The bedsprings protested my movements but didn't awaken Matilda or Jacques.

A pungent odor made me gasp. Tied around my ribcage was a wet bag of herbs and ointment that smelled like a dead animal. I untied the bandage and slid the smelly poultice off my body.

My stomach protested its hunger. The other aches and pains in my body were minimal. The herbs might have helped, but I was also a fast healer.

"You're finally awake," my father whispered in his hoarse voice. He eased forward in the chair where he sat wrapped in a blanket. "You had us worried."

"How long have I been asleep?"

"Four days now."

Shaking my head, I closed my eyes and rubbed my bearded chin.

"How are you feeling, son?"

"Rested but hungry."

"We could go eat breakfast," he said, sliding the blanket off his lap and rising.

"I can wait until they're awake."

"Jacques!" Father said. "Forrest's awake."

"Father, you needn't do that."

Jacques and Matilda jerked and opened their eyes.

Jacques yawned, rubbed his eyes, and rolled out of the bed. He gave a relieved smile to see me sitting up. "How are you faring, Forrest?"

"Pain isn't what I last remember."

"I should hope not," Jacques replied. "A lesser individual would have died. But since you're a Hunter, it looks like you've healed quite well. Matilda made a poultice for you."

I nodded and scrunched my nose. "It's a wonder I didn't have worse nightmares. The smell caught my attention when I awakened."

"It's been hard to breathe in here," Father said softly.

"It has helped him heal," she said, sitting on the edge of the bed. Her eyes narrowed.

"That's a matter for debate," Father replied.

I nodded toward her. "I'm certain it did its purpose."

She smiled, grabbed her clothes, and stepped inside the small changing room. "Thank you, Forrest."

Jacques walked to the washbasin and poured fresh water into it. He glanced at me in the mirror. "You had some bad dreams?"

I shrugged. "They weren't pleasant by any means."

"What were they about?"

"None really made any sense. All of them were about dark places with creatures hiding in the shadows that I never saw, but I knew they were there, waiting for me."

"That occurs sometimes when your body is healing. It's happened to me several times. But you had us worried those first two days. I wondered if you'd survive," Jacques said.

"Why?"

He sighed. "You burned with fever. You sounded like phlegm was building up inside your chest. Occasionally you stopped breathing. I was afraid you were coming down with pneumonia. Sometimes you even cried out in your sleep."

I stood and grabbed one corner post of the bed. "I've really been asleep four days?"

"Yes." Jacques put his face over the basin and washed his face. After a vigorous scrubbing, he patted his face with a towel.

Glancing around the room, I said, "I'm surprised we're still at this inn. We should almost be out of funds, shouldn't we?"

"Interesting thing about that," he said.

Cocking a brow, I said, "What?"

"Remember that the vampire never offered his name?"

"Yes."

Jacques nodded toward my father. "Show him, John."

Father reached under the side of the bed, brought out a leather pouch, and set it on the bed.

"What's that?"

Father grinned. "A reward."

"Reward for what?"

"Killing the vampire."

"Who left it?" I asked.

Jacques and Father shrugged.

"You don't know?"

Jacques shook his head and reached inside the pouch. "No name was left. But a short message was tucked inside. 'For freeing us from Trenton's terror, please accept our thanks.' Three hundred British pounds."

"His name was Trenton?"

"That's really all we can guess from the note, but apparently he had caused quite a bit of problems. For someone to leave such a high reward, when they didn't even have to leave one at all, he must have wreaked havoc for a long time," Jacques replied. "But we won't need to worry about food or lodging for weeks."

Father shook his head. "Let's hope we don't have to wait around that long."

"This means that whoever left the money probably witnessed Trenton's demise," I said.

"I agree."

Father nodded. "At least you know the name of who pummeled you."

"That I do," I said with narrowed eyes.

Jacques slid his arms into his shirtsleeves and slowly buttoned the shirt. "Shields has been by the past three days to check on you."

"Any news on the duke?" I asked.

Jacques shook his head. "No. Nothing new."

"You've not found any evidence while I was asleep?"

"We've not gone out during the night, Forrest," Jacques replied. "It was best for us to make certain you recovered."

"What did you tell Shields about my condition?" I asked.

"The truth," Father said.

"About the vampire?"

Jacques nodded.

"Why?"

"He already knows our purpose for being here. Telling him lets him know that Duke Raginwulf isn't the only vampire in London."

"We had already told him of the possibilities," I said.

"Yes, and now he has undeniable proof. It helps him prepare for future situations, so he can decide if he needs to tell other constables about what they might eventually face."

"When a vampire is killed, there's not much proof left behind."

"Shields trusts us."

"Do you think he left the reward?"

Jacques shrugged. "It's possible. But it could have been any wealthy individual who had suffered loss to Trenton."

"It could be the duke," I said.

Jacques gave me an odd stare. "What makes you think that?"

"Trenton was trying to get me to help kill the duke, remember?"

Jacques chuckled.

"What?" I asked.

"Vampires hiring bounty hunters to kill their competition. That's a market I had never anticipated."

"Me, either, but you have to admit, it's not totally out of the question," I said. "The one hiring an assassin can hide in the shadows until his enemies are dead, thus expanding his territory."

"Vampires are secretive and trust a selective few, if anyone at all. They have opposing hierarchies like werewolves do. Since they're territorial, most won't intrude upon another leader's ambit. Duke Raginwulf has encroached upon every vampire, human, and werewolf hierarchy within London. His presence is drawing out all of his unknown enemies. He's greatly outnumbered. He's a fool for being here. When they find him, they will kill him."

"He has a reason for coming to London. I don't think it was to invade other vampire territories. Perhaps he hadn't considered those risks before he arrived, but he seems to be pursuing a sole purpose."

"Like what exactly?" Jacques asked.

"That's what I want to know. Have you visited Esmeralda again?"

Jacques frowned. "No. Why would we do that? She refused to offer us further information."

"I think Raginwulf is in London specifically because of her."

"What makes you think that?"

"I've not figured it out yet, but why would a master vampire with his wealth pursue her family?" I asked. "She told us her story, but how much of it is true? What did she *not* tell us? What is she lying about?"

"She might not be lying about anything," Matilda said, walking back into the room. "But I do agree with you that she's hiding something."

I grabbed my boots and sat in a chair. While putting them on, I glanced at Jacques. "After we eat, I think we should pay her community a visit during the daylight hours this time."

"That's a long walk," Jacques said. "Do you feel up to it?"

I glanced into the mirror. "Other than the fading bruises, I feel much better than I look."

"What do you expect to find?"

"I don't know. Something in my spirit is prompting me that we will find some answers to this puzzle there. We might discover useful evidence, but we also need to pay careful attention to how everyone acts. If good fortune sides with us, we might gain vital information to aid us in killing Duke Raginwulf. Like you've hinted many times, we are going to need a lot of allies to join together against the duke to be successful."

"No argument here," Jacques replied.

"Then let's get going."

CHAPTER 26

I overindulged at breakfast, eating three times more than normal, but after not eating for four days, I figured my body had some catching up to do. My body had healed rapidly in spite of being deprived of food. Not only did my ravenous appetite capture the attention of the wait staff, the cook, and all the patrons inside the dining room, even my family members stared at me with slightly disturbed expressions on their faces. But my urge to eat controlled me. I couldn't satiate the need.

After I had finished eating the pound of steak, a half-pound of potatoes, a quarter block of sharp cheddar, and a whole rye loaf, we left the dining house. I expected my stomach to become bloated but it didn't. My senses were keener, my muscles swelled thicker, and energy pulsed through me. I had never known such vigor.

Jacques clasped my shoulder, shook his head, and grinned. "That was eventful, cousin."

I blushed with a slight smile.

"It's a good thing you earned a hefty reward for killing that vampire, Forrest. Otherwise, we'd all be sleeping on the street tonight," he said. "Your meal cost what all of ours did together."

"Let him be. His body needs sustenance," Matilda said softly. "He's healing."

Jacques nodded. "I realize that, but I've never seen anyone eat with such cravings, and *I'm* a werewolf."

Father regarded me with a side-glance as we walked. His eyes widened. "You seem taller and broader."

I laughed softly, shaking my head. "I've been lying down for four days. It's been a few days since you've seen me on my feet."

"He's right," Jacques said. "You're at least two inches taller. Stop. Stand toe to toe with me for a few seconds so we can measure you."

I did as he requested. We stood face to face. I was taller than before. He had to look up slightly.

"You were already gigantic in my mind," Jacques said. "Especially for your tender age. You're not just tall. You have girth. But remember what I told you the other day. Don't think because you're enormous that you're slow. I've never met a Hunter who was not agile. You have incredible strength, but I assure you, you've been gifted with speed, too."

"I've always been a clumsy runner," I replied. "Because of my huge feet."

"Use your size to your advantage. Don't convince yourself that you can't do something or you become your biggest enemy. You might need to practice running but since you're one of the Chosen, you won't have such a handicap."

A soured expression creased Father's face. "He's *not* infallible."

"No one is," Jacques replied. "But I've yet seen a Hunter with his frame and build, which thwarts away any doubt of him *not* being Chosen."

Father cleared his throat to mask his grumbling, but it didn't slip unnoticed by me. I found it odd that he was jealous of his own son. At times I truly wondered if Baron Randolph had not nearly killed my father if I'd have ever learned about my calling. Jacques might have eventually told me, but Father had tried to keep it hidden from me. Perhaps the loss of Momma wasn't the only reason he drank too much. Self-pity might be another reason.

Rather than draw attention to Father's resentment, I strode past him

FORREST WOLLINSKY: BLOOD MISTS OF LONDON

and walked in the center of our group. Most of the traders and produce vendors were setting up their tables under the awnings, but the middle of the cobblestone street remained fairly clear. Since few horses and wagons occupied the street, it allowed us to walk faster. It didn't take long for us to get a half block ahead of Father. Matilda lingered behind with him, so he didn't walk alone. She hated to see him alone and regarded him like a daughter would a father.

Once he was out of hearing distance I glanced toward Jacques. "Did Father get drunk during the four days I slept?"

He shook his head. "No. In fact, he never left your bedside other than to do nature's bidding. He was genuinely concerned about you. A few times I awoke during each night to find him on his knees at the side of your bed praying. As badly as his legs ache, Forrest, you can imagine what kind of suffering he did to perform such a task."

I nodded and felt partially ashamed for thinking he'd have slipped off to drink again.

"That surprises you?" Jacques asked.

"It does."

"It shouldn't."

"For a long time he's acted offended that I was chosen to be a real Hunter. He gets resentful of any success I've had slaying vampires. I can see it in his face and hear it in his voice."

Jacques smiled gently. "Would you like me to tell you about the strife that often occurs between sons and fathers?"

"Sure."

"Most men grow up in the shadows of their fathers constantly berating themselves because they don't measure up to their father's accomplishments. Until their fathers pass away, they cannot become successful. They feel like nothing they do can come close to equaling the success of their fathers. But you, Forrest, you have a different situation altogether."

I frowned. "How's that?"

"Your father believes he can never measure up to what you are. Sadly, though, he's correct. He never will. He knows it. You see, he's conflicted inside. He's truly proud of you and what you are. His resentment isn't toward you, although I'm certain you feel that it is. His contention is with himself. His harbored bitterness is toward whatever power chose you and not him. Since he has no way to lash out at that force or *those forces*, his emotions come out whenever he's around you, though unintended."

"Is there anything I can do to alleviate this?"

Jacques shook his head. "I'm afraid not."

"I'm glad to know he didn't drink while I was sleeping. I hated losing my temper with him the other day. The things I said—"

"Were the truth, Forrest. Never shame yourself for being honest even when the honesty stings. That means with me, your father, or whomever you fall in love with one day. That's not to say you should thrash others with your words. Never do that. Be kind and loving and as understanding as possible, but always be honest if what the person is doing is self-destructive or causing harm to others."

"I thought he was going to strike me."

"I did, too, Forrest. But you're large enough to defend yourself if the situation ever arises again. Has he ever lifted his hand toward you before?"

I shook my head. "Only in admonishment but when I deserved it. But he never did when he was angry or drunk."

Jacques smiled. "I never pictured him doing so, nor would I have thought he'd ever abuse you, but after seeing his threatening behavior the other day, I needed to ask you. He has always seemed loving and protective."

"He was before Momma died."

"Believe me, Forrest, if he had ever mistreated you or your mother, he'd have answered for it, even though he's my cousin. I assure you, I'd have made sure it never occurred again."

I smiled, in spite of the tears burning to be released. There was no greater feeling than knowing someone else was willing to fight to protect you because he loved and cared about you.

"I appreciate that," I said softly.

"Since I've never had a child, you're the closest I have," Jacques said with a broad smile.

"You'll be a great father someday, I'm certain. You're like a second father to me," I said. "You've helped build my knowledge in how to slay vampires and the issues in life that a young man doesn't understand. Father has never done that."

"Most of life's knowledge is gained only through experience. We tend to remember more from our mistakes than our successes."

I nodded. "I have bruises to back up that statement."

"I have scars," he said with a grin. "Both physical and mental. But the truth be known, I'll take the physical ones over the mental any time."

"I agree. I have some of those, too."

"No one escapes them, but we will have more than our fair share of them since we hunt and slay vampires. Losses come regardless of how hard we fight to protect those we love."

What he said was indeed the truth. I determined that I would continue pursuing the undead. No matter how many of them I slayed or destroyed, I'd never feel vindicated.

"Seems you've rekindled love," I said.

Jacques blushed a deep red. A nervous smile parted his beard and he glanced away.

"Is she the reason why you returned to London?"

He sighed. "Truthfully, I had never expected to find her."

"But you were hopeful?"

Jacques shrugged. "Deep down, I suppose I was, but I didn't get my hopes up. I thought she had moved on. Besides the odds of running into her were next to none, considering how heavily populated London is."

"Perhaps she found you."

"What do you mean?"

"Magic."

He nodded. "Possibly."

"It was obvious she had things pressing upon her mind that she needed to resolve."

"We both did," he said.

After an hour of walking through the crowding streets we stopped short of the Gypsy community. A hand carved wooden sign displayed the name: Lowbey.

"What's wrong?" Jacques asked.

"I wonder if any underground tunnels run beneath their streets?"

"Why?"

"We might have a better chance of discovering what Esmeralda's hiding if they don't see us."

Jacques shook his head. "I'm certain with their established reputation they will frown upon our snooping instead of us being forthright with them."

"She didn't divulge any further information when we had asked," I replied.

"And should they catch us trespassing underneath the streets, what type of punishment do you think she'll decree? They were ready to cut us to pieces the other night."

Father looked worried. "He's right, son."

"Perhaps you should wait here," I said.

He frowned, offended. "You keep leaving me behind."

"I'm sorry. You're welcome to come, but you're on your own should we be discovered."

"I'm aware of the risks," he said evenly.

I didn't think he really was, but I wasn't about to waste time with useless arguing. "You have a weapon?"

He nodded and smiled. "Always."

We eased to the edge of the first building on the street. I peered around the corner. Few people were moving about. The trader tables were vacant.

"Have they left?" I asked.

Father, Matilda, and Jacques stepped out onto the street and looked.

Jacques shrugged. "I think they're late risers. Their nightly festivities might go late into the morning hours."

"Psst!"

I glanced toward the side of the building. Peering out from the street drain were two sets of reddish eyes. The were-rats? One pushed a metal square door partway up at the building's edge. Jacques and I hurried to it and slid the door off the opening.

Matilda walked down the ladder first, followed by my father, and then Jacques and I.

"Lord Albert sent us to find you," Clyde said in his small rat-human form. His whiskers twitched. "We've looked for you for days and thought you might have left London."

I shook my head. "No. We had some setbacks."

George held up his lantern, studying my face with eager excited eyes. "As we understand it, you killed Trenton."

"He nearly killed me, which is why I've not been hunting at night. I've been recuperating."

Clyde smiled. "Lord Albert's offer still stands."

"What offer?"

"You becoming one of us."

I shook my head. "No thanks."

"You'd have healed much quicker," Clyde said. His beady red eyes beamed. "Less than a day instead of over half a week."

"Come on," George said. He walked back in the direction of Whitechapel.

"Where are you going?" I asked.

"To see Lord Albert," Clyde replied.

"No," Jacques replied. "We're heading under Lowbey."

George and Clyde exchanged nervous glances.

"You don't want to do that," George said, shaking his head.

"Why not?"

Clyde exhaled a shuddering breath. "Because of the evil that hides there."

"What evil?" Matilda asked.

"We're not certain," Clyde replied. "But we have accidentally stumbled upon whatever it is. Lord Albert has forbidden our entering Lowbey."

"He hasn't us," I replied.

"I don't sense anything," Matilda said, looking at Jacques.

George handed his lantern to Jacques and turned to walk away. "Enter at your own risks. Should you survive, Lord Albert insists it's urgent you meet with him."

He and Clyde walked into the dark tunnel, their long rat-tails swaying back and forth with each step.

"What does he want?" I asked.

Neither boy looked back. "We don't know. He doesn't give us information. We're just his messengers."

I glanced toward Jacques. "Should we go with them?"

He shrugged. "That'd be my preference since I don't like the idea of sneaking around Gypsy territory, but since we're already here, we might as well. Perhaps Matilda can sense this *source* of evil."

"I don't at this moment," she said. "But we may not be close enough for me to pinpoint it."

"To ease all our minds, we'll do a quick scour of the tunnel, but the building Esmeralda was using is in the center of the community," I said.

"That might be too difficult to get to," Jacques said.

I nodded. "Since we only have one light, we should stick together."

"Should we run into trouble and get divided," Jacques said, "I will stay with John. Matilda keep close to Forrest since we can see without added light."

She nodded.

I held the lantern in my left hand and walked under Lowbey's main street. Esmeralda was hiding something. I just didn't know what it was. We might discover what it was or encounter whatever evil George and Clyde had warned us about. We'd never know unless we searched.

CHAPTER 27

The tunnel we followed wasn't like those we had explored before. It was dank and reeked of urine and fecal matter, which was a great deterrent to prevent anyone from using the tunnels to gain access to other sections of Lowbey. The center of the tunnel was filled with ankle-deep brown sludgy water, so we walked along the narrow edge to avoid it.

My father gagged and coughed. "Son, I don't think we're going to find anything useful in this tunnel."

Tears welled at the edges of my stinging eyes. "I agree that it's horrible down here. We'll go just a bit farther."

An occasional bat flitted past us. The wet domed walls and ceiling glistened in the lantern's light. Water dripped like scattered raindrops. Father staggered behind me and leaned against the wall to prevent falling into the water. He took a sharp gasp of air.

"You okay?" I asked.

He held a handkerchief over his nose and mouth. "It's hard to breathe."

My throat and lungs burned from breathing in the acrid air, so I understood exactly what he was feeling. I also took into consideration of his feebleness, too. His lack of strength was why I had wished he'd stayed above and waited for us. But I couldn't continue to make him feel inadequate because doing so would only increase his resentment toward me. Eventually, he'd accept the fact that he couldn't keep up or his stubbornness would insist that he died trying. Knowing my father, the latter seemed the most likely.

"He's not going to make it back to where we started," Jacques said.

I nodded ahead of us. "There's a ladder leading up."

Jacques shook his head. "Forrest, we have no idea where that leads. The men regarded us as enemies the other night, and we had walked down the street in plain sight. Imagine how it will look for us to emerge from beneath the village midway down one of their streets. Do you really want to chance their reaction to our unexpected arrival?"

"Are you indicating that you'll carry Father back?"

He shook his head. "Only if it becomes necessary."

"Then what do you suggest?" I asked.

"An alternate route if we happen upon one soon."

I shrugged. "I'm good with that. There's only so much of this stench any of us can tolerate."

"Wait," Matilda said in a near whisper.

"What?" Jacques said.

"I feel a faint pulse of magic, but I'm uncertain of its source or whether it's good or evil." She placed a cloth over her nose and mouth. "I think it's farther down the tunnel."

"Straight ahead or down that side tunnel?"

Matilda shrugged. "I can't be certain until we get closer."

If she had detected magic, her sensitivity was far greater than my own. Of course since she was a witch, she was more attuned the mystic realm than I could ever be. But if Matilda was able to locate the magic, then the one responsible for this magic probably already knew Matilda and the rest of us were in the tunnel.

Since Esmeralda practiced magic, too, I automatically assumed she was behind the source deeper in the tunnel. But my mere speculations about magic were not always accurate.

"Be wary," Matilda said softly. "This witch has probably set magical traps."

Father gagged until he vomited. He leaned against the wall, trying to catch his breath. The retching sound grated on my gag reflex, but I kept my resolve not to repeat his performance.

"Here," she said, handing him an extra cloth from her pocket. "Put this over your nose and mouth. The herbs will counteract the stench."

Father took the cloth and did as she instructed. His breathing stabilized. Jacques gripped Father's left elbow and walked alongside him.

I hurried my pace, trying to get closer to the source of magic before we found it necessary to return to the streets above. Being underground had not exactly kept us unnoticed, in spite of my hopes that we could sneak into their village unobserved. Someone was watching us. Anytime I got the feeling of eyes studying me, the impulse had never been wrong.

After walking two more blocks underneath the village, a prickling sensation crept around my neck, causing the hairs on the nape of my neck to stiffen. A pocket of cold air settled around me, chilling me to the bone. I stopped and looked toward Matilda. "Do you feel that?"

She nodded. "We're close. Keep going."

I took a deep breath of acrid air and swallowed hard, bracing myself for my next step forward. The air felt thicker and heavier. Each step I took was like wading in waist-deep seawater, even though we weren't standing in water at all.

"Careful, Forrest. She doesn't want us going any farther."

"I agree with whoever *she* is," Father said through the cloth.

I gave Father a shrewd stare before I attempted one more step and found myself standing against an invisible wall that was cold like ice. I pressed and pushed, but it was impassable.

Jacques touched the wall and winced, pulling back his hand. "It's painfully cold. What do you make of this, Matilda?"

She placed both hands against the barrier and closed her eyes, concentrating. "This is Esmeralda's magic. I sense her presence upon it."

"Can you break through it?" he asked.

She ran both hands across the barrier, feeling and chanting softly. After a few seconds she shook her head. "No. She's quite powerful in her magic, like most Gypsy witches are. I don't detect a hanging curse spell."

We didn't have any other choice except to turn back. Before I could even make the suggestion we were greeted by an unexpected group of men.

"We had hoped you understood you weren't welcome several nights ago," one man said, holding his crude metal weapon that was shaped like a curved scythe blade.

Perhaps *greeted* wasn't the best word for our encounter. They exhibited nothing friendly in their approach. We turned and faced them.

The man looked at me. "Esmeralda isn't pleased that you've returned unannounced. She demands to see you. So come along with us peacefully and there'll be no bloodshed."

Anger flared Jacques' nostrils. His eyes narrowed. It's never wise to threaten a werewolf, even in his human form. Matilda stared at the man coldly. Her jaw tightened and her lips formed a partial snarl.

I pressed my back against the invisible wall. An idea whispered into my mind. An old Hunter's insight? I didn't know, but I weighted the suggestion and obeyed. I slid my silver cross from my pocket and placed it against the magical barrier behind me. Where the cross touched the cold barrier, the wall retreated slightly and allowed my hand a pocket of space.

"Your crosses," I whispered. "Place them against the wall."

Father turned and placed his against the wall.

"What are you doing?" the man asked. He held the scythe back above his head, ready to swing at us. "Come along with us. *Now.*"

Matilda and Jacques pressed their gold crosses against the wall.

"Stop them!" Esmeralda's desperate voice echoed through the tunnel. She was nowhere to be seen.

The cold wall opened and congealed around us, pushing us through to the other side. I visibly shivered from the icy chill that shot through my body, as did the rest of my company.

The men advanced but the magical barrier didn't budge for them. The man swung the scythe but the wall's magic prevented him from striking it. We could see one another through the wall, but we couldn't touch.

"Open the wall!" the man shouted, looking up. I assumed he was yelling at Esmeralda. "We cannot pass!"

"I cannot," came her firm reply. "Doing so opens it for worse things to enter."

"How did you know the crosses would let us through?" Matilda asked.

I shrugged. "I didn't, really. My cross was what caused Esmeralda to lower her guard the other night. I suppose this barrier is set to prevent a vampire from passing through. Since we have crosses, the magic recognizes that we're not vampires."

The men stared at us with hardened gazes. They no longer appeared to be willing to peacefully escort us to Esmeralda, even if we agreed to go with them. They'd rather kill us if they could get to us.

I wondered if the barrier was to keep Duke Raginwulf out or was it to contain what was on this side? Of course there was another possibility. The wall might protect whatever Esmeralda was hiding from outsiders or protect the outsiders from it. Based upon her control over the rest of her village and their undying loyalty to her, I got the impression that she wasn't too concerned about the fate of anyone outside of her tightknit society.

A tendril of magic pricked my hand that held the cross. My hand shook but source of magic didn't attempt to force me to drop the cross.

"Do you feel its presence?" Matilda asked, looking at me.

"Yes."

Father lowered the cloth from his face and took a deep breath. The air was cleaner here. The sludgy water stopped at the other side of the invisible wall. The center of the floor was dry as were the walls and ceiling. Apparently we had gotten past two of her deterrents.

"Shall we proceed?" I asked.

Jacques glanced back at the angry men. "I don't think that it's any safer for us to turn back."

Looking at Matilda, I said, "What do you sense about what lies ahead?"

"It's still distant. It could be masked by another magical barrier though."

"I wonder what it is?"

She sighed. "We're bound to find out if we keep going."

Murderer! whispered harshly in my ear.

I glanced around. "Anyone else hear that?"

"What?"

"A voice?"

Each of them shook their heads.

Blood is on your hands.

"How about that time?" I asked.

"No," Jacques said with a concerned frown. "*What* are you hearing?"

"Just accusations."

"What kind?" Matilda asked.

I shrugged.

Laughter echoed softly near my ear. I handed the lantern to Jacques. I lowered my cross, placing it into my left hand. Then I took my dagger from my pocket. Warmth flowed from the blade's handle and traveled to my elbow. The blade could thwart the power of a master vampire, allowing me to take control of him, but I didn't expect any master vampire to be hiding somewhere within these tunnels, especially not since Duke Raginwulf was Esmeralda's foremost enemy. But there could be other masters.

The dagger, however, was a useful weapon even against humans, whereas a stake produced deep punctured wounds, which were effective in slowing down a mortal enemy but offered a slow painful death.

I had never killed another human, and Jacques had warned insistently that I shouldn't because of how it would affect my young mind. I agreed. I never wanted to kill anything that wasn't supernatural or undead. Albert, on the other hand, had warned me that it was inevitable. Eventually I'd be forced beyond my control to carry out such an unwanted deed. We were at war against dark supernatural creatures. Sometimes they controlled humans, as I had witnessed firsthand. War always had its casualties, and the Civil War stories Dominus had told me also confirmed that.

Even though I was the youngest, I led the others down the tunnel. Jacques seldom protested having me ahead of the group. My size was intimidating, but I suspected he allowed me at the front so he could watch for enemies approaching from the rear. And with his extreme speed, he could always attack an enemy ahead of us before our adversary or I even blinked.

The tunnel remained quiet other than our slow advance. No water dripped. No rats or bats stirred. It was too quiet. Like death. Matilda had mentioned magic traps and to be wary. I detected nothing magical except for the faint pulse of magic deeper in the tunnel. But then it happened.

A large black shadow draped across the tunnel ahead of us, moving like a windswept curtain, preventing us from seeing anything beyond it.

"What now?" I asked.

Matilda's dark eyes narrowed, and she nodded ahead. The black veil had vanished. In its place stood Esmeralda and the three Gypsy men from the other night. None held weapons, but the expressions on their faces indicated they didn't have need of any.

"You were warned!" she said in a low menacing tone that chilled to the bone.

I held her gaze without blinking. "As I recall, *you* welcomed us in."

"To my shop, yes. Here, *no*. My men gave you my wishes to come see me. Instead you defied their order."

"My allegiance isn't to them, or to you. They don't tell me what to do. They might fear your power—"

"*Forrest!*" Matilda hissed in a stern whisper. She shook her head.

"I assume you're the one accusing me of murder?" I asked, unflinching. "That's a bold allegation, even for you."

Her eyes narrowed, growing dark. "But you murdered him."

"Who?"

"Trenton."

My lips curled into a slight smirk. "He was a vampire. It's my duty and calling to slay vampires. *Any* vampire."

"He was an ally, not our enemy," she replied.

Jacques frowned. "You aligned your people with a vampire? Do you understand how dangerous that is?"

"Not as dangerous for us than when Duke Raginwulf finds us."

"A vampire acts only in his or her best interests. Mortals are never benefited by any proposed agreements," I said. "They view mortals either as a potential food source or an expansion of the hierarchy."

"Not all—"

Through gritted teeth, I said, "*All.*"

Father said, "Forrest was paid handsomely for killing Trenton, which means someone apparently viewed the vampire as a major threat to the residents of Whitechapel. How could you not sense his evil?"

She regarded my father with a harsh frown, but didn't answer his pointed question. Instead she turned her attention back to me. "A bounty?"

I nodded. "I suppose one might consider it such, but none was offered ahead of time. No one offered me a bounty to kill him."

"Perhaps a price should be placed upon *your* head," Esmeralda said in a near whisper. Her piercing dark eyes were colder than a venomous serpent coiled to strike.

"Careful," Jacques said. "Any threat placed against Forrest is directed toward all of us."

She pursed her lips before releasing a small laugh. "You're all fools to think you can ever intimidate me."

"The duke has come for you, and you hold great fear of him," Jacques said.

Her brow furrowed.

"See?" Jacques said. "I'm certain if Matilda worked the proper set of spells, she could release your hold on the hedgerow, allowing him direct access to Lowbey."

"You'd side with that vampire?" she asked.

"Why not?" Jacques replied. "You had allied with one."

"To rid ourselves of a more powerful one."

"That didn't work in your favor, did it?" Father said. "The last thing you want to do is kill us. We are probably the best allies you could ever have. Don't make us your enemies. Trust me. It won't end well for you."

For several moments I stood in awe at my father's sudden bold words. Over the past few months, during our travels and pursuits of other lesser vampires, he had seldom spoken a word, allowing Jacques and myself to speak while he stood quietly in the background.

"I'd rather not have you as enemies, but you tried to enter our village unseen like thieves slipping through the shadows. Trespassing in areas where you're not welcome is not the action of an ally or a friend. We lack trust between us now, and that's difficult to rebuild."

"What are you hiding?" I asked.

"Whatever do you mean, Hunter?" She feigned childlike innocence. "You uttered similar words the other night. Tell me why?"

I slid my dagger into its sheath, placed the cross in my pocket, and crossed my arms. I stood in long silence until her discomfort caused her to shift her feet. She kept our gaze, but her nervousness increased. Her body became restless. The men standing behind her became uneasy. They looked about, like they hoped to find weapons.

"For a man who is from Romania, you dare challenge a Gypsy witch by staring into her eyes? Have you no fear of the consequences? Misfortunes befall those foolish enough to engage us," she said. Her tone and boldness didn't back her warning.

I grinned and shook my head slightly but stared intently into her eyes. After my extended silence, she bit her lower lip. Her building fear caused her to look away. "Perhaps you stared into Trenton's eyes too long, Gypsy. A vampire can enslave humans to do his bidding. It's foolish for most anyone to gaze into a vampire's eyes, but I am one who is capable of doing so without the fear of being seized by his charm. That's because I'm a Hunter. I have no fear of gazing into their eyes, nor do I have any fear of looking into yours. I can perceive one's nature and her lies."

"I've not lied to you," she said in a quiet voice.

"Perhaps not, but you haven't told us everything," I replied.

"Our affairs aren't your business."

"A master vampire has traveled across several countries because of something you have done. He's killing innocent people, which makes it our business, especially if you want our aid in killing him."

Esmeralda frowned. "I've never requested your help."

"No? Apparently before the duke is finished, you're going to need it.

Eventually, he'll find a way past your magical barriers and when he does, he will slaughter dozens of your people. Maybe even hundreds of them. Is that something you wish to risk?"

She broke our gaze and swallowed hard.

"Let us pass and find what it is that you're hiding," I said.

"No," she said evenly. Her eyes grew fierce again. "If you wish to speak with us, then come above to my shop. But you're not welcome beneath our village."

I smiled and looked past her. "Then what you're hiding *is* in that direction."

"Go!" She pointed toward a ladder with her thin crooked finger. "If you return to this tunnel, horrible unspeakable things will befall you."

A wave of dark energy washed across me, but I pretended not to notice. I fixed my gaze on her, but she still refused to yield additional information or hold my gaze. Finally, I said, "The longer you withhold what you're hiding, the stronger you're making him. You do realize that, don't you?"

Esmeralda looked away uneasily. "I said, 'Go.'"

"As you wish." I walked past her to the ladder leading to the street above. Jacques, Matilda, and Father followed. "Now may be the only chance you have to reveal your secret because there's a good chance we might leave London before this vampire is ever slain."

"You're a Hunter. You'd let him stalk the people of Whitechapel rather than destroy him?"

"Isn't that what you're currently doing?" I asked. "It seems you want me to rid you of a problem you've incited. Duke Raginwulf has come to Whitechapel for one purpose. Vengeance. He wants to punish you for whatever you've done and have refused to disclose to us. It's not necessary that I kill him anytime soon. I can hunt him later, *after* he has completed his vendetta by killing you."

Tears of frustration welled in her eyes, but she held her silence. I shrugged and went up the ladder. We all exited onto the street in Lowbey without her calling after us. Other than rude cold stares from peddlers, we suffered no threats or harassment as we left the village.

CHAPTER 28

*L*ord Albert greeted us inside his underground chambers when we entered. George stood to the right of Albert's crude throne and Clyde to the left. The other three sat in front of Albert. The four of us stood before him like meager humans before a rat king.

Albert smiled, resting his chin upon his slender, rat-fingered bridge. "I see you got my message."

I nodded.

"The boys told me of your interests in what lies beneath the Gypsy village. Did you find what you were seeking?"

"No," I replied.

"What prompted you to enter where those of us refuse to tread?"

"Esmeralda."

His eyes widened slightly. "The Gypsy witch?"

"Yes."

"Why do you seek her? I thought your primary interest was in killing this murderous vampire."

"She's the reason Raginwulf is here."

Albert eased back in his chair. He ran a slender hand along his long goatee, pulling it straighter before twirling the end of it around his index finger. "That's an interesting assumption. What is your logic behind that line of thinking?"

"Because her niece was married to him, and according to Esmeralda, they unwittingly killed her, not knowing she was a vampire," I replied.

"Do you believe her?"

"I believe she's hiding more than what's she telling us. It's under Lowbey in one of the tunnels."

Albert frowned. "What do you think it is?"

I shrugged. "I'm not certain, but whatever it is, she has bound magic to shroud and protect it."

Albert glanced toward Matilda. "Is this true?"

She nodded. "I have sensed the presence of magic deeper in the tunnel, but we weren't able to get near it. She has used magic to set up barriers along the tunnel to prevent anyone from sneaking underground."

"You do realize the dangers that come from provoking the anger of a Gypsy witch? The curses they can bestow upon those they view as enemies are unsurpassed and unrelentingly cruel. A Gypsy carries a grudge forever, and the curse continues long after her death. These are some of the reasons I have forbade my boys from setting foot within Lowbey's village borders."

"I have no fear of her," I said.

Albert studied me long and hard. "You should have respect of their powers, if nothing else. Just because you're a Hunter doesn't mean you can traipse through any territory unscathed. With your excessive size I tend to view you as a man, but your mind is still soft and learning, like my boys. Mischief tempts you to take unwarranted risks. And although you killed Trenton, your fight with that vampire almost killed you."

Humility overcame me, and I nodded.

"Now, you're stalking into the Gypsy community, and with a defiant supreme attitude nonetheless, if I had my guess. That's a foolish endeavor for you or any shape-shifter. Anyone outside of their village they do not trust. Often outsiders are betrayed, robbed, or swindled, as Gypsies *are* the masters for the slight of hand."

I glanced toward the smallest were-rat who had tried to still my

Hunter box upon our first encounter. "Perhaps the little one there should seek a Gypsy trainer in Lowbey. His stealing skills are lacking."

Albert's eyes narrowed. "Impudent—"

"*Forrest!*" Jacques scolded, grabbing the crook of my left arm.

I yanked my arm away and pointed at Albert. "Honesty, remember? He has no right to lecture me when he's allowing his own boys to roam the streets to steal from vendors and unsuspecting visitors. A thief is a thief, regardless of his cultural upbringing."

Albert snarled his upper lip and bared his teeth. Anger stirred in those red eyes. His hands tightened on the armrests of his chair, and he appeared ready to spring forward to attack. I braced myself, placing my hand on my dagger. After a few moments, he expelled a long sigh and forced a nod. "Quite right, Forrest. We shouldn't steal, but look at us. What occupation can we have on the surface? I'm cursed like this for the rest of my days. The boys can appear as humans for a few hours during the day, but they have no forewarning of when they will transform into their rat form. The older they become, the less time their bodies will look human. In time they will be like me, nothing more than sewer scavengers, living off the scraps of society."

"My apologies," I said.

Albert gave a nonchalant wave of his hand. The soured expression on his narrowed mouth signified he held no interest in my regret. "Not necessary. We've more important matters to discuss."

"Why do you fear the Gypsies so much?" I asked. "Do you think Esmeralda could curse you more than what you already say you are?"

Albert scratched at his neck and chin. "Most Gypsies are wanderers. They stay a short time in a place before moving on. Generally before their true tactics are discovered by the less fortunate. Lowbey is actually the first settlement I've ever seen where they've not set up a temporary camp of wagons. They're occupying buildings and setting up businesses."

Father nodded. "I had wondered about that behavior myself. I remember wagon caravans."

Albert looked at his boys affectionately and then he glanced to me. "Myself, I have no fear of them or Esmeralda for that matter. But when it comes to my boys? Think about it. The traveling caravans of Gypsies not only have fortune-tellers and healers, but they have freak shows where, for a price, people can view bizarre humans and animals. Imagine what they'd do if they captured one of my boys. He'd be nothing but an animal to make them money. A prisoner for people to gawk at."

"They have shows like that in Lowbey?" I asked.

He shrugged. "It's doubtful. I've seen no placards promoting such shows in Whitechapel. But that wouldn't stop them from selling a were-rat child to their relatives passing through in a caravan."

"That's true," I replied.

Matilda shook her head. "It's disgusting."

"Mortifying," Albert said. "And yet, it happens. Forrest, may I ask you something? It's actually the reason I requested you to come here."

"Sure."

"Why did you face Trenton alone?"

"I was not looking for him," I replied. "I wasn't planning to confront any vampire. I had gone for a walk."

"Was he, perhaps, *looking* for you?" Albert asked, folding his long fingers together.

I thought about that for a few moments. Our encounter didn't seem by accident. Trenton had been watching me out in the open. "Now that I think about it, that's possible."

Jacques cocked a brow, looking at me. "You think so?"

"He appeared on the street beneath a lamppost, and he was watching me." A sudden revelation came to me. "*She* sent him."

"Who?" Albert asked.

"Esmeralda."

The were-rat's brow furrowed. "Why would a Gypsy witch have any association with a vampire?"

Jacques said, "She told us she had allied herself with Trenton."

"To fight Duke Raginwulf," I said. "But Trenton confronted me soon after we left Lowbey. She knew I was a Hunter."

"You said that he wanted you to help him kill Raginwulf," Father said.

I nodded. "He did."

"I speculate," Jacques said, "that he knew you'd refuse to befriend him. He wanted you to attack."

"Either she wanted to eliminate you," Albert said, "*or* she was testing you."

I glanced toward Jacques. "When we had talked to her earlier and she learned I had gotten a bounty for killing Trenton, she said a price should be set upon me. But perhaps she had already set one."

Albert shook his head and chuckled.

"What?" I asked.

"Can you see the treachery of offering your trust to a Gypsy? Perhaps she was testing both of you. For Trenton to defeat you meant it was possible for him to kill Duke Raginwulf. If he failed, London had one less vampire to worry about."

I grinned. "And yet, she was the one who actually killed Trenton."

"How's that?" Albert asked with a curious stare.

"The stake that killed him was from a hedge she had enchanted to attack and slay vampires. The magic on the stake propelled it into the air and through his heart."

"The irony," Albert said with a shrewd smile that made him appear even more sinister than normal. He rubbed his slender hands together briskly.

"How do we discern her true motive?" Jacques asked.

"I don't think we can," I replied. "She pitted us against one another. Since we don't know if she was trying to have Trenton kill me or me kill him, we cannot trust her."

"Her anger increased when she acknowledged you had killed Trenton. That's a good sign she wanted you dead," he said.

I shrugged. "That and the hinted bounty on me indicate she's not an ally. And besides that, she remains defiant in revealing what she's hiding. I believe she possesses an item of great value that Raginwulf refuses to abandon."

Albert rose from his throne and stretched. His long gray robe flowed around his ankles. "None of you have any idea what that item might be?"

"No," I replied.

"What makes you think that's his actual reason for being in London?"

"Because he's a master vampire. He's abandoned his social status, his lair, and everything else in his pursuit of Esmeralda."

Albert nodded, thinking. "It's actually a good theory. During your absence, we've not seen any trace of Raginwulf though. I've not found any more human feedbags or neophytes. I've not entered the abandoned workhouse though. I'd rather not investigate that alone. The boys aren't experienced enough yet, either."

"We should inspect it as a group," Jacques said.

Albert smiled. "When you decide on a date, please inform me. I'd be most interested in going."

"We'd be fortunate to have you with us," I replied. "Thanks for the invitation today. But it's time we must leave."

"Very well," Albert said. "A word of caution though. With the speculation of Esmeralda plotting to kill you, other vampires might be hunting you now."

I nodded.

"Watch your back," he said.

CHAPTER 29

When we returned to the inn, Constable Shields was waiting for us with another gentleman outside our door. Shields tipped his hat and slightly bowed toward Matilda with a kind smile. The stranger did the same. Jacques unlocked and opened the door.

Once we were all inside the room, Shields studied me and shook his head. "Quite a remarkable thing to see you out and about, Forrest. You had all of us concerned about your welfare. But other than faint bruising, you appear as though nothing had ever happened."

"I heal fast," I replied.

"Quite obviously you do." He smiled.

I glanced toward the man with him. The stranger was thin and wiry. His head seemed too big for his shoulders, and he sported a thick moustache that didn't look right on such a boyish face.

"Oh, forgive me for my rudeness," Shields said. "This is Warren Wellington, a reporter with one of the papers. He has been keenly interested in meeting you."

I eyed the reporter suspiciously. "Why exactly?"

Warren removed his hat, smiled, and offered his hand. I politely shook it. "It's an honor, Forrest."

"How's that?"

"To meet someone who does what you do."

My gaze flicked toward Shields, which made the constable nervous. "Care to elaborate?"

"Killing the night demons," Warren replied.

I shook my head. "I'm afraid you're mistaken."

"Come now," he said. "You kill these demons of the night. No sense denying it. I . . . I witnessed you slaying the one that almost killed you a few nights ago."

"Did you?" I asked with a slight frown.

Seeing my agitation, Warren smiled with less vigor and adjusted his necktie.

"What I killed *wasn't* a demon," I said. "That's a different monster altogether."

"Oh? I thought vampires were demons."

I shook my head. "What exactly is it that you want?"

"A headline of a story that no one else has ever written. A firsthand account of these monsters you slay will sell more papers than—"

I placed a firm hand on his shoulder and glared down at him. "You cannot print such things. Constable Shields, explain to him the dangers of reporting about these vampires to the public."

"I've tried," Shields replied. "He won't listen to me."

Jacques glared at Warren. "Forrest is right. You can't write about these creatures."

"And why not?" Warren asked. "People have the right to know."

I squeezed his shoulder tightly until pain showed on his face. "The people of Whitechapel and London are terrified of the murderous stalker who has slain women on the streets in the dead of night," I said. "Even when the murderer hasn't killed again, speculation about him gets reported daily. You report about blood-craving vampires, and you'll send the entire area into a panic they'll never recover from."

Warren jerked from my painful grasp and rubbed his shoulder. His eyes moistened. "But isn't that what the murderer is? A vampire?"

Shields' face reddened, and he turned away.

"What's this all about, Shields?" I asked.

Shields didn't reply.

Warren grinned. "If you'll grant me an interview explaining what these creatures are and how you hunt them down—"

My voice deepened. "You write *anything* about me or these vampires, and I will hunt *you* down. Do you understand?"

He shook at my threat.

"And when I do, I'll perform upon you what is necessary to kill a vampire. But since you're human, it might *not* kill you. I imagine the pain is more than you can handle though. Now, get out!" I towered over him, forming huge fists and glaring at him.

Warren stumbled backwards over his feet, nearly tripping and falling before his hand found the doorknob, allowing him to correct his balance. Once he opened the door, he darted down the hall.

Shields removed his hat, shook his head, and stood at the open door. "Forrest, my apologies."

Father and Jacques scowled at the constable, too.

"*What* did you tell him?" I asked.

"More than I ever intended," Shields replied. "Truly I'm sorry. The day after you slew Trenton, Warren stopped by the station and spoke to me, telling me what he had witnessed. The only reason he had questions, which is something I'd like to know too, was how the vampire's body vanished except for a pile of dust or ash. I didn't know, but since I was busy with the murder investigations he offered to buy me drinks later if I'd sit down and talk with him."

"And you did?" Father asked.

Shields offered an embarrassed nod. "I did. Due to the grisly nature of that last murder and having to sort through all the drawings and pictures, I drank too much. The images of that poor butchered woman wouldn't leave my mind. I suppose after I was drunk I had told him far more information about you than I remembered telling. I'm so sorry, Forrest. I've betrayed our friendship."

"You have, constable. In spite of my father's protest, I told you what I am. That was to remain confidential and secret. I trusted you to keep it so. We don't simply reveal to people what it is we do. If that information is published for the whole city to know, we'll have more problems than we already have, and they're increasing without added publicity."

Shields fought tears like an admonished child but kept his silence.

I crossed my arms. "You tell Warren that I meant what I said. If he has a story printed about my role in slaying vampires, I'm coming after him. I don't make idle threats."

"I'll inform him. As I said earlier, I'm thankful to see you on your feet and getting around. No words can ever express how sorry I am."

I nodded. "You've said the words. Future actions will reveal whether you mean them or not. I do have a question for you."

"Sure. What?"

"Did you leave a reward for us after Trenton was slain?"

He shook his head. "No. Why?"

"Just curious."

"Someone did?" Shields asked.

"Yes. When we talked days ago, you seemed unaware that any vampires existed in London. Were you aware that Trenton was one?"

"Honestly, no. All I knew about him was that he owned a lot of the slum houses. He was wealthy, and he did little to improve the living conditions of his rundown buildings."

What a convenient occupation for a vampire to oversee? A slumlord.

"Have you learned more about the women?" Jacques asked. "Any motive?"

Shields shook his head. He paled. "No. I can't understand how anyone could kill so brutally. Any murder is a bad thing . . . but—"

He hurried out of the room with his hand over his mouth.

"I suppose I have no choice but to keep a low profile for several days," I said.

Jacques nodded. "All of us will, which is a shame. It prevents us from finding the duke before he kills again."

"We know where he is probably hiding," I said.

"That's too risky."

"Not during the day," I replied. "And Albert is willing to help us."

Jacques shook his head. "Look, Forrest, to get there, we either take the underground passageway where we killed four of Raginwulf's offspring or we walk through Lowbey where Esmeralda has undoubtedly set more traps. Either direction is risky. And if Warren witnessed you slaying Trenton, you can be assured he wasn't the *only* witness. Trenton's master or siblings might have seen it, too."

"I understand that, but—"

"Here's what we're possibly facing," Jacques said. "Most of the tunnels are dark and absent of any light, so vampires can wait for us during the day. Human servants can be watching for us anywhere. On the streets or underground. And not only that, the duke might have found another place to hide during the day since we know where he is. Keeping a low profile for a few days is actually not a bad idea."

I grunted. "It seems cowardice."

"It keeps all of us alive."

I took off my hat and set it on the dresser. I ran a hand through my long brown hair and sighed. "I hate thinking we're giving him a keen advantage by staying off the streets."

"I understand your frustration, Forrest. Don't think of it as hiding. Think of it as strategy. It gives us time to plan, too. I will pay the constable a visit to see if he can give me a better-detailed street map of Whitechapel. We need to know these streets and the alleyways better than we already do. It's like a labyrinth. While we're learning that, Matilda can get supplies to enchant charms and cast spells."

I nodded.

Father grinned. "Plus, it gives another advantage."

"What?" I asked.

"Right now, the duke, the Gypsy witch, and possibly other vampires are waiting for us. After a few days of not seeing us, they will lower their guard. When we finally emerge they won't be expecting us. It's less likely we'll be seen."

"That's true. I can see how that definitely benefits us," I said. "So it's agreed that we wait a while before returning to the hunt?"

Jacques nodded, as did Father and Matilda.

"We check the papers each day. The first sign that the duke's stalking the streets, we return to hunting for him."

"Only if it's at least a week from now. Any sooner than that, and we're the targets," Jacques replied.

Reluctantly I agreed, but I ached inside to find Raginwulf and stop his murder spree before he added more victims to the list. But prematurely killing the duke prevented us from discovering what had prompted his pursuit of Esmeralda. The longer we waited actually gave us a better chance of discovering what Esmeralda was hiding. It also allowed Raginwulf additional time to confront the witch. If he didn't succeed in killing, I held no doubt she'd seek our help, but the only way we'd do that was by her telling us what she was hiding.

She had already given every indication that what she had hidden was farther down the side tunnel. I didn't doubt that she expected us to return. In fact, she was probably hoping we did. I didn't view her as a forgiving person or someone I'd ever trust. But without any contact from us for several days, she'd become worried, especially if Raginwulf killed more people.

Waiting was the best solution, but not so much for an impatient person like me.

CHAPTER 30

 ctober 1st, 1888

OVER TWO WEEKS had passed without us hearing any new reports of Whitechapel murders. Like we had agreed amongst ourselves, we didn't grace the night looking for Raginwulf. We never ventured back to the Gypsy village either.

The long days and even longer nights were overall uneventful for me at the least. Matilda worked on her spells and studied the magic bound to the enchanted hedge branch to see if she could duplicate it. She had also made charms for each of us to deflect any dark magic Esmeralda might attempt to curse us with.

Father spent his time working the word riddles in the daily papers. Jacques was almost as bored as I was, except that we practiced sparing one another each day. Like he had insisted several times before, I was more agile and swifter than I thought I could be. He challenged me to footraces each day in empty narrow alleyways. I never beat him, but for me it wasn't about the speed. I wanted to run without tripping over my huge feet. It took a lot of practice and concentration, but eventually my clumsiness was almost nonexistent.

All of us learned where each street and alleyway was located on the map Shields had been kind enough to give us. Jacques had made rough sketches of the underground tunnels that led to the old workhouse where we believe Raginwulf slept during the day. He also drew a map for the underground tunnel of Lowbey and the streets overhead. We didn't have enough knowledge of the village's layout, but at least what little we did know, he had written it down.

Panicked knocks came at our door.

Jacques opened the door. Constable Shields peered in. Dread filled his eyes and his skin was ashen white. Dark bags hung beneath his eyes. "Come in."

Shields graciously nodded. "I had hoped to find you at breakfast this morning."

"We're behind schedule this morning," I replied. "Thought about waiting until lunch before eating. What brings you by?"

He pulled the folded newspaper from beneath his arm and handed it to me.

I spread the paper open on the desk. I read the headline and looked at him. "Jack the Ripper?"

Shields nodded. "That's what the papers are calling him now."

"Why?" Matilda asked, walking over to read the paper.

Shields cleared his throat, pulled out his handkerchief, and wiped beading sweat from his brow. He handed me a folder. "We received a letter the other day from a man claiming to be responsible for the murders. Honestly we thought the letter was a hoax until the two murders last night."

"Two?" Jacques and I said at the same time, exchanging glances.

"Yes. Unfortunately so."

I opened the folder to see a handwritten letter. "Written in red ink?"

"To symbolize blood, I suppose," Shields said.

I read through the letter and carefully placed it back into the folder. "I don't think the actual killer wrote it."

"Why not?"

"These aren't words this killer would use."

Shields frowned. "Why do you say that?"

"They're too much in jest. Not the proper words a person of his caliber would use. He wishes to strike terror into the hearts of London. *That's* his game. This letter is silly and unfounded and not that of a vampire with high social status. This is a mockery to him."

"So you really think the killer is a vampire."

"We're certain of it," I replied. "And this letter isn't something he'd write."

"When's the last time you hunted for him?" Shields asked.

"The night before you brought Warren in to see me."

"That long?"

I nodded.

"For God's sake—"

"God has nothing to do with this," I said evenly.

He frowned. "Why delay your hunt this long?"

"You put our lives in risk by telling Warren information he should never have known."

"I apologized."

"I know, but that didn't change our circumstances. We already put our lives in jeopardy every time we hunt any vampire. We don't need extra attention placed on us."

"He didn't print anything," Shields said.

"I realize that, but he did witness me slay Trenton, and he wanted a story. I have no doubt he'd have been watching and following us from a rooftop or in the shadows so he could write about it."

"I don't think he will go anywhere near you."

"Why's that?"

Shields smiled. "I relayed your message to him. He quit the post."

"He quit?"

"You have this unique ability to drive fear into a man's soul. He truly believed you'd stake him."

"I would have."

Shields cocked an eyebrow. "Not *really*."

"Ask anyone in the room," I said.

Shields glanced around. Jacques and Father readily nodded. Matilda acquiesced a gentle nod.

"You look serious even when you're not. I assumed you were jesting."

I shook my head. "About these two women, what do you know?"

"Both were prostitutes. One's throat was slashed open, and the other . . . she was butchered worse than Annie had been. She was gutted like livestock."

Jacques scanned the newspaper with his finger. "Are you certain both were killed by the same person?"

"It's an assumption at best. Why?"

"He only slashed the one's throat. All the other murders were more severe."

"We believe someone happened upon him right after he slashed Elizabeth's throat. A witness said that blood was pulsing from her throat when she was found. The murderer fled without being seen," Shields said.

I glanced at Jacques. He nodded.

"What?" Shields asked.

"A vampire can move that fast. Since he killed two women this time, he wants to heighten everyone's fear," I said.

"When will you return to hunting him?"

"Tonight," Jacques replied.

"Thank you."

I shrugged. "After killing two people, he'll probably go into hiding for a while."

"Why?" Shields asked.

"Prolong the fear. Increase the hunt by Scotland Yard. While I don't think he's high on the publicity, he thrives on terror."

Shields sat in the desk chair. "Then how do you plan to find him? We've had no success. Our best detectives are on these cases. No clues have narrowed down our search. He definitely has a way of eluding us. Even last night, Elizabeth was killed in a place where a lot of people were leaving a club meeting. Her murderer should have been seen, but he wasn't. He had slipped away unnoticed. That's why I believe your theory is better than ours. He has to be something *not* human. The ghastly ways he has butchered these women makes me consider changing my profession altogether."

"Our line of work isn't any better," Father replied. "When you're hired to kill a vampire that is a little child . . . it's not a duty you think you'll ever encounter."

"A child?" Shields' eyebrows rose, causing him to adjust his glasses. "Vampires turn children into vampires?"

Father shook his head. Sadness claimed his gaze. "I've only seen it one time, and I pray I never endure such again."

"Usually children aren't turned," Jacques said. "Their blood is poisonous to a vampire. I suppose there are rare exceptions if the vampire is strong enough to survive the poison."

"Poisonous? How?" the constable asked.

"The way it was explained to me is that children are the most pure and innocent in God's creation and since vampires are vile, unholy creatures, they are unable to partake of such purity. It's like the children are blessed and protected from being cursed like the undead, at least for a while, until the age of accountability when they should know right from wrong."

Shields looked stunned. "I've been a Catholic all my life. We've been taught about the devil, his demons, and other types of fallen angels, but nothing is ever mentioned about these undead creatures. Why has it been hidden from us?"

Jacques shrugged. "I can't tell you why. Maybe we're blind to a lot of our surroundings. Otherwise we'd all go insane."

"I'm teetering on the edge now," Shields said, staring at the wall. "I hope you find this vampire soon. Tonight is preferable."

Jacques placed a hand on the constable's shoulder. "We promise we'll do our best. Tracking the undead isn't easy. Killing them once you find them is even harder."

Shields nodded and gave a gentle smile. He reached inside his suit jacket and slid out a bright gold cross. "Even though I was skeptical in the beginning, I'm taking your advice. I suppose a gold cross will work?"

Jacques nodded.

"I didn't want to use a silver one since you and Matilda have difficulty with silver."

"We appreciate that," Jacques replied, smiling.

"I sincerely apologize for excusing myself, but I do need to get back to the investigation," Shields said, walking to the door. "Believe me, I'd rather be here talking to you. And more so, I wish I was in a world where such cruel, evil violence didn't occur."

"We all do," I said.

Shields tipped his hat graciously before exiting.

After Jacques closed the door he returned to the newspaper. "As a werewolf I've come across a lot of grim kills where victims have lost appendages, but the last murder Shields showed us is worse than any of them."

"If we don't stop Raginwulf, I'll wager the next murder will be even worse," I said.

"Why?" Matilda asked.

"He's deliberately displaying his threat to Esmeralda. As his agitation increases, his aggression escalates. He's letting her know that when he finds her, what he does to her will be far worse. The earlier news of his victims had frightened her, but if she's aware of how bad this last one was, she's probably terrified now. Her magic can't protect her from him much longer."

Father looked at me. "She might seek us out now."

"If she waits too long, she may not have enough time to find us," I said. "Depending upon why he has come for her, she might beyond anyone's help. He's proven to her she has no safe place to hide because he can find her."

"That's determination," Jacques said.

"It must be something of extreme value."

"But what?"

I shook my head. "That's the mystery we need to unravel."

CHAPTER 31

*A*ll the newspapers now characterized this vampire as Jack the Ripper. His hunting grounds were on the streets of Whitechapel. Our hunting grounds were the same as his, only *he* was our target. But we knew the actual truth about him, what he actually was, and his true name. We understood a *part* of his purpose for his slayings, and Esmeralda knew exactly *why* he was here, choosing to keep the reasons to herself.

After sunset, the four of us walked through the worst of the slum housing districts where Trenton had once been the owner and overseer. The destitute residents were absent from the streets and alleys. While the vast majority of them couldn't read or even afford to buy a newspaper, the news of the double murder the night before was known by almost everyone, traveling faster than the wind. These poor people had little to live for, but even poverty-stricken, they hid indoors because they still valued their meager lives. Such rugged hearts held the hope for another day, seeking any sustenance to survive.

Candles and lanterns glowed faintly through the thin curtains in the upper windows. No footsteps other than ours struck the cobblestone. The night air was still but chilly with few clouds in the sky.

We stopped at a bench near a streetlamp and sat down. I hunched forward, resting my elbows atop my knees and clasping my hands together. I stared ahead, watching the street before us.

"It's incredibly quiet tonight," Matilda said. "For the streets to be so vacant, the tension is still obvious."

Father nodded. "I agree. It adds to the eeriness."

The absence of people was chilling. The shadows appeared darker than normal. With the increased silence I almost expected a sudden rushing creature to erupt with high-pitched shrieks and attack.

I glanced toward my cousin. "Jacques, you mentioned werewolves have hierarchies, too. Where do you fall within yours?"

Jacques faced me. "I'm an outlier. I'm certainly not an Alpha, but thanks to your father, I was able to escape the pack of mammoth wolves. But the pack to which I had belonged isn't typical of what might have been in London."

"Why? What's the difference?"

"Our pack didn't hold true hierarchy levels since Dracula's grandson held our allegiance and controlled us. We were his property and an extension of his power."

"An extension?"

Jacques nodded. "As mammoth wolves we guarded his castle during the day while he and his vampire offspring slept. We also kept guard of the perimeter at night. We considered ourselves siblings and equals. We didn't have ranks. As a true pack in the wild, we'd have fought for position."

"Rusk was one of your pack?"

He nodded. "Yes."

"If you remember, son, he was the one who gave me the talisman to turn Jacques back to his human form."

"A talisman?" Matilda said, looking at Father.

Father nodded.

I smiled at Father. "I remember, but why did Rusk return to Ploiesti instead of staying with us?"

Jacques smiled. "He and I would like to forget our past together when we were at the mercy of Dracula. Seeing one another we'd always be reminded."

"But if you're like brothers—"

"While under the master vampire, we *were* like siblings, almost like we had been mentally neutered so no rivalry ever occurred amongst us. In a sense it prevented us from having a wolf leader to plot for an escape."

"And coexistence as equals has changed now?"

He nodded. "We'd be forced to fight."

"Why?"

"It's a part of our primal beasts. At some point it would happen even if we tried to avoid it. One has to be supreme and the other must become submissive," he replied.

"So that's part of the hierarchy?"

He chuckled. "No, it *is* the hierarchy. It's nature's pecking order."

"That makes better sense," I replied. "Why hasn't Dracula's grandson ever attempted to recapture you and Rusk?"

"I don't know that it's worth his time. He could send lesser vampires to track us, but they don't have the strength over us that he does. Essentially, he'd find it easier to make new mammoth wolves for his pack than seek us."

"So how does such an order work with the vampires? Since we're fairly certain Raginwulf is a master, why didn't he bring his vampire servants with him?"

"Because every master vampire between Romania and London would have viewed his approach as an act of war. It's doubtful he'd have even reached London. Essentially, his servants would be his army, and no master wants another master to encroach upon his or her territory. With such numbers, hiding a sleeping army during the daylight hours would have been too difficult for any vampire. That's why he's siring new vampires, but they are weaker and harder to rein in. Plus, the vampire hierarchy is much broader than a werewolf hierarchy."

"How?" I asked.

"The tiers accumulate into hundreds of branches all around the world, but every tier can be traced back to one vampire."

"Dracula?"

"Yes, but no one knows where he resides after he fled his castle, leaving his grandson to reside within. The two generations beneath Dracula, his actual children and grandchildren, are the most powerful masters. His sons and daughters rule as princes and princesses around the world. Their power almost equals his except that their bloodlust has given them more to dispensing cruelties to the crofters they rule over. You've yet to witness a master vampire with the authority and control these prominent vampires of the purest bloodline maintain. Let's hope at your tender age you never do. Their supernatural physical and mental strength are why I fear Dracula's grandson and his ability to leash me under his power again. Believe me, he'd punish me severely before returning me to the pack. He'd make an example of me to the others. Death would be more desirable."

Matilda took his hand into hers and leaned her head against his shoulder.

I took his warning to heart. Trenton had nearly killed me, and his bloodline wasn't pure. Probably far from it. I couldn't imagine what those directly descended from Dracula and his children were capable of doing. The uneasiness Jacques had displayed convinced me not to pursue the highest vampire ranks for many years even though I was one of the Chosen.

Glancing toward my father, I noticed his eyes were distant in thought. It occurred to me that even though Father wasn't a Chosen Hunter, he had risked his own life to confront Dracula's grandson to rescue Jacques and free my mother from the vampire's control. I marveled at his bravery. Had he not succeeded I would never have been born. Possibly his boldness was why his only son had become destined to be a Vampire Hunter.

His eyes peered into mine. While his stiff aging body continued degenerating, his inner strength and courage raged onward. I wanted to say something in regards to his valor but words seemed too inadequate. I understood his anger and frustration more than ever. His inability to get around and fight vampires like he once had was the biggest reason for his resentment, not of me, but like Jacques had hinted, Father was bitter at himself for his shortcomings. His criticalness toward me wasn't necessarily to discourage me but to prevent me from being overconfident, which had nearly caused my death at the hands of Trenton.

We sat in silence for a quarter hour. No strangers ever emerged on the street.

Finally, I stood. "I don't think he will make an appearance tonight."

"We should make one quick round through the streets though," Jacques said. "If other streets are dead like this one, there's no reason to continue watch tonight."

"Tomorrow we should investigate the abandoned workhouse," I said.

"It's risky."

"Not as bad as these streets without any light at all."

Jacques nodded. "I suppose that's true. The darkness doesn't affect my vision. We'll do a quick tour and head back to the inn."

CHAPTER 32

The following morning's breakfast was light and fast. We wanted to get to the abandoned workhouse before midday when it was less likely the Gypsies would be more active on that side of their village where they might witness us entering. The Gypsies weren't early risers. They seemed to congregate toward the center of Lowbey and the main street during the day to set up their vendor carts and tents.

Since we had purposely abstained from going near Lowbey, Esmeralda either figured she had scared us away, *doubtful*, or she was worried about what our next move would be. With her skeptical nature she probably viewed us as the type of folks who prodded until we got what we wanted. I was, but not Jacques, Matilda, or my father. The more time she spent fretting about Raginwulf and us, the less concentration she had to focus on spells and curses.

I had spent a vast amount of my time considering the benefits of allowing the situation between Esmeralda and Raginwulf to unfold between them. Since my suspicions remained that she had done far more to provoke his wrath than what she had told us, she had brought this burden upon herself. I wanted to see who would be victorious. For some reason I believed her magic wasn't any match for Raginwulf's aggressive dominance. He'd become the ultimate victor and take whatever she was keeping to herself.

However, after the most gruesome murder yet, we couldn't allow the *Ripper* to continue terrorizing the blameless victims who had nothing to do with Esmeralda. This vampire needed slain before he killed more innocents.

We crossed the street where we had first met the were-rat boys and descended into the underground tunnel system. After climbing down the short ladder and lighting the lantern, we made our way toward Albert's chambers since he wanted to accompany us to the workhouse. But he and his boys met us before we were even halfway to his room.

"Ah," Albert said with a toothy smile. "I was just going to send a couple of the boys to the surface to find you. Are you ready to hunt for the duke in the workhouse?"

I pulled a stake from my pocket and nodded.

"Good," he said with an eager smile. "I'm interested in seeing that enchanted hedgerow you had mentioned."

"You might have to view it from afar," Matilda said.

"Why's that?" he asked.

"We're trying to keep our distance from Esmeralda."

"Still?"

I nodded. "For now. To keep her on edge."

Albert offered a solemn nod. "Come. The boys will lead the way."

The were-rats paced eagerly ahead of us with their long tails swaying behind them. Two of the boys carried lanterns. After several turns through the tunnels we came to the room where we had slain the four vampires. No undead lurked within the shadows. The boys hurried up the narrow stairs almost racing one another. We walked brisk steps with Father following from the rear. Stairs were rough for him, but his determination got him to the top.

After we emerged in the overgrown garden, Albert called for the boys to wait for my father to emerge. Father reddened when he came through the door, partially from the exhaustion of climbing and partially due to embarrassment of his inability to keep up.

Albert crossed his arms, looking at Matilda. "Where are those hedges?"

She looked in the direction where we had discovered them, but some of the larger garden shrubs, dry brittle weeds bearing sticker seeds, and the wide trees blocked the hedges from view. "It's not possible to see them from where we are."

"Ah," Albert said, nodding. "Perhaps after we have inspected the old workhouse?"

Father stepped beside me and wiped sweat from his brow, even though the outside temperatures were moderately cool. "Let's move along. I'm ready."

Clyde and George were the largest of the five rat boys, and they greatly resembled giant rats. The other three, also furry with their long tails dragging behind them, looked more human in their faces. They kept slightly behind their larger siblings, not necessarily ostracized by the two larger were-rats, but the differences in their appearances showed obvious separation between them.

"Boys," Albert said.

They slowed and looked over their shoulders toward him.

"Don't enter the building first. Allow us. If Duke Raginwulf is inside, it's too dangerous."

They nodded.

"Be watchful for large holes in the ground," I said. "It's a long way down."

They chattered whispers amongst themselves but otherwise ignored me. I realized they could heal from severe injuries and possibly such a fall was inconsequential for them, but who wants to suffer through the grueling pain of healing when it's avoidable?

"Albert," Matilda said. He glanced back, and she pointed down the hill toward the green branches that stood like a natural fence line. "That's the enchanted hedgerow."

He grinned. "Splendid. Of course, I can't go to them during the daylight. I can't chance someone seeing me. I'll come back during the night for a few cuttings."

"Perhaps one of us can do that," I replied.

"I'd be gracious, if you could."

I nodded. "Let's see what we discover inside the workhouse first."

"Agreed."

At the far edge of the old rundown building the rat boys stood and waited. The side door had already been splintered open. This was near the spot where we had seen the growing mist that first evening after we had discovered the overgrown garden.

"It's been a long time since I've been inside this old building," Albert said. "Before it was shut down, it had been a good place for me to find tidbits of food. They dumped the scraps into old barrels on the other side of the building."

Matilda scrunched her nose in disgust. "You ate the leftover garbage?"

He shrugged and offered a sly grin. "Another reason I don't refer to myself as a *king*. I've never feasted at what I'd call a King's Table."

"I'm sorry," she said softly.

He waved his hands. "When you look like I do, you make due. Now, follow along *quietly*, and I'll show you what remains of the house where the destitute people fed and slept. It wasn't much, but it was better than being hungry and sleeping on the street, especially in the winter or on cold rainy nights."

"Why did they close it?" I asked.

"As you noticed below in the cellar, the foundation is poor, sinking, and falling through in places. It's not a good situation when living on the streets is safer than being inside a building that might collapse."

Albert entered and motioned for the boys to stay at the doorway. I pulled a stake from my pocket and my father did as well. The morning light beamed through the cracked broken windows, spilling yellow pools and strange shadows across the floor. The modest light didn't fully illuminate the floor or the small side rooms.

The large center of the ground floor was rows of dusty old crude tables and benches where people had sat and ate. They almost resembled the pews in the cathedrals except these weren't fancy polished benches. Some of these rough tables were missing boards where vagrants had pried and stolen them to burn as firewood in corners of the room. Others had been toppled. A few overhead beams had collapsed, crushing through lines of tables, forming a slight path of obstacles.

"Where do you think he'd hide?" I whispered.

Albert shrugged. "The beds are on the floor above and it's darker there."

Jacques gave him an odd glance. "How do you know that?"

"I lived here for a while after it shut down."

"Why don't you stay here now?"

He made an odd face and pointed at the fallen beams. "Even though it's closed, you have the occasional homeless groups that stagger their way through the winter snow to hide for the night. Thus, the burnt boards. Besides, the dark underground tunnels are better places to hide and it's less likely people will explore after dark. And when some do, they're quite timid and easy to scare away."

At the center of the ground floor, boards creaked overhead. Part of the ceiling sagged in places that the support beams had secured. Dust leaked through cracks in the ceiling and filtered slowly down.

"Shh!" Jacques said.

"What is it?" Father asked. "Is someone else here?"

"I don't know, but I smell blood," he replied.

Matilda nodded. "So do I."

"Fresh?" I watched Matilda and Jacques sniff the air and walk in the direction of the scent.

"Recent," Jacques replied in a whisper. He took out a wooden stake.

I walked along the opposite side of the room in between the table rows and the wall. Broken window glass crunched beneath my boots. Names were carved into the wooden tabletops. Fragments of old broken plates and bent forks lay on the floor. Empty tobacco pouches and other bits of garbage littered the room.

Between the dust and the building stench of something decaying, breathing was becoming more difficult. It wasn't as bad as the tunnels beneath Lowbey, but the pungent odor was far from pleasant.

Matilda coughed and gagged, placing her hand over her nose. "Over here."

I eased my way over to her to join the others. Two men lay crumpled over one another with large bite marks on their necks. Their skin was ashen gray. Dried blood streaked down their throats onto the collars of their shirts.

"Stake them?" I asked, moving closer.

Jacques knelt, pried open their stiff jaws, and shook his head. "No. They were drained and no blood is in their mouths. He didn't turn them. He feasted upon them."

"How can we be completely certain?" I asked.

"Place your cross to their flesh. If it burns them or bolts them awake, then I'm wrong," Jacques replied.

I took my silver cross and pressed it against the one man's forehead. Nothing occurred. I did the same to the other man. Still nothing. "You're right, cousin. He didn't turn them."

"Nor would he," I said.

"Why's that?" Albert asked.

"The one that is a Gypsy," I replied, pointing at the one man. "That's the fiddler from the night we entered their town."

"The other one is Warren, the reporter," I said.

Jacques recognized them and nodded. "I think Raginwulf purposely left them like this as a testament for Esmeralda."

Albert knelt and examined the men. "You think she'd even come here?"

"She wouldn't," I said. "But once she realizes the fiddler is missing and that Raginwulf had been attacked by the hedges, she will probably send someone to search for them."

Matilda glanced at me. "How'd he get the fiddler?"

"He's found a way into Lowbey," I said.

"Or he lured him past the hedgerow," Jacques said.

"Seems most likely," I said, reconsidering. "She has set many traps. The hedges are the closest, and he knows they're there."

"The hedges cannot affect him if he turns to mist," Albert said.

"Mist?" I asked.

Albert nodded. "It's one of the most effective ways for a vampire to pass through barriers or to escape. But there is also a great downside."

"What's that?"

"A vampire who undergoes such a transformation becomes quite exhausted. He must feed quickly. But in his mist form, you cannot kill him. As a mist, should he intend to flee, you cannot stop him. However, depending upon what type of power he has, touching the mist can actually poison you, though such is rare."

I had never realized all the abilities vampires were capable of performing. "I wonder if Raginwulf is actually the one who has been killing the women in Whitechapel."

"Why?" Jacques asked.

"Some of the women were butchered with absolute pure hatred. But these two men only have bite marks? It isn't consistent."

A loud crash echoed on the floor above.

Jacques stared sternly at Albert. "I think he's still here."

Albert smiled. "If he is, he cannot flee outdoors since the sun has risen."

I headed toward the stairs. "Then we have him trapped."

"Forrest," Jacques said sternly. "I realize you believe this is a good situation, but don't be hasty. A trapped vampire often becomes far more dangerous than one who has a clear route of escape. Remember what he's done to me twice."

"I understand. But he's up there. We must stop him. Not for Esmeralda's sake but to prevent him from killing more people."

"Noted, but proceed with extreme attentiveness, Forrest," Jacques said.

I nodded and stared toward my father. His brow furrowed and determination set in his eyes. It was a wordless expression I understood where he pressed me to stand my ground and obey my instincts. Although Jacques had spent far more time teaching me how to kill vampires, Father had taught me to listen to my faint inner voice, even before I knew I was a Hunter. Often, he had told me those whispers came from a higher source and when properly heeded, they allowed one to survive unexpected dangers.

Dominus expanded upon those quiet spoken warnings as instinctive premonitions given by the spirits of former Hunters. Many times while fighting vampires I can attest that such forewarnings have saved my life. While this is indeed a gift, unfortunately, they were only warnings and never outright steps detailing how to kill a specific vampire. I suppose that would be too easy.

With my massive size I was unable to step silently up the steps. The boards creaked and moaned beneath each heavy step I took. Several of the steps had become partially rotted and decayed from a leak in the roof. I stepped over them and the awkward movement caused even more protest from the weakened boards. With only a few more steps to climb, I grabbed a handrail and gripped it, using it for leverage to help lighten my steps.

Jacques followed with more nimble graceful steps, barely making a sound. Matilda did as well. Albert, in what I'd say was an incredible scurrying display, was at the top of the stairs in front of me without having made a sound. I knew Jacques could move fast when it became necessary, but the only times I had ever seen such speed from him was outdoors. He gave Albert a slight envious frown.

Turning at the top of the stairs, I was overtaken by my bewilderment. Sunlight filtered through a narrow line of windows, lighting up the far end of the room. Rows upon rows of what appeared to be caskets without lids occupied the floor. Narrow aisles separated the rows. In the poor lighting, it was difficult distinguishing what the objects were.

"What are these?" I asked.

"Beds," Albert replied softly.

There must have been over a hundred of them, possibly more, and they lined from one wall to the other and were covered with heavy layers of dust and cobwebs.

"They look like caskets," I said.

Albert nodded. "They are called 'coffin beds.'"

Old dusty blankets were in a few of these beds nearest me. Some reeked of mildew where water had leaked through the ceiling, soaking the bedding. I held the lantern over a few of the drier beds. "He could be hiding in one of these."

"Only where the sunlight doesn't reach," Albert whispered.

That eliminated the far side of the room. The light grew dimmer where we stood and toward the wall opposite the windows, several coffin beds were in complete darkness. "There?"

"It looks like the best place," Jacques said.

I placed the lantern into my left hand and took a stake from my pocket. The others took out their stakes and crosses. Father had finally reached the top of the stairs. He took out his weapons, too. Albert stepped across one of the beds and down onto the next aisle. Matilda moved to a different aisle with Jacques. Father stayed behind me.

The three aisles between the beds met at the darkest part of the second floor. I wondered where this vampire was hiding. While we were downstairs something had fallen inside this enormous room, but none of the beds seemed to have been disturbed or overturned.

A square of light washed over the coffin beds as I carried the lantern toward the darkest corner of the room. I gripped my stake tightly, preparing for the moment the light revealed Raginwulf lying in one of the beds. Matilda and Jacques kept their attention focused on where I walked. They held their medallions in their left hands along with their golden crosses. By the way their ears slightly moved and their noses flared, they were using their keen senses to locate the vampire.

We walked to the dark corner, looking into each bed, but he wasn't inside any of them. A pale face peered from the rafter above the darkened beds. He was at least ten feet above us like he was clinging to the rafters but he wasn't touching them. He was levitating.

His eyes narrowed with scorn. A second later he revealed his fangs. There wasn't any path for us to take to get near him. He looked rather pleased by that and a sense of triumph gleamed in his eyes. The enchanted branch that had killed Trenton was on the table in our room where Matilda had been trying to figure out the spell bound to it. I had forgotten to take it with me.

"Fools," he said with a harsh whisper. "You dare hunt me within my den where I have the most power?"

I set the lantern onto the side of a bed and eased my hand into my left coat pocket. I grinned at him, staring directly into his eyes. I laughed. "Your power doesn't reside here. You left your stronghold to come to London where you are far weaker."

"Forrest," Jacques whispered. "Don't taunt him."

"Advice you should heed, young Hunter," Raginwulf replied. "My battle does not involve you, but yet, the lot of you continue to pursue and interfere."

"That's because you're killing women on the streets of Whitechapel," I replied.

"I have my reasons for ridding the world of these bawdy women."

"Esmeralda would be one of them?" I glared at him.

His eyes regarded me with sudden interest. His thick Romania accent was identical to mine. "What do you know of the Gypsy witch?"

"Only that she's perturbed you by something she's done and she's withholding whatever that information is from us," I said.

"Bring her to me," Raginwulf said. "And the murders will cease. You have my word."

I shook my head. "Sorry, but I don't align myself with the undead."

"Such a fool."

I shrugged. "For mankind to survive, the undead blight must be removed from amongst us."

"Is that so?" Raginwulf asked. "Were it not for us, mankind would cease to exist. Isn't that right, were-rat?"

I glanced toward Albert. He didn't take his attention off the vampire. Instead, Albert's eyes reddened, and he gnashed his teeth.

"So, Hunter, don't be so presumptuous to believe the living are worth more than the undead. We all have purpose on this earth. Yet, you regard us as the lowest life forms when in actuality we're the supreme beings."

"Life form? You're unliving, undead. Cursed above all else." My hand tightened around the stake. "Soulless creatures destined to abide in Hell."

Father and Jacques each regarded me with an odd stare.

I shrugged.

Raginwulf's intense gaze bore into mine. He lashed toward me with a coaxing wave, attempting to sway me with his glamour, hoping to compel me to do his bidding, but his urging was abated and dashed away in seconds. He frowned with curiosity. "Hunter, I ask that you

LEONARD D. HILLEY II

dismiss your obsessed need to kill me at least for a while. Until justice is wrought."

"I cannot."

Raginwulf glanced toward Jacques. "Can you not persuade him to abstain from his driven urge to slay me? After all, you know my strength and that I've spared your life twice, wolf. I have no quarrel with your group. Even though this Hunter has made my situation a bit better by killing Trenton, he needs to realize I'm far more powerful than that whelp. If he refuses to concede this morn, I will show no mercy. Instead, I will have no choice but to kill all of you, including the female wolf at your side. Is that what you want?"

Emotions struggled on Jacques' face for several long seconds. He had been determined to kill Raginwulf until he threatened Matilda. Now he didn't seem as certain.

I looked at Jacques. "Take the others with you. I'll fight him alone."

Jacques frowned and shook his head, placing his fingers on his medallion. "No. We came as a team, and we will fight as one."

"Agreed," Albert said with a shrewd stare.

"Then I shall dismember all of you and feast upon your broken bodies." He withdrew a long serrated blade, his fangs lengthened, but before he moved, I lobbed a glass globe of holy water toward him.

The glass shattered against the rafter beside him, spraying holy water across his face. His angered growl was hellishly frightening and unlike anything I'd ever heard. Jacques lunged over the bed toward the vampire.

Raginwulf's skin peeled, and he dropped to the floor behind a line of the beds. I rushed over several beds with my cross and my stake. Before I climbed over the next row of beds, he was gone.

"Behind you!" Albert shouted.

I turned to see Raginwulf only feet away from where I stood. I lifted the silver cross in my left hand. His gaze flicked toward it, causing him to cringe and cower backwards. The holy water continued burning his face, but he seemed unbothered by it. He continued recoiling as I walked toward him with the cross. He hissed and gnashed his fangs in a threatening manner. Then he winced, touching the festering blisters on his face.

Albert nimbly crossed several beds and brought up his stake. He looked twice his normal size, heavier, and rage loomed in his red eyes. His claws had lengthened, and he snarled.

Raginwulf darted toward the stairs incredibly fast. I grinned. The downstairs was brighter with a lot more windows. When he realized what I smiling about, he ran past me with blinding speed toward the darkest corner where we'd first seen him. By the time I turned again, he became a floating crimson mist of blood, hovering momentarily before touching the wall and drifting down between the cracks in the floorboards.

"Should we rip up the boards?" I asked.

Jacques glanced at Albert.

Albert shook his head. "No. It will do us no good. While he is mist we have no way to cause him any harm, whereas he might have the ability to poison us. We should go. I need to get the boys back underground where they're safe."

"Fire won't work?" I asked, taking the lantern toward the dark corner.

"This building might be abandoned," Albert said, "but do you really wish to suffer the repercussions for setting it ablaze? The prisons in London are not hospitable. Besides, the vampire can move faster than the fire can burn."

"But he'd be forced to go into the sunlight."

"No. The basement beneath this building connects to the cellar near the garden. As mist, he can make his way through the collapsed section." Albert bowed and smiled. "I appreciate you allowing me to come here with you, but it is essential I get the boys back to the safety of my den. I cannot risk the Gypsies seeing them."

Jacques clasped a gentle hand on Albert's shoulder. "Sure. I think we all need to get back. Should Esmeralda find the bodies downstairs while we're here, there's no way to convince her that we didn't kill them."

We began walking single file down the creaky stairs.

"I agree. At least we know where Raginwulf is now," I said.

"It's doubtful he'll remain in this building," Jacques said. "Like you mentioned to Raginwulf, he's not as strong in London as he is at his lair in Romania."

"What stopped him from attacking us?" I asked. "He had drawn his blade."

"The holy water weakened him," Albert said. "With his strength subsiding, the increasing sunlight, and our crosses, I believe he realized he was cornered. A solitary vampire most often flees. He has no effective defense when cornered. While they are fearsome creatures, the older ones have brittle bones. Injuries are not escapable. He simply reevaluated his situation and fled."

At the foot of the stairs, Albert bolted through the tables toward the door where the boys were supposed to be waiting. Jacques and I hurried after him. Matilda remained behind with my father, so he didn't have to walk alone.

When we reached the door, Albert took a deep breath and released a long sigh. The five boys sat in the high grass aggravating a large nest of angry ants with dead twigs.

"Okay, boys," Albert said. "It's time to go."

CHAPTER 33

*W*e had been so close to slaying Duke Raginwulf. He had stood only feet away from us. Albert modestly downplayed the vampire's fear of the large were-rat, but as I thought about the situation, Raginwulf had fled from Albert, not me or our crosses. The were-rat was possibly our best ally in destroying the master vampire, and he had mentioned Raginwulf had fled from him during their first encounter. Albert had even mentioned that he could kill the vampire. But how?

"We should return to the workhouse tomorrow," I said.

"No, Forrest," Jacques said. "I've warned you about becoming too arrogant. I understand you can't help most of it because of your age. You're so young and have this unbelievable gift . . . but you're *not* invincible. I'd like to see you live another seventy years or so, but you won't live to see your teens if you don't learn to better evaluate the surrounding dangers. You were taunting a master vampire that has bested me twice."

"I know, but—"

"No, understand, what he said was true. It doesn't matter that he's a vampire. He wasn't lying to you. He could have killed me both times I had encountered him. He didn't."

"But that doesn't make him our ally," I replied. "We cannot ignore what he is or what he has done."

"No, again, *listen*. He was powerful enough to thwart the nine of us when we had encountered him weeks ago."

"Five were children," I said.

"*Six* were children," Jacques said with an intense glare. In spite of my size, his gaze peered into my adolescent mind and shook me. He put me in my place and rightly so.

"Listen to your cousin," Father said. "Arrogance is going to get you killed, Forrest. You'll have wasted the gift given to you, not to mention, greatly disappoint the ones who have blessed you with it. That's not the way to thank them."

Tears heated my eyes, and I was thankful we were in the darkness of an underground tunnel, heading to Albert's lair. My rash behavior was not only endangering me, but everyone in our party. Being scolded like the inner child I was, wasn't easy for me to swallow. But I couldn't deny the truth.

"Trenton was not anywhere near as strong as this master. Raginwulf wasn't boasting about his might. I'm not certain that he's an elder vampire, Forrest, but he's at *least* a couple hundred years old," Jacques said. "You're no match for him. Trenton wasn't either. At least *he* was attuned to understand that. That's part of the reason Trenton sought your help. Continue to be reckless and you will find an early death, and . . . I don't wish to witness that or ever receive such news."

"My apologies," I said. I swallowed hard, trying to push the giant lump down my throat, but it wouldn't budge. I fought not to let my voice crackle as I spoke. "I put all our lives at risk, and I didn't realize that at the time. I promise to be more careful in the future."

"It's easy to allow your passion to overpower rationality, Forrest," Jacques said. "I hate to admonish you in front of the others—"

"But it's the best way," Father said sternly. "It stings to be embarrassed while your peers are watching, and children tend to remember it longer."

I sighed. "You're both right, and I appreciate you calling it to my attention."

"We won't always be here to point it out," Father said softly. "So grasp it early."

"Thanks, Father."

After walking through the tunnels for nearly a half hour, we came to Albert's sconce-lit chambers. He was already seated with his head leaned back and his eyes closed. "So what are your plans now?"

I glanced toward Jacques and shrugged. I decided to let Jacques take charge since I had been thinking prematurely about everything.

"Not certain," he replied.

"I doubt Raginwulf will roam the streets tonight," Albert said.

"Why?" I asked.

"He'll need time to recover after he expended vital energy to take the form of a blood mist. Adding that to his injuries, he won't venture far."

"Which means he will need to feed," I said.

"Feed, yes. Hunt, no. He will seek the first weak person to compel and feed from. He won't prolong his time on the streets and alleys. He might suspect we'll be looking for him."

I sat down on a large square block near a burning fire pit. "Can you explain something to me?"

"What?" he asked.

"What did Raginwulf mean that mankind wouldn't be here without the aid of vampires? He directed the statement to you as though you know exactly what he's talking about."

Albert's tired eyes opened. "He's correct."

"Tell me how?"

"Vampires spared us from the Black Death several centuries ago. With over a fourth of the mortal human population dead from the plague, the vampires realized their source for survival was coming to an end. If all the humans died, eventually they'd cease to exist."

"Can't vampires feed off livestock? Cattle? Horses?"

"They could but most prefer human blood over draining livestock."

"Why?"

"The challenge to compel or glamour mortals into obedience enlivens many vampires. For some, it's the intimacy of enticing a beautiful male or female and partaking the human's blood. The rush is more exciting than . . . shall I say *amorous* activities. And since most vampires rule over territories, how can they rule without humans?"

"So how did they stop the plague?"

Albert grinned. "They were the cure."

Jacques said, "How?"

"Vampires have a unique healing agent in their blood, which can heal other humans when they consume it."

I frowned. "But won't that turn them into vampires?"

"Only if the person's blood is drained until he dies. But for a mere mortal, drinking a vampire's blood has other temporarily added effects. Not only does it heal a person of his ailments, but also it boosts his strength and all his senses. After a few days, the blood is completely out of his system, so if he died, he'd be a corpse and no one need fear he rise as a vampire."

"So the vampires fed the plagued victims their blood in order to heal them?" Matilda asked.

Albert nodded. "They did it out of necessity. And the vampires compelled the people not to remember the act and returned to their positions of power. Like I said, they have a psychological need to rule, so they need the lower classes. Even though vampires are parasites, they have aided humans during extreme sicknesses for centuries."

"But it's self-serving," Jacques said.

"I agree," Albert said. "No doubt about that."

"Are you suggesting humans need the vampires?" I asked.

"Not at all. But it's doubtful, Forrest, that no matter how hard you try, you'll never rid the world of these bloodthirsty beasts."

"Then why did he direct the question to you?" I asked.

Albert folded his long fingers into a prayer-like manner. His eyes studied each of us for several moments while he thought. "Because I was alive when it happened."

We stared at him with stunned expressions.

He smiled, apparently expecting our reaction. "It was before my curse. I was a human then."

"So you're half a millennium old?" Jacques asked.

"Fairly close."

"Then what caused the curse?"

Albert lowered his hands into his lap. "I was a prisoner suffering from the plague. I was in its final stages, and death was imminent. All the prison cells had been opened. The guards who didn't have the plague fled the prisons. Those of us who did, we didn't have the strength to leave. Dozens died in their cells. I forced myself out of the prison. I wanted to see the sunlight once more before I died. But it was dead of night when I got outside. Vampires had besieged the city, trying to heal all who still breathed. Seemingly one found me, compelled me, and when I regained my senses I was healed."

"As a rat?" I asked.

He shook his head. "No. I was human but since there weren't any guards for those of us who had survived to place us back into our prison cells, I accepted the entire ordeal as a pardon and was ready to leave London forever."

Matilda studied him with keen interest. "And what stopped you?"

"The witch who had accused me of my crime. Her lies were why I was jailed."

"What was your crime?"

"None. She accused *me* of being a witch."

"When *she* was the witch?" Matilda asked.

Albert nodded. "Exactly. At trial when the judge asked what magic I had done, she made vivid accusations. When I protested that I could do no such thing, what she accused me of doing occurred before the judge and court. But it wasn't me. *She* was the one who made it happen."

"Why would she go to such trouble to have you imprisoned?" Jacques asked.

"She was my jilted lover. I knew what she was. I had witnessed her evil deeds. She had sworn to me that if I ever left her, she would make me suffer. When I escaped the prison, she was why I had sought to leave London altogether. But she found me before I got to the port and placed this curse upon me." He smiled. "A few weeks later, she died from the plague. I suppose justice was served, even though her curse remains."

"Do you harbor bitterness toward witches?" Matilda asked.

"My dear lady, no. Just like everywhere else, there are good and evil people in this world. Some witches practice to heal and aid the unfortunate with blessings during their times of need. But those with dark souls cast evil spells out of spite, pure selfishness, or unfounded vengeance. This is why the Gypsy witch must be stopped, too. I discern a long veil of darkness surrounding her. Not only must Raginwulf be stopped, she needs to be as well."

"And these boys?" I asked. "Your actual children?"

"*Adoptive*," Albert said. "They were outcast and unwanted because of how they were born. I have taken them as my own."

"Born this way?" Matilda asked.

He nodded.

"Why?" I stared at the five were-rats and back to Albert.

"I don't rightly know, Forrest. Why are you a Hunter? How can the unliving roam the Earth? So many situations occur in life that we'll never find the answers to explain them. Either our knowledge cannot comprehend the reasoning or else it is not for us to question."

"When you heard of my mother's death," I said, "you said that such losses are known here."

"Yes," Albert replied. "The boys' mothers died during childbirth. Blood sickness was what the midwives had explained their deaths to be. The boys were sent to a cathedral, but I intercepted their arrival, taking them for my own to protect them from the priests."

"They'd harm them?" Matilda asked.

Albert nodded. "In the process of excising the *demons* inside the boys, the priests would knowingly *kill* them. Their deaths would be recorded as successes, sparing them from everlasting Hell."

"They have demons?" I asked.

"No. They were born with the same innocence as any child is. But priests attempt to explain away the unknown or altered as ungodly, thus ridding the world of what others view as unsightly to behold." He glanced at Matilda. "Think to how the witch mania extended throughout England. Few *real* witches were ever killed. But those labeled as such were due to physical disfigurements like moles, birthmarks, and other deformities, as a sure sign of the devil. This is why I agree with your spiritual approach in life, Forrest. I have witnessed the treachery from some of those who are in highest holy places for myself and they believe themselves to be gods. What offense had these boys done to deserve death? Not a thing. Nothing is more sinister than harming an innocent child."

"I agree," Matilda said.

I thought about what Albert had said about their births. "So if they bite or scratch a human, like you threatened before, the person becomes a were-rat?"

Albert offered a sly grin. "By all means, allow one of them to do so. You'll have firsthand results."

My jaw tightened and I frowned. "So they've turned others?"

"They are cautious, as I have taught them. A few *accidents* have occurred."

"Then they *can* infect others?" I asked with a firm stare.

"Yes. As can I. It is the curse I carry. The boys suffer from it, too, and I have no definitive answer as to why. But none of us seek to plague other individuals with what we're burdened to carry."

"What accidents?" Jacques asked.

"Clyde and George were the two I saved from being killed by the priests. The other three—Jeffrey, Oscar, and Charles—were infected while they were playing tag with George and Clyde. From scratches. At least I don't *believe* it was deliberate."

I stared at Albert for a long while. It was difficult to believe he was over five hundred years old. I couldn't imagine living that long.

His gaze caught mine. He smiled. "You have lingering questions on your mind, don't you? Ask them."

"Do you really consider the curse a curse? After all, you've lived to see so many changes in London. You could have traveled the world several times."

"With my appearance, it's difficult to travel to other countries and great cities. I have journeyed to Paris, St. Petersburg, and Spain, but even wearing a hooded cloak, it's almost impossible to conceal what I am. The long tail is hard to hide. But is it a curse? Yes, in many ways, just as the witch had intended."

"How so?"

Albert offered a tired sigh. "Because the witch was jilted, and I stand by my decision that I was safer putting distance between us, her main intention was to ensure that I'd never find true love. She succeeded because I've never met a woman who'd marry an actual rat. I doubt such a woman exists. Sure, some women assert their men are just that, *rats*, but far from the physical sense of the word. But in many other ways, I have watched the evolution of society, albeit mainly from underground or during the dead of night. I've been blessed to behold such things, but I'd cherish them even more with a soul-mate to share the pastimes with."

Jacques stared at Matilda. They exchanged warm smiles. Father lowered his head and closed his eyes like he was in prayer.

Albert forced a smile. "Of course, the boys' shenanigans keep me quite busy nowadays."

The rat boys chattered amongst themselves with smiles and little bursts of laughter. Their noses scrunched and whiskers twitched.

"So what are your plans?" Albert asked.

I glanced at Jacques and shrugged. I didn't know what we should do next. I had proven I was too overconfident in my attacks, so I wanted to know what Jacques thought our next set of actions should be. Neither of us was able to offer quick responses.

"Good," Albert said with a broad smile while staring at me.

"What?" I asked.

"No hasty decisions?"

I shook my head.

"As I mentioned earlier," Albert said. "I don't think Raginwulf will remain in the workhouse. He will seek a new place to hide during the day. He won't chance us returning for him during the daylight again. Finding him now might be nearly impossible, especially if he delays killing more victims and leaving them for the constables to find. He has deliberately not set up a predictable pattern."

"That's true," Jacques said.

"Then how will we find him?" I asked.

Father cleared his throat. "We're going to have to draw him out."

Albert's brow rose with keen interest. "How do you propose we do that?"

"We find Esmeralda and take what it is that he seeks," Father replied.

"You really think it will be that easy?" I asked.

He shook his head. "Son, there won't be *anything* easy about it."

CHAPTER 34

ovember 9th, 1888

EIGHT DAYS HAD PASSED while we mapped out a plan on how to enter the tunnel that ran beneath Lowbey's main street. Actually the map and details of what we planned to do was the easiest part. The hardest part was what we had placed upon Matilda. We needed protection from whatever magic the Gypsy witch hurled at us.

Matilda worked on warding spells, but these weren't simple to fabricate. They were quite thorough, down to every exact detail, if done correctly. To perfect her enchants and hanging spells took a lot of meditation and the proper rituals, most of which she needed to do in total isolation without any interruptions.

While she agonized working through the spells, Jacques, Father, and I spent a lot of time hunting for various herbs, ointments, and oils from various vendors. What herbs we couldn't find in shops, we searched the wooded areas and meadows farther out from Whitechapel. Since it was late fall, a lot of them had dried up and gone to seed, so we dug up the roots. Finding all the proper herbs took over half a week to obtain.

During this time nothing new was reported about Jack the Ripper, at least no more murders had made the headlines. There was plenty of speculation and hoax letters circulating, some of which found their ways into the newspapers. Rumors were rampant on the streets, in the pubs, and amongst the vendors. Panic mesmerized the general public.

Constable Shields had visited us numerous times over coffee, almost pleading for us to find the Ripper. Albert wore a hood and searched the streets and alleys nightly with us to no avail. No new clues had surfaced. Raginwulf was a master vampire *and* a master at concealment.

I believed Father was correct. The only way to get Raginwulf was to lure him out into the open with whatever Esmeralda was hiding or had stolen. We couldn't even attempt to bait him until Matilda had finished the spells and enchantments to thwart the Gypsy witch's magic attacks once we reentered the underground tunnel.

The evening air was crisp and cold, almost hinting of winter's early frost when Jacques, Father, and I left the pub. Father had abstained from liquor or beer and had instead drunk hot tea. He had not given into his cravings since the night he and I had nearly come to blows. Even though I had suggested a place other than the pub, he insisted he needed to prove his desires for spirits had been conquered. Not thoroughly, I must add. His hands trembled while others drank at nearby tables, but he resisted his urges. The thick sheen of sweat on his brow signified his internal struggle was far from over.

"We need to check Matilda's progress," Jacques said. "She told me this morning that she expected to be finished by this evening."

"I hope so," I replied. "It's been over a week since we saw Raginwulf. He's killed no one."

"None publicly," Jacques said.

"Which means he could strike at any time," Father said.

Jacques nodded. "He's been feeding somewhere. With the number of homeless people, some could disappear and never get reported to the constables. He doesn't need to kill them. He only needs to feed from them."

When we reached our room, Father knocked softly at the inn room door.

"Yes?" Matilda asked through the door.

"It's John."

She opened the door. Fatigued hung on her face. Her eyes looked tired and her hair was soaked with sweat. When she saw Jacques she gave a nod of great relief and smiled.

"So we can explore the tunnels under Lowbey tomorrow?" Jacques asked.

"Yes."

They embraced, and he kissed her forehead.

I glanced at Jacques. "Do we search for Raginwulf tonight?"

He shook his head. "We need our sleep tonight so we'll be more alert tomorrow. Even with Matilda's magic, it's best to have clear faculties about us."

Seeing how worn out Matilda was, I agreed. She, more than the rest of us, needed sleep. After being scolded about how my zeal had endangered us when we found Raginwulf, I wasn't about to argue about any actions we should or shouldn't take. Tomorrow brought its own amount of risks and dangers without our being weary from scouring the streets, looking for Raginwulf.

Father had combed the streets with Jacques and I during the past week, even though he ached and complained. He didn't possess enough stamina to patrol tonight and then stand alongside us in the morning to confront Esmeralda, provided we found ourselves in such a position.

In many ways I wished it hadn't taken so long for Matilda to prepare the incantations and enchants for her charms because I was confident Esmeralda would have been more fearful of us a week ago than she probably was now. After the gruesomely displayed murder that shattered the resolve of Whitechapel and Scotland Yard, she should have been prey to her own fear and worry, and an easier adversary for us to conquer. We had no way to predict her mindset.

Of course, we were certain that she knew about the deaths of the fiddler and the reporter. While she might be afraid, she'd be cautious and set up stronger measures to keep out intruders.

When I finally lay down on the quilt pallet on the floor, I expected my engrossed mind to prevent me from falling to sleep. Instead, the moment my eyes closed, sleep sucked me into its deep embrace. Often I have wondered if our dreams betray reality or is our reality an actual nightmare we are doomed to endure, leaving our dreams to be the only luxuries for escape. Throughout my life, I've seen unusual things that must have traveled through a rift in the dream realm to invade my conscious life. Some of these things have refused to die, and took an excessively long time to kill until I found the adequate weapon.

Before the following sunrise my mind drifted in that state between sleep and awakening. An uneasy feeling washed over me, but I didn't bolt upright in spite of the dread quaking through me. No vision came, but I couldn't shake Esmeralda and Raginwulf from my mind. I felt both of them struggling against one another for supremacy. One or both of them would die.

Today.

I didn't foresee the details or whom else might die along with them or how the events would even transpire. In the edges of this near dreamlike state, another dark force loomed in the background, building its strength and steadily approaching as an additional threat. Something unexpected I had never sensed before but knew was coming. Our group was caught in the center of these three assemblages. Each of them sought to align with us to turn on the others, but I was confident none of them could be trusted. I wished for clarity, but it never came.

Our plans to seek what Raginwulf had traveled to London to retrieve were dangerous, more so than our entering the abandoned workhouse to find Raginwulf. The level of risks involved was beyond reasonable. The outcome seemed bleak.

A hand grabbed my shoulder and shook me. Blindly, out of instinct, my fist swung upward but was grasped with incredible force and pushed back before it struck its intended mark.

"Forrest!"

I shook my head and opened my eyes. Jacques stared at me for a few moments.

"Are you okay?" he asked.

I relaxed and loosened my fist. Peering around the room, realizing I was safe, I nodded.

"Bad dream?"

"More an unclear premonition than anything else."

"Forewarning of today's events?"

I shrugged. "Perhaps. But whatever we face, it won't be pleasant."

Jacques grinned. "Why do you think Matilda has worked so hard this week?"

She had worked nonstop in hope to shield us from our imminent confrontation, but after the stressful feeling that had dominated my pre-waking moments, I worried that she might not have done enough. There were some things you couldn't prepare for. I hoped the events of this day weren't some of them.

A knock came at the door.

Jacques and I exchanged glances. Neither of us needed to say a word. We both knew who stood on the other side of the door. Constable Shields. His news most likely would not be pleasant. Of course, after he had shared evidence of the murders with us, no visits afterwards had ever been cheery news. Instead, his horrified mind sought our council, not only to find the murderer, but to also alleviate his mind from the building nightmares plaguing him.

Father opened the door.

Shields was paler and more distraught than ever before. His hand shook as he removed his hat.

"Come in," Father said.

"Sorry for such an early intrusion."

Jacques offered his hand and helped me to my feet. We met Shields near the door. "Another murder?"

Shields wiped his mouth with his handkerchief. "Worst one yet. Did you search the streets last night?"

We shook our heads.

"Why in the heavens not?"

"We have another pressing matter to attend this morning," Jacques said.

"What could be more important?" Shields asked.

"We have a lead."

Shields' eyes glistened with tears that could be hopeful or sorrowful.

He lifted his glasses and rubbed his eyes. Readjusting his glasses, he nodded. "I hope your lead is the one that will stop all this."

"We do, too," I replied.

"The previous murder . . . I truly never believed I'd ever see anything worse than Catherine's butchered body. But this one? Even the devil has more compassion. It was the most violent murder scene I've ever investigated. She was savagely hacked to death and dismembered."

Matilda cringed and placed a hand over her mouth, excusing herself from the room. She retched in a pail repeatedly.

"Oh, my apologies," Shields said, cringing. "I brought you today's post."

I nodded my appreciation.

"And I have photographs of the crime scene to show you," he said. "But I warn you, it's a bloody mess."

While Jacques, Father, and I looked through the photographs, Shields turned away. It was more than he could stomach. He took his handkerchief and wiped his brow. The color of his face made me wonder if he was seconds away from joining Matilda in the other room.

These photographs were indeed graphic images that never escaped one's mind after viewing them. Since Shields wasn't looking, I slid one photograph from the others and tucked it inside the folded newspaper. I neatly stacked the rest of the photographs and offered them facedown to Shields.

"You're right," I said. "Horrible. Simply appalling."

Without sorting through the photographs, he tucked them under his arm. "I don't mean to keep you from whatever you have scheduled for today. I'll be on my way. If your lead proves beneficial, *please* let me know."

"We will," Jacques said.

Father opened the door.

"I think today we shall find what is necessary to stop this," I said.

"I truly hope so. I cannot survive seeing another butchered human. I'll be intoxicated before lunch," Shields said, walking out the door. "Good day, gentlemen."

After he left and Father closed the door, Matilda returned from the adjacent room. Father gave me a curious stare. "*Why* did you take that horrible photograph?"

"To show Esmeralda," I replied. "If that doesn't convince her what Raginwulf intends to do to her, nothing else will. Between it and the news story, she should believe she needs our assistance."

Jacques held a grim expression on his face. "You cannot trust turning your back on her anymore than you could Duke Raginwulf."

"I don't trust either of them, but we need her to draw Raginwulf out of hiding," I replied.

"She may force us to kill her, rather than offer any help at all," Matilda said.

"If we do kill her, we'll never find this vampire. We will have done him a great courtesy. He might leave London without our knowledge."

Jacques grabbed his coat. "We cannot worry about what hasn't even happened yet. We need to get started while the day is still early."

I opened my Hunter box and sorted through the contents. While they were packing their equipment, I picked up the gun Dominus had given me as a departing gift, and slid it into my coat pocket. I grabbed a handful of silver bullets and tucked them into my trouser pocket. The gun was a last resort since silver bullets didn't kill vampires. But Dominus had told me the bullets slowed them down. We needed any extra leverage we could obtain.

I placed my Hunter hat on my head. Silver bullets were tucked beneath the leather perimeter band for easy access should I need them.

Father tucked three stakes into his pocket. His aged hands trembled slightly. When he gazed toward me, he placed his hands inside his pockets. He turned so I wouldn't acknowledge the worry in his eyes, which was something I had seldom ever seen him suffer.

As most children, I viewed my father as the strongest man alive, not knowing fear and always fighting to protect me in the grimmest times. He had faced death and triumphed. But the sudden reality of seeing his fear and worry proved that he was only a human like me and subjected to all the shortcomings we all face. We all lived on borrowed time.

CHAPTER 35

*A*bout midway across Whitechapel, George stood at an alleyway. I nodded, and he hurried underground to inform Albert that we were on our way to Lowbey.

We were about a block from where the Lowbey borough began when an unexpected person stepped into our path and confronted us.

Rusk.

"Brother," Rusk said to Jacques with a broad smile. "It has been a while. You've not been an easy wolf to find."

"Rusk?" Jacques smiled, but he was hesitant to approach.

"Hunter," Rusk said, nodding toward me.

"Rusk," I replied.

Rusk studied our group with intense curiosity. "Off to slay a vampire?"

"As a matter of fact," I said with a slight grin, "we are."

"A master vampire?"

Father and I nodded.

"Good to know." Rusk smiled and turned his attention to Jacques.

Jacques cautiously extended his hand, and Rusk heartily shook it. "I never expected to see you in London."

Rusk offered a tired smile that parted his grayish black beard. "We lost you when you docked across the English Channel. With London's vast population it took us a while to pick up your scent."

"We?" Jacques asked.

Two men stepped out from behind a vendor table. One was blonde, tall, and rugged. His golden-brown eyes reflected the wolfish beast inside. The leather overcoat he wore was shredded down one side with what looked like jagged claw marks. His short beard was orange-brown. His hardened glare hinted of no smile to follow.

"Ulrich?" Jacques offered his hand, but Ulrich replied with a glazed expression. His cold gaze sent a shiver down my spine. The unspoken threat was there. I slid my hand into my pocket, searching for a weapon. After politely waiting a few seconds, Jacques lowered his hand, giving a side-glance to Rusk.

Rusk whispered. "This was not *my* doing."

The other man stepped forward and looked directly into Jacques' eyes. He was the same height as Jacques but thicker in the chest and shoulders. His burly beard was more silver than black. His pupils were blacker than coal. From the anger stirring in his gaze, his soul was probably even darker. His upper lip rose into a slight intimidating snarl, exposing his yellowed teeth.

Jacques held the man's gaze for a few moments but didn't step back. He held his ground, showing no fear or submission.

"Luther, too?" Jacques said to Rusk.

Rusk nodded. "Yes. Two more of our former pack are awaiting us at the dock. Yuri and Denis."

"Why?" Jacques asked.

Luther stared at Matilda with hunger blazing in his eyes. He took deep breaths sniffing the air while looking at her. "Who's the she-wolf?"

She refused to keep his gaze, not from being submissive but because he obviously made her uncomfortable. Luther smiled as his eyes studied her. He couldn't stop eyeing at her.

Jacques gently took Matilda by the wrist and pulled her directly behind him. He didn't answer the question. "Why are you here, Luther?"

A low guttural growl rumbled in Luther's throat. His voice was deeper than any human I'd heard before, almost thunderous when he spoke. "To bring the escaped members of our pack back together. We're stronger as a group."

"We've never been a roaming pack," Jacques said. "We went our separate directions. You know that."

"We were foolish and naïve and desperate to be free of our master. It's essential we become a pack to increase our strength and ensure our survival."

"I'm not interested."

Luther cocked a brow. He snarled, revealing more teeth. "Looks like you're already putting one together, Jacques. A young she-wolf to bear children. Perhaps we should fight for her."

"I have chosen who I wish to be with," Matilda said in an icy tone. "Fighting doesn't change my decision."

"That's not how a pack works," Luther replied.

Jacques narrowed his eyes. "I'm not in your pack, nor do I ever intend to be. You cannot force someone to—"

"You are already our brother. Leaving didn't change that. You are still one of us." Luther placed his hand on Jacques' shoulder to push him aside to get closer to Matilda, but Jacques didn't budge. His hand tightened on his silver cane, and he moved it closer to his medallion.

Ulrich stepped forward. Jacques faced both men without flinching or any fear in his eyes. I imagined he could handle himself sufficiently in a fight against either one, but his chances for success diminished quickly should he be forced to fight both men at the same time. Unlike Jacques and Matilda, these werewolves didn't have enchanted medallions to hold their beasts at bay.

Some of the vendors and passersby saw the contention and formed a circle around us, hoping to watch the tension escalate into a street brawl.

Rusk uneasily stepped away from Jacques and came near where I stood. He shook his head and mumbled obscenities.

Jacques frowned and his hands clenched into tight fists. The eyes of the two opposing werewolves darkened. They looked to be only moments away from changing in spite of it being broad daylight with people watching.

Jacques leaned forward and whispered, "I must warn you two, being discovered as a werewolf in London is a capital offense. The constables are armed with silver bullets and will shoot to kill werewolves without any hesitation. They won't take you into custody. You'll be dead. This is *not* a place where you want to reveal what you truly are."

Two constables stood at a vendor table across the street. Their backs were turned toward us, but if the gathering crowd increased much more, the rising noise of the eager spectators would capture the officers' attention, too.

Ulrich apparently noticed the officers and took a step back, thinking about the situation. Luther peered into Jacques' eyes. Sensing Jacques wasn't lying, Luther calmed slightly but was too stubborn to step aside.

Rusk approached Ulrich and Luther. "Jacques and his friends are preparing to slay a master vampire."

Luther's expression reversed from anger to slight elation. "Is this true?"

Jacques nodded.

A coarse rumble of laughter rattled in Luther's throat. "Brother, we'd be honored to fight alongside you to kill this vampire."

"I appreciate the offer, but another matter demands our attention first," Jacques replied.

"Like what?"

"Finding a Gypsy witch."

Luther frowned. "Why?"

"She's the key to finding him," I said.

Luther stepped back from Jacques. Part of the crowd dispersed releasing slight groans of disappointment since an obvious unspoken truce had been met and the potential of seeing a fight was gone.

Luther's mood brightened. Perhaps it was because he hoped to kill *something* today. Jacques began walking again with all of us following except for Luther. Luther walked alongside Jacques and offered an enthusiastic side-glance. "The discussion of you joining our pack isn't over."

"It is for me," Jacques replied.

Instead of offering an argument, Luther grinned. "Once you see the power of our numbers fighting together for a mutual objective, you'll understand *why* we still need one another."

"I've done well on my own for some time now," Jacques replied. "I believe *you* need me more than I need you."

Luther's jaw tightened. His moods changed swifter than the wind.

"Besides, Luther, you mentioned us fighting together toward a mutual cause, but we'd have to fight one another for domination to be in the same pack. There's nothing mutual about that."

"Afraid to get beaten by me?"

"No. There isn't any reason for us to fight. Perhaps we can come together to fight against our enemies, like now, but it doesn't mean we should always stay together. When did you escape?"

"About a year after you and Rusk did," Luther replied.

"Is Dracula's grandson still the overseer of the castle?"

"Yes."

"Then how did you flee?"

"A group of aristocrats visited the castle and kept the younger Dracula occupied for days with a feast of some sort. That's when several of us took the opportunity to escape."

"But you'd have stayed mammoth wolves unless—"

Rusk nodded. "They sought me out in the same pub where John found me. I recognized them and of course found the old Gypsy woman to make talismans for them."

"Lovely," Jacques whispered.

Once we passed the Lowbey Village sign, George and Clyde motioned us toward the passageway that led to the underground tunnel. We hurried down the ladder into the tunnel. George and Clyde each held a lighted lantern.

After everyone was in the passageway, I glanced toward Rusk. "This Gypsy witch isn't anything like the woman who made the talismans for all of you. She's already threatened us with great harm if we ever returned."

Luther frowned. "Then why did you?"

I told the story that Esmeralda had told us, but that we believed she was the reason why Raginwulf had come to London. While I spoke,

Matilda slipped something into Jacques' pocket, then into Father's. She rubbed an oily substance on their foreheads with her thumb in a quick X-like motion and another substance beneath their noses. Then she did the same to herself.

"Then we kill this witch?" Luther asked.

Jacques shook his head. "No. Not unless she gives us no other choice."

"Why not, if she's a danger to us?" Ulrich asked.

From the shadows, Albert said, "We need whatever it is that she possesses."

Ulrich and Luther turned sharply toward Albert. While they were turned, Matilda quickly did the X ritual on my forehead, rubbed a different gel beneath my nose, and tucked something into my coat pocket. Then she hurried to the were-rat boys and performed the same rituals.

Rusk looked at her questionably. She smiled and shrugged but did not approach him or give the blessing over him. Although I wasn't exactly certain why she didn't bless him, she had spent the entire week preparing only for our group of four and the were-rats. Whatever she had placed into our pockets must have been all she had made. She didn't have any extras. And if she was hanging protective spells over us, she had spent the majority of her time focused on our protection, not the other three werewolves.

Jacques faced me. "If you will precede, Forrest?"

I was stunned that he was putting in the lead position again.

He must have noticed my confusion. He smiled and nodded, motioning me to go. After the other werewolves focused on me, Matilda hurried to Albert and slipped an object into his vest pocket and blessed his forehead with the oil. He nodded graciously.

After I took my first step I realized that these werewolves were the third group I had sensed in my near dreamlike state. Things were about to get nasty in ways we had never anticipated.

CHAPTER 36

Several weeks had passed since we had last entered this underground tunnel, giving Esmeralda more than ample time to set new snares unless she had been too preoccupied worrying about the revenge Raginwulf was most likely plotting.

The drainage groove in the center of the tunnel was filled with seeping sludge. Water dripped from the ceiling and the acrid odor remained but barely noticeable. I wondered if the gel Matilda had wiped beneath our noses had blocked the stench. It must have been because Ulrich, Rusk, and Luther kept covering their noses and glancing around in disgust.

When we reached the section of the tunnel where the invisible wall had previously slowed our advance, no magical barrier obstructed the path. I stopped walking and inspected the walls. The last time we were here this part of the tunnel was dry, but the entire channel was now filled with feces and urine. Water dripped from these walls and the ceiling.

"Matilda?" I asked.

"Yes?"

"Unless I'm wrong, whatever she had protected with magic is no longer down here. What do you think?" I turned and faced her.

Matilda closed her eyes and placed her hands before her. "These traps have been removed, but the faint magic I had detected before is still ahead of us."

I placed my hand against the wall where the invisible wall had previously connected. It was cold and wet, but no sensation of magic lingered. For a few moments, this seemed more a trap than not, if only to get us to lower our guard before she attacked full force.

"Let's go," I said, walking farther into the tunnel. "Keep watch around you. She's allowing us passage through, but that's not necessarily a good thing."

"Agreed," Jacques said.

The frigid air hurt my lungs and made my hands ached. Luther stepped between Jacques and myself, which seemed a deliberate hostile motion to flaunt his unearned dominance over Jacques. Surprisingly, Jacques held his peace and ignored Luther.

"So where is this witch?" Luther asked. "Perhaps if the Hunter walked faster, we could find her before nightfall."

"When you enter the place where a witch has forbidden you to enter, you take precautions," I said. "She's powerful, and we encountered many traps the last time."

"Where are they now?"

"The old traps are gone, but that doesn't mean she hasn't placed any new ones."

"Seems your Hunter is cowardice," Luther said, stepping beside me to pass.

I placed a hand on his shoulder and turned him. He snarled and his eyes darkened. He pushed me but my hand caught him around the throat. I lifted him and shoved his back against the cold wet wall.

"You've just made a deadly mistake," Luther said, showing his teeth. His eyes changed. I squeezed tightly, causing him to choke. His face turned red.

"Forrest," Jacques said. "Set him down."

I ignored Jacques. Luther gripped my forearm with both hands and attempted to pry my hand off his throat, but I was much stronger than he had anticipated. Ulrich stepped forward with his fists raised. Before he reached me, I held my silver cross in my left hand and held it where both werewolves could see it. Although it was a cross, the lower part was a sharp-tipped dagger.

I glared at Luther. "A vampire will flee from a pure silver cross because it burns his flesh, but this silver cross can kill a werewolf in seconds. All I need to do is *stab* you with it."

Luther studied the dagger blade of the cross and his eyes widened. He eased his grip on my forearm and lowered his hands loosely at his sides. When the flicker of his wolf's gleam in his eyes retreated, I lowered him to the floor. He massaged his throat. "You lead for now, Hunter. But—"

Jacques stepped between Luther and I. He pointed a stern finger at Luther. "You verbalize a threat toward Forrest, and I let him kill you right now."

"Finally," Luther said with a broad grin. "Jacques' wolf is surfacing. I see the Hunter and the she-wolf are your weaknesses, so now I know what it takes to get you to fight me."

"If I fight you, it's not for pack leadership, Luther. It will be to kill you."

Luther laughed. "We shall see, Jacques."

Luther gazed at Matilda with an odd smile. Matilda scoffed and turned away.

Jacques nodded toward me to continue. He stepped in behind me and Luther took the third spot in the line. Luther looked over his shoulder, apparently trying to locate Matilda, but he became uneasy when Albert suddenly moved from the rear of the line and stood directly behind Luther. Albert held a silver dagger that gleamed in the flickering light of the lanterns.

I returned to a slow walking pace, hoping to sense a magic trap before stepping into one. But everyone behind me continued talking softly, which made concentrating on the path more difficult.

Albert sighed. "No pack can have two Alphas, Luther."

"I realize that."

"Then why press Jacques into a fight when you both have Alpha personalities. Neither of you would ever settle to have the other rule the pack. You're too strong-willed."

"Besides, I'm *not* interested," Jacques said.

Albert chuckled. "And there's that issue as well."

"But we're unique werewolves," Luther said with a tinge of disappointment in his voice. "Brought together as a unified pack by Dracula's bidding."

"His curse," Jacques said evenly.

"How can you call what we are a curse?"

"His bondage was a curse. We didn't have control over our senses or our personalities. He wanted to keep us bound to him, and it worked for a while. At least a few of us have escaped. We recognize one another from our wolf bonds but not for who are as humans. A veil hid our true selves. That's why you and I clash. It's why we have hostility toward one another. We always will."

"And Matilda?" Luther said. "She's one of us because of you. Is she not?"

"By accident."

Luther smiled back at her. "That's convenient, Jacques. Infect the most beautiful of women to keep her drawn to you out of necessity."

"That's not how it occurred," Jacques said.

"All the same, you've increased our number."

"We are not—"

"Silence!" Matilda said. "Do you not even care that we're trespassing where a witch has explicitly warned us not to return? Forrest and I cannot focus with all this contention. Settle this *after* we're finished here."

"I like her," Luther said softly, giving her a quick wink. "I think her personality is far too strong for you, Jacques. She's better suited for me."

Jacques didn't reply, but he released a slight low growl.

Ahead was the side tunnel we had noticed during our previous journey but Esmeralda had prevented us from reaching it. In our conversation with the Gypsy, she had indicated something of great importance was in that direction. Since she had partially betrayed herself with the slip of her tongue, she'd expect us to explore that route whenever we returned. Without any magical snares as of yet, her bait was most likely well protected. I'd have been a fool to think otherwise.

After crossing the narrow trench of sludge, I stopped at the edge of the side tunnel and glanced at the people lined behind me. Everyone stood ready and waited for me to start walking. George hurried toward me with his lantern, ready to walk beside me. He grinned from eagerness.

This tunnel was drier, darker, and narrower. No water dripped from overhead, but the walls sweated. The slight stench of the sludge channel decreased. I stepped into the tunnel and immediately sensed the pulsating magic I had felt the last time we were here, but it was a lot stronger than then.

"Something's down here," I said.

George glanced up at me. His eyes narrowed from curiosity.

"Yes," Matilda said. "I felt it earlier, but it's much greater here."

My body tingled. Chills crept along my skin, but not from what was farther down the tunnel. Whatever protective blessings Matilda had placed upon us flourished around me, as did something else. We were approaching danger or it was coming toward us.

Thwack!

Hunter instinct beckoned me to duck, and I dropped, using my body to shield George. A horrible wolf yelp echoed in the tunnel behind me. With all the werewolves behind me, I didn't know who had been injured except that it was a male.

I grabbed George's lantern and hurried toward the scream. Ulrich lay on the damp floor clutching an arrow sticking out the center of his chest. He writhed in severe pain. The agony caused his body to begin transformation. His eyes widened and his body shook. He gasped several times, and then his mouth opened wide. His alteration into wolf form stopped and his body stiffened. He no longer breathed.

Ulrich was dead.

Jacques reached for the arrow.

"No," I said, pushing his hand aside. I yanked the arrow out to satisfy my own suspicion and inspected the arrow in the light. "It's silver tipped."

Jacques' eyes became grim with rising anger. His nostrils flared.

"It's more than just being silver," Matilda said. "It is coated with wolfsbane."

Father came forward, shaking his head. He took the arrow from me.

"I can go alone. In case there are other traps," I said, looking at Jacques and Matilda. "Esmeralda expected our return, and she intended to kill a werewolf."

"She didn't know what we are," Matilda said.

Father held the arrow and glanced at her. "I think she did but acted like she didn't know. Why else would she use a silver arrow tip *and* wolfsbane? That first night when we met her, she hinted that she sensed something different about you. Remember?"

Matilda nodded. Her dark eyes narrowed, looking past me toward what more we might face next.

Jacques glanced toward me and shook his head. "It's too dangerous for you to go alone, Forrest."

"She deliberately sought to kill one of you. I doubt she has only one trap laced with poison and silver," I replied.

"I and my boys can go with Forrest," Albert said. "Silver doesn't affect us."

Luther and Rusk knelt beside Ulrich. Sorrow filled their gazes.

Luther looked at us. His jaw tightened. He pointed at Ulrich's body. "*This* wasn't due to magic. The Hunter must have hit a trigger that released the arrow."

"I never saw any trigger."

"You don't have to see it to release it."

"I felt nothing. No wires or levers," I replied.

He glared at me. "You dove for cover immediately. I suspect none of us could have reacted so quickly without some kind of forewarning."

"I was warned," I replied. "But not from tripping a mechanism. I am a Hunter and often receive premonitions from spiritual elders. I had less than a second to duck, which wasn't enough time to shout a warning."

Luther stepped toward me, but not in a threatening manner. His eyes searched the stone floor. He pointed. One stone was pressed a few inches lower than the surrounding ones. "There. Did that stone sink beneath your foot?"

"No."

"It had to."

George offered a nervous nod. "It sunk when I stepped on it."

Luther rose with rage in his eyes. His hands tightened into fists.

George cowered and Albert walked forward with his dagger in hand. His intent gaze was set on Luther.

Luther snarled. "Any of you who wish to remain behind, do so, but I'm going forward with the Hunter. This witch will suffer for Ulrich's death."

His boast was heartfelt, but its undertone was to ensure that Jacques continued moving forward, too. Although at that point in my life, I was too young to understand the depths a conniving jealous heart could undertake. I sensed disloyalty more than unity in Luther's actions. In hindsight, I realize he had been lusting to have Matilda for his own and was hoping Jacques was the next one killed. Luther's false valor to go after Esmeralda was only a subtle challenge to keep Jacques searching for the witch. He knew if Jacques remained behind, it showed weakness, and since Jacques was an alpha at heart, he'd never give Luther the opportunity to show him up. Jacques would continue to prove his boldness, if nothing else.

"You were right about this witch being nothing like the one who made our talismans," Luther said. "She's evil. I will avenge Ulrich's death."

"Don't be hasty," Jacques said. "That was a physical trap, not a magical one."

"I'm aware of the differences."

"Shh!" Matilda said. "Lest you're wanting to reap the same fate as Ulrich."

I walked ahead of the group and thought about how easily Ulrich had died. Werewolves were difficult to kill with ordinary weapons. They can survive devastating injuries and heal rapidly. Had the arrow been steel-tipped without the wolfsbane, Ulrich could have yanked out the arrow shaft and would still be alive. But the silver . . . pierced his flesh, poisoning him, and less than a minute later, he was dead.

My father had told me how deadly silver was to werewolves, but until I had actually witnessed Ulrich's quick death, I never realized the true hazard. Now, I thought twice about carrying my silver cross, not to mention that I was carrying a loaded gun and toting a pocketful of silver bullets. It might not have bothered me at all except that my cousin and Matilda were werewolves. I didn't like the idea of how one mistake on my part could be fatal for either of them.

Since the other tunnel was directly under the main street, I guessed this one must lead to Esmeralda's shop. Perhaps not, but the sensation of magic slowly increased the farther I walked. The protective shield around me sent more shivers through my body. A small crackling sound radiated around me like a burst of static energy, which I took to mean I had just passed through one of Esmeralda's magical barriers. I wasn't certain, but if I had, Matilda's spell had worked effectively to thwart its intent.

Glancing over my shoulder, I caught Jacques' bewildered reaction when he passed through the pulse, too. But when Luther stepped into the witch's magic pool, he wailed. Small bursts of fire shot around his boots and climbed his legs. Rusk removed his overcoat and wrapped it around Luther's legs, smothering the flames, but then the same thing happened to Rusk. He had stepped into the hidden magical fire. Neither of them had Matilda's protective blessing.

Hair sprouted on Luther's face. His eyes turned wolf-like. The tips of his ears changed. His fingers sprouted thick, yellow claws.

"Calm yourself," Jacques said.

Luther snarled. His jaw and teeth were changing. "No. She killed our brother and now has assaulted us. She dies."

Luther continued to change, but Rusk fought and resisted his instinctive urges. Even Jacques was having difficulty staying human. His hand tightened on his medallion when Luther got on all fours and howled. Luther's bones snapped and sinews popped, which sounded brutally painful, but his growls didn't echo any pain but reverberated his elated anticipation of allowing his inner beast to emerge. Matilda placed her hand upon Jacques' and shook her head.

"Luther," Jacques said.

The werewolf stared strangely at Jacques for a moment, recognizing his name. He howled and then turned toward Matilda, sniffing her. Albert stepped between her and Luther. He was ready to plunge the tip of his silver dagger into Luther. Luther rose and ran past me.

"Keep up with him, Forrest," Jacques said.

"You're certain that's a good idea?"

"We know we're buffered. But we need to find Esmeralda before Luther kills her. She needs to remain alive until she reveals why Raginwulf is in London."

"What about Rusk?" I asked. "He's not protected."

"He needs to turn back, unless he wishes to risk following," Jacques replied. "That's a decision he needs to make."

"There's a good chance that Luther's rush through the tunnel has triggered any other snares she has set," Matilda said. "She won't have enough time to reset them, especially if she senses his approach."

"What about my father?" I asked.

The question disgruntled my father since it called attention to his handicap.

Rusk said, "I'll stay with him as the rest of you hurry ahead."

I nodded and smiled. Apparently he remembered my father's physical problems.

CHAPTER 37

By the time we reached the end of the tunnel, angry snarls and growls were followed by wails of agony. Loud cracks snapped the air. Several Gypsy men in drab suits lay dead in the corner. Pools of blood formed beneath their severed throats. Three more men stood with large bullwhips and thrashed at Luther, snapping him, but only increasing his bloodthirsty anger.

One whip flung forward, wrapping around Luther's arm. He secured it in his hand and yanked, propelling the man toward him. Luther's long claws pierced through the man's chest and out the other side. He lifted the man and used his limp body as a shield, rushing toward the other two men with whips.

Esmeralda appeared at the top of a stairwell. Seeing us, she said, "Enough! Truce?"

Jacques watched Luther for a few more moments and then said, "That's up to him since you've decided to provoke him."

Worry creased her face. "I didn't realize he was with you."

Luther ripped the whip from another man and charged him, slashing through his gut deep enough to eviscerate him.

"He isn't, really," I said.

"Please?" she said. She looked much older than when we had last seen her. Fatigue plagued her. "I thought he was sent by—"

"The duke?" Jacques asked.

"Yes. Please call him off?"

"I don't think he'll be too forgiving since your arrow killed one of his pack members."

Esmeralda closed her eyes and leaned back against the doorframe. "That was meant for Raginwulf."

"Silver doesn't kill vampires," Albert said solemnly. "And even you should know better than to cast such a lie before us. I'm a discerner of the truth, and your intention was to kill these people who had only offered to aid you against a common enemy. Now, you've become our enemy."

Her eyes widened at his appearance. She seemed far more terrified of Albert than the werewolf. "Forgive me."

"What is it that you're hiding from us?" I asked.

Esmeralda sobbed and sat on the stairs, leaning her head against the wall. "I—I cannot tell you."

"Is it worth losing your life?"

Rusk and my father finally caught up to us.

"Rusk," Jacques said. "Go calm Luther down. We have things to discuss with her."

Rusk nodded.

"So you know about the fiddler's death?" I asked.

"Yes."

Luther rushed the last man with a whip and swiped his claws through the man's overcoat and undershirt. Deep grooves cut through his flesh, quickly filling with crimson. Luther placed his hand on the injured man's shoulder and glanced toward Esmeralda. "He does not die."

Esmeralda's eyes widened, but she kept the side of her face against the wall. "You've cursed him?"

"To replace the brother of mine that your trap killed. He leaves with me."

She slid her hand behind her, reaching through the doorway. A second later she hurled a glass bottle to the floor. It burst in the center of where we stood.

"Wolfsbane!" Luther growled. He grabbed the man he had infected and sprinted back in the direction we had come.

Matilda and Jacques fled, too, covering their faces. Rusk hurried behind them.

Esmeralda rose and descended the stairs with another bottle of liquid. I held my dagger to my side and waited. Albert told his boys to follow the werewolves. He approached her with bold confident steps. When she noticed his approach, she stopped at the bottom step.

Albert smiled. "I'm resistant to your magic, witch. And wolfsbane has no affect on me. But you're aware of *what* I can do to you. Aren't you?"

She lowered the bottle, offering a feeble nod. "Please? Have mercy."

His eyes narrowed. "No mercy unless you cooperate."

Albert and I approached her.

Esmeralda sat on the bottom step and shook her head. "I just can't."

I reached inside my overcoat and pulled out the newspaper Shields had given me. I took the photograph from inside the paper. "Esmeralda, Duke Raginwulf isn't going to stop pursuing you. He's already found a way to kill some of your people, like the fiddler."

She shook her head. Her voice trembled with sobs. "No, he didn't get into our village. They went to the workhouse to stake him during the day, but they failed."

"Look at this photograph. This was his last murder and the most brutal one yet. He plans to do this or much worse to you. I don't know what he seeks, but his passion to get it back has driven him to rage-filled violence unlike anything the constables of Scotland Yard have ever seen." I handed the photograph to her. She shook. Her moist eyes filled with horror. "We want to slay Raginwulf, but we need to know *why* he is here."

"What good is that information to you?"

"He's no longer in the abandoned workhouse, so we need to lure him to us. I believe we can, provided you share with us the real reason why he has pursued you across several countries. We can use it as leverage or bait to trap him."

"You can't," she said softly.

I tapped a finger firmly on the photograph. "That will be you. Then he'll get what he has come here for anyway. We can help you."

Rusk, Jacques, and Matilda stepped through the door at the top of the stairs and stood, staring down at us.

Esmeralda glanced toward Matilda. "You don't understand. I'd rather sacrifice my own life than allow him to—"

Matilda walked down the steps and sat beside her. Matilda placed her hand on Esmeralda's back and gently rubbed her hand across her shoulders. "Whatever it is, we promise that he won't be victorious. We can keep you safe. But unless you're willing to help snare him, we're ready to move on. Forrest and his father have stayed in London much longer than they've intended. They've slain many vampires in other countries, so I'd safely wager my life on their success."

"Eventually," I said, "he's going to find a way into Lowbey. With his rage and strength, he's not going to be satisfied by killing only you. He'll make a bloodbath of your people."

Esmeralda's wrung her aged hands together. "Other than immediate family, I have placed trust in few people throughout my life, and I've been less inclined to put faith in anyone after what happened with the duke and his deception."

Jacques said, "Either you start today by trusting us, or we leave you to whatever fate befalls you."

She looked into Matilda's eyes for several seconds before she rose to her feet. "I hope you're correct that you're able to defeat him. His death would greatly diminish my burdened heart, but if you fail . . . nothing can ever ease the pain. Come, follow me."

Esmeralda walked up the stairs and wisps of magic intensified beyond the doorway. Jacques and Rusk stepped aside. I followed Matilda and Albert carried up the rear behind my father. I had no idea where Luther had gone, but I felt certain that the rat boys had left the village and headed back to their underground chambers.

She led us to the building where we had first met her. The magical power we had been sensing was inside her shop. After we went inside she stood still with her back to us. Her body shook. "You're certain you'll do everything to prevent him from taking what I value more than my own life?"

Pulses of energy radiated from behind a door where the table was set. For some reason I had never noticed it during our previous visit.

"Is what you've done that has enraged him truly justifiable?" I asked.

Esmeralda was silent for almost a minute. "Yes. I believe I had no other choice."

"Good. I give you my word that we will slay him," I said. It was too bold of a statement for someone my age to promise, but the words left me without hesitation. An urging inside spoke through me, controlled me, and that made me slightly nervous. Even Jacques looked at me questionably.

Esmeralda pulled the chain of her necklace from her blouse, which secured a large key. She walked to the door, stuck in the key, and unlocked it. She hesitated before finally pushing it open.

A wave of magical energy rushed through the door and washed over me. From the way the others reacted, they had all felt it, too.

"You've set a magical fortress around this room?" Matilda asked.

"Yes," Esmeralda replied. "Which has taxed my health dearly. I've aged twenty years trying to maintain this protective shield."

Several oil lamps lit the room. A young woman sat in a rocking chair nursing an infant. We exchanged glances, unsure of whom the magic shield was protecting.

Esmeralda turned and faced us, cupping her hands at her waist. "When I shared the accounts of what had happened with my niece on the night we first learned she was a vampire, I withheld significant information. This child is who Duke Raginwulf seeks to obtain."

"Why?" Jacques said.

"He is the duke's son," she replied. "That's why he has abandoned everything to find me. He wants Varak back."

CHAPTER 38

"*D*uke Raginwulf's son?" Father asked. "How is this even possible?"

Jacques frowned. "Only those who are direct descendants of Dracula can father children like living mortals. At least that has always been my understanding. Otherwise vampires sire offspring by feeding their blood to their victims and then draining their life's blood until death. Then they rise as vampires. Is Raginwulf directly related to Dracula?"

"Not to my knowledge," Esmeralda said.

Albert stepped closer to the child, and Esmeralda became visibly upset by his approach. "It is extremely rare for a vampire to father a child the natural way, but it does happen."

"You know of this happening?" I asked.

Albert grinned. "Live over five hundred years and your chances of seeing rarities proliferates quite a lot."

"I suppose so."

Matilda walked to the side of the rocking chair. The baby opened his eyes, looking at her. "Sky-blue eyes."

"He has his father's eyes," Esmeralda said.

"So tell us what else had happened?" I said.

"When Fifika had arrived at our homestead, the time for her to give birth was near. She insisted that she stay with us. After she had discovered Raginwulf's true nature, she left the duke because she feared what his influence on her child would reap. She informed us of the duke's tyranny over their servants and those beneath his immediate rule, which was something none of the rest our family had ever seen. Her accusations seemed groundless."

"Due to his glamour?" Jacques asked.

"I suppose, but she was mortified to let him near the child."

"When did she give birth then?" Father asked.

Sorrow filled Esmeralda's eyes. Her brow furrowed. "After she attacked us and we cornered her with the crosses, she began having pains across her stomach. Each time one of us tried to help her, she tried to bite us, so we couldn't do anything to relieve her pain. That's why we had hoped to get her to a priest the next morning. Not just for her, but for the baby's sake."

"But that didn't happen?" Matilda asked.

Esmeralda shook her head.

"So she gave birth while you had her cornered?"

"No. When we walked her outside and she burst into flames, the baby lay on the ground unharmed," Esmeralda replied.

Albert frowned. "The sunlight has no effect on the child?"

She shook her head.

"Interesting," he said.

"What does that mean?" Jacques asked.

"It means she was pregnant *before* Raginwulf turned her," Albert replied.

Esmeralda glared at him. "How *dare* you make such an accusation."

The were-rat offered a slight smile. "Sorry, but there's no other explanation. Sunlight would have engulfed the child along with the mother, if he was a vampire."

"So he's *not* a vampire?" I asked.

"Worse," Albert said. "He's a hybrid, half human and half vampire. Oh, Raginwulf is definitely the father, or he'd have killed Fifika for her infidelity well before the child was due to be born. He wanted her pregnant before turning her so the child would be a hybrid."

"A hybrid?" I glanced at the infant.

"Yes. He is capable of withstanding the sunlight unharmed, which is probably why the duke wants this child so badly. Imagine the power a vampire can wield if sunlight has no affect on him, and he has no direct ties to Dracula. Hunters know the best time to slay a vampire is during the day when vampires are the most vulnerable. A hybrid doesn't need to fear this weakness, and because he could go outside in the sunlight, most people would never suspect him to be a vampire."

I held the photograph out for Esmeralda to see again. "I'm beginning to understand why his murders were so graphic and why he cut out some of those women's wombs. He wanted you to know he was the murderer and it testified to what he plans to do to you since you ripped his child away from him. He's going to come after you regardless, so we need to find a place where we can trap and slay him."

She looked away from the picture and back toward the baby. She shook her head. "Are you implying I should have let Raginwulf take Varak?"

"No."

"We cannot allow him to have Varak," she said.

Albert looked at her reassuringly. "Believe me, there's no way we're going to allow him to take this child. The world is in grave danger if he rears him. Even Dracula's clan would fear his rule."

"Why?" I asked.

"Elder vampires can glamour, making themselves appear gorgeous to the overall human population, but Hunters are gifted with insight that allows them to see through the guise. A hybrid or half-blood can go undetected even by Hunters, which is why they are far more dangerous than normal vampires. They thirst for blood, like the vampires, and their overenthusiastic bloodlust is often what makes them careless, giving a Hunter a trail to follow. By then the carnage is so bad, Hunters are often blamed for not acting sooner."

"Why would Dracula and his children fear these hybrids?"

"Half-bloods despise other vampires and view the direct descendants of Dracula as the most vile for having increased the undead population. Since the hybrids walk in the sunlight and have incredible strength, they can kill those protecting a Dracula's tomb during the daylight and slay the royal vampires while they are the most vulnerable."

Esmeralda took Varak from the wet-nurse, and the look on the woman's face held the gravest concern, as though the child she was nursing was hers and not orphaned. Her hands remained outstretched toward the Gypsy witch like she longed to hold the child close to her breast and keep him warm and safe.

"I'd give my life to save him," Esmeralda said.

"As would I," the wet-nurse whispered.

"I'm afraid it may come to that," Albert replied.

I regarded the child with great curiosity. There was power surrounding the infant, something I had never felt emitting from a baby before. I had experienced such from Baron Randolph and Duke Ragin-wulf, but for radiance to come from a baby struck fear deep inside of me. His aura was strong, such that Esmeralda was willing to sacrifice her life to save his, but this was the child's prompting more so than her own rationality. I sensed his control pulsing toward her and the wet-nurse, demanding their protection and desire to remain within his presence.

The look in Matilda's eyes altered. She smiled, coming closer to the baby. "He is beautiful."

Father, Jacques, and Rusk nodded their agreement, also smiling and under complete enthrallment. The child had mesmerized them, too, I realized. Gentle stirrings manifested around me, trying to draw my loyalty, my affections, toward the child. I suppose, since I am a Hunter, I was able to resist being spellbound by Varak.

I feared how powerful his charisma would eventually blossom as he aged. He held great power now, but he didn't have full control. After years of practicing, however, there wasn't any way of knowing what his limits would become. And while I had promised Esmeralda I would ensure the child's protection, I found myself worried about the dangers humanity faced should he be allowed to live.

But who could kill a child, even if destiny ruled that he'd become pure evil?

Not me. Not even with the strength of the premonition warning me, *screaming* at me, I couldn't do it. The dangers the world eventually faced concerned me, but due to my conscience of him being an infant, I could only hope that my instinct was misleading me. Perhaps the child could eschew evil tendencies and cling to the high morals to make the world a better place. I doubted either Esmeralda or Matilda could discern this child's proper future. Would his nature be different with a virtuous person than with his own father? Or did it matter? Was he predestined to perform wicked evil deeds regardless?

I glanced toward Albert with a shrewd stare. He shrugged and shook his head. He was like me, in that the child couldn't sway Albert under his control.

"We need to discuss the best place to draw Raginwulf so we can slay him," I said.

My deep voice jarred Jacques. He turned toward me and nodded. "I'd say right here, but this room is too small. We need a larger place."

"How about right out in the open?" I asked.

"Like the village square?" Esmeralda suggested.

Albert folded his hands together. "That would be a good place, but he's fast. Trapping him might be more difficult in the open."

"Are you certain he will come into Lowbey?" I asked.

Albert nodded. "He wants his child, so yes. He will not hesitate to come for him, but something else must be done first."

"What?" Esmeralda asked.

"You'll have to remove your protection spells surrounding the village."

The Gypsy witch looked worried and frail.

"It's the only way, Esmeralda," Albert said. "Your magic has kept him at bay for quite some time. You remove those shields, and he'll sense it immediately, which is why you cannot remove those spells until we're absolutely ready."

"You guarantee that you can slay him?"

Matilda smiled at her. "It's early afternoon. We have plenty of time to get everything into place and be prepared."

"Besides," Albert said, "Raginwulf's attention will be so focused on Varak that he'll be blind to our ambush."

Jacques glanced toward Rusk. "This vampire has far more strength than Randolph. We cannot afford to make one mistake, or some of us might be killed."

"Esmeralda," Albert said. "You need to make certain none of your folks interfere. In fact, it's probably safest if they resided as far from the village center as possible tonight."

She nodded.

"I forewarn you because should we weaken him, he will attempt to feed upon anyone to gain back his strength. Since the majority of us are not mere mortals, he would have less difficulty if any of your folks were within striking distance. The longer we prevent him from getting to Varak, the more his rage will increase."

"I will let them know," she replied.

"Can you do something else?" I asked.

Esmeralda gave me a curious stare and partway shrugged. "Depends upon what you're asking."

"Have someone cut ten sharp stakes from that enchanted hedge."

She frowned. "Why?"

I explained how the one branch had pierced Trenton's heart.

Albert glanced toward me. "When she disenchants all of her magic traps, her magic will drain from those stakes as well."

"I realize that, but if Esmeralda teaches Matilda the spell, Matilda's magic will remain once Esmeralda has cancelled hers."

Albert smiled at the idea.

"I can do that," Esmeralda said. She motioned to a man standing right outside the door, told him what to do, and then the man ran out the door.

"It's time we get things prepared for tonight," Albert said, glancing toward Jacques and me.

Jacques and Rusk joined me near the door. "We should inspect the village square to find the best places to hide and set traps."

Rusk nodded. "We should stash extra stakes and crosses in case he overpowers us."

"Are you ready, Esmeralda?" Albert asked.

Esmeralda cradled Varak in her arm and swayed back and forth, rocking him. Her moist eyes fastened on the baby's. The wet-nurse rose and stood at Esmeralda's side desperately holding out her hands to take the baby back. Esmeralda refused to release him. "We'll keep you safe, Varak."

CHAPTER 39

*D*usk slowly settled. The ominous cloudy sky hung low over the city, foreshadowing the mood of the night and casting thick gloom over our hopes for success. We waited for hours, and my patience waned to less than the moon's tiniest sliver. When the city clock tower struck midnight and the reverberating gongs echoed, the impending confrontation with Raginwulf was at hand. I sensed his presence nearing.

Esmeralda had removed her magical barriers around the outskirts of Lowbey, opening the door for the duke to waltz into our midst.

Whereas I could detect his approach, I wondered if he realized he was walking into a trap? Did he know we awaited his arrival? He seemed too intelligent to be fall victim so easily, but he wanted Varak, his son and heir, more than he wanted to reign in his eternal undead life alone. He understood the power his son beheld and had deliberately made certain of the child's birth in the manner he had been conceived. He wanted a half-blood child, and I seriously doubted he had ever wished the demise of Fifika, and perhaps that was another reason for dispelling his rage toward Esmeralda and her immediate family. He was coming, not just for the sake of his child, but also for vengeance, to make them pay for the loss of his beloved wife and his son's mother.

I had already sensed how dangerous this influential child was, but more frightening was what Varak would become if Raginwulf managed to flee with the child. Raginwulf would ensure the child was molded into something far worse than himself and Varak would rise into high leadership. Together they'd cause endless bloodshed and possibly remain unchallenged for decades, if not centuries. Once he reached maturity, even I with a dozen or more Hunters faced the impossible task of killing them. Their sway over their glamoured minions would force us to kill hundreds of innocent servants and townspeople in order to get anywhere near their lair. Killing mortals was something I had sworn never to do unless in self-defense.

The chill of the night air swept over me. I stood beneath an awning inside the doorway of a closed shop where I had a clear view of the village center. The water fountain was a pool of dark liquid that shimmered its mirrored surface, which reflected the only lit streetlamp. Father stood somewhere in the shadows to the east of my position. Jacques and Rusk, already werewolves, were across the street on the other side of the fountain in an alley. Albert had hidden so well that I didn't have any idea where he was.

Three curved benches outlined the fountain in the village center. Esmeralda sat on the bench facing me. She wore a wool coat with a hood pulled over her head. In her arms she held what appeared to be a bundled child. On the other two benches Matilda and the wet-nurse sat dressed like Esmeralda, and they each cradled bundles in their arms as well. Decoys.

Varak was in one of the bundles, but I wasn't certain which woman held him. I assumed he was with Esmeralda, but that was an easiest assumption for Raginwulf to make and certainly expect, so the wet-nurse possibly held him. None of us outside of the women sitting around the water fountain actually knew which woman cradled Varak in her arms. The other two held dolls in tight bundles, so no children were at risk.

Since the duke had tracked his son across many countries he sensed where Varak was. We hoped the decoys imposed enough of a distraction for us to attack Raginwulf while he was off guard and trying to determine where Varak was. I thought it odd that the duke's surname was more suitable for a werewolf than a vampire, but his actions made him worthy of carrying it. He was indeed like a *raging wolf* tearing through obstacles to protect his own.

The night air suddenly plummeted. At the main street a billowing of fog slinked between the buildings. My hand gripped a stake tightly. Raginwulf was here.

I shook my head. It was hard enough to fight him in the dead of night, but he favored the additional cloak of thick fog, which reduced visibility far worse, especially for my father and me since we relied upon our human visibility. Rusk, Jacques, and Matilda were able to see through the moving mists.

The women seated on the benches were risking their lives to lure Raginwulf toward them. It was our responsibility to ensure their safety, but with the growing fog, I worried that we might not be able to keep them alive.

The cloud of fog swirled, growing thicker, and easing slowly forward like a narrow wall. It occurred to me that if the fog reached the fountain, he'd kill the women and escape with Varak before we took the opportunity to stake him.

I slipped along the edge of the building, staying beneath the shadows of the awning, but with my massive size, I was far from invisible. I balanced my weight upon the toes of my feet without stomping down upon my heels to prevent making clomping noises. Jacques had shown me how this method allowed someone to walk almost silently, and since I had practiced to reduce my clumsiness, this manner of walking aided my approach without drawing immediate attention to me.

While I wasn't quite certain how Raginwulf was able to manipulate the weather elements, I imagined it required a great deal of focus on his part, and since his attention was probably on the fountain benches, he was less likely to be watching the buildings at the edges of the street.

I made it to the corner of the square and pressed my back to the wall of another building. The fog flowed in soft pillows, rising and building, forming into the shape of a cube. I crept along the building's edge toward the main street where he stood outside the village center.

My hand gripped the stake, but with my apprehension sweat moistened my palm. Even if I had a clear opportunity to drive the stake into his heart, the moisture on my grip would probably prevent me from piercing through his overcoat and ribcage to reach his heart. A pair of gloves would have come in handy, but more and more I was wishing I had a crossbow like Dominus. Indeed this was a weapon I needed to acquire. I needed range.

Nearing the main street, the smell of frankincense flowed from the fog. Was that his fragrance? It had to be. Some of the vampires I had slain had used perfumes or herbs to mask their unpleasant odor of decay, which was slight to a human, especially from a distance, but a vampire was more cognizant to his own death smell and self-conscious that unsuspecting acquaintances could readily detect him as a living corpse. I had yet encountered a vampire who didn't enjoy fraternizing with the higher elements of society. Even Dracula had been known on occasion to host some extravagant festivities with the royal members of other countries without selfishly feasting off his guests. Vampires craved attention and prominence more than most humans.

Until Fifika's death and Varak being snatched away, Raginwulf was probably highly regarded by those he ruled over and those who ruled over him. The bloodbath he had performed on the streets of Whitechapel was merely done to satiate his need for retaliation until he was able to reach Esmeralda. He had lost all control and rationality, which was why he and all vampires were evil. No good vampires existed. Once rage escalated inside their minds, vampires possessed no control over the carnage that ensued. They no longer cared who they killed or why. That was the true danger of any creature that roamed the earth without a soul. No soul meant no conscience, and that's why a greater power summoned Hunters to rid the world of the vampire plague.

The frankincense became stronger, which was the only hint I held of how close Raginwulf stood near me. Vampires didn't need to breathe, and what heartbeat they had was so slight that it was practically unnoticeable. But with the growing fog, I was unable to see him. A rush toward the scent was dangerous and foolish. He could kill me before I saw him. However, an attack would probably stop him from producing the wall of fog that he longed to use for cover to get to the fountain.

I slipped my left hand into my coat pocket and grabbed a globe-shaped bottle of garlic juice. While it worked more as a repellant than a killing agent, it should break his focus, but unfortunately turn his attention directly at me. Since I had used the darkness and shadows to my advantage to move to this position, my father, Jacques, and the others had no idea I had moved. But if I didn't act now, the situation we faced would become far more dangerous.

I lobbed the glass globe toward the center of the adjoining main street, hoping he was standing in the center. When the glass shattered, an aggravated growl emitted. "Fool!"

Before he moved, I took a vial of holy water and doused it over my face, throat, and the front of my overcoat. He rushed toward me, from the cube of fog, and gripped my throat tightly, but only for a moment.

Blisters puffed on his fingers, popping, and oozing as he yanked away. I drove forward with the stake, but he noticed my advance and backhanded me hard enough to pivot me into the air. I dropped hard to the cobblestone square and my stake rolled out of reach.

"Now!" I yelled.

From the shadows, Jacques and Rusk snarled and ran toward Raginwulf. My jaw ached and my head spun with dizziness. I crawled toward my stake, shaking my head, trying to clear my vision. When I grabbed the stake, I rolled to my side to see Rusk being flung into the air.

Jacques gnashed his teeth and raked his sharp claws through Raginwulf's overcoat, apparently slicing all the way through the cloth, his vest, and into the vampire's flesh. The vampire shrieked, clutched his chest, and backed away, feeling and examining his injury.

Rusk brushed himself off and in a blur he was at Jacques' side, trying to corner the vampire. Raginwulf was gone in a blink's time. Jacques and Rusk turned and looked around, trying to find him.

I pushed myself to my feet, staggering slightly. Trenton had hit me relentlessly but never with such impact.

My father stood beside me. "You okay, son?"

I nodded. "I'm standing. Where'd he go?"

Before anyone offered a reply, the wet-nurse screamed. We rushed toward the fountain. Raginwulf yanked the bundle from her arms, but she didn't have Varak. He hefted her with one hand and thrust her into the pool. Water splashed and he turned, approaching Matilda. Before he reached her, she burst from her seat. He jerked back in surprise when she lunged forward, snarling. She bit his left arm and slashed across his abdomen with a vicious swipe, nearly gutting him.

He grabbed her hair at the back of her head and yanked with such force that she yelped in pain. In a flash, he had drawn his long serrated dagger and plunged it into her gut, twisting it in rage while growling.

"No!" Jacques shouted. He tore into a sprint, striking Raginwulf dead center in his back, propelling the vampire forward.

Matilda fell to the cobblestone, clutching the knife in her stomach. Pain twisted her wolfish face as she ripped the blade out. She lay there, panting and whimpering.

Raginwulf staggered, trying to fling Jacques off his back, but couldn't. Jacques snarled, biting into Raginwulf's shoulder and shaking his head like a dog with a toy. The vampire wailed, turned, and slammed Jacques hard against the wall of the closest building. The impact jarred Jacques enough for him to release his hold. A look of triumph loomed on the vampire's face for a moment. Then one of the magical stakes we had hidden shot through the air toward him.

Raginwulf was fast. Before the stake struck his heart, he turned enough that it missed its mark. Instead, it spiked into his left biceps, almost tearing his arm in half. He winced and flashed fangs.

Jacques reeled in pain, rising slowly to his feet. He shook his head and glanced at the vampire with pure hatred. Matilda lay sprawled near the fountain, blood pouring from her gut. Jacques took two steps toward Raginwulf, but the vampire shot forward with incredible speed, clutching Esmeralda's throat and lifting her off the ground.

"I will take my son now," Raginwulf said in a near hiss. His eyes glowed crimson red.

She spat in his face, clutching Varak tightly in both arms. "I'll die first, but not before you."

Another magical stake shot from a statue near the square. He lowered her slightly and the stake caught her right calf. She cried out in pain.

Raginwulf laughed. "I will feast off you after you have suffered death."

Esmeralda stared into his eyes with sudden boldness, laughing as well, which confused the vampire. Several more stakes shot through the air. He lowered her and vanished. The stakes halted midair and dropped into the water fountain where the wet-nurse thrashed, trying to get to her feet.

Father and I neared the fountain where Esmeralda limped back to the bench and sat down. She reached down and gripped the stake, yanking it out. Strangely, it didn't appear to have gone very deep.

"Where did he go?" I asked.

Blood droplets hung in the air on the other side of the fountain like a soft moving mist. A blood mist like we had seen in the abandoned warehouse. In this form, we couldn't harm him, but he couldn't take the child, either.

Jacques knelt beside Matilda. She wasn't moving or breathing.

I swallowed at the lump rising in my throat and hurried to them.

Hurt and anger claimed Jacques. He pulled her to him, closing his eyes tightly, squeezing out tears.

"Is she dead?" I asked.

He clung to her and shook his head. "No, but she nearly died."

Father picked up the blade off the street. "It's not silver."

I released a sharp sigh.

"She'll heal," Jacques whispered. "But whatever magic she has used for enchants on the stakes and our medallions are gone."

Esmeralda leaned over Varak, rocking him slightly. Even with all the disturbances, the child had never cried. The wet-nurse stood from the water and stepped onto the cobblestone beside the bench where Esmeralda rocked the child. Water cascaded off her soaked clothes. Her eyes focused on Varak.

On the other side of the fountain the blood mist hung, slowly beading together like rain droplets collect and connect on a glass pane.

I nudged my father and nodded toward the accumulating mass. In minutes I expected Raginwulf would reappear and return to his pursuit of killing Esmeralda to get Varak. Rusk joined us. "Get ready. He's not gone."

Rusk frowned. "That's him?"

I nodded.

Matilda opened her eyes. Jacques placed a gentle hand on her cheek. "Is he dead?"

Jacques shook his head. "Not yet. When he reappears, he'll be much weaker though. He sustained a lot of injuries and turned to a blood mist. Both have sapped his energy."

"Which means he'll need to feed," I said softly.

Father nodded.

Matilda coughed. "I'm okay. You need to help them slay Raginwulf. His carnage ends tonight."

Jacques leaned down and kissed her lips. Gently, he set her down on the cobblestone and rose to his feet. We stood as a united front while Esmeralda and the woman watched over the infant.

CHAPTER 40

A half hour passed before Raginwulf's form began materializing. From what I could see, all his injuries were gone, but he was still in an in-between state.

I gripped my stake and took a step forward.

Jacques grabbed my shoulder and shook his head. "No, Forrest, allow me. I deserve this honor."

I glanced toward Matilda. She lay in human form with her eyes closed, but her bleeding had stopped. Her skin slowly stitched together. I understood his need for revenge, not just for what had happened to his love, but for the previous taunting encounters with Raginwulf. I nodded.

Jacques smiled. "Thanks."

He hurried to the other side of the fountain. His claws lengthened. The moment the vampire was in solid form, his body was intact without obvious injuries. Jacques clutched Raginwulf by the throat and growled. He brought back his left clawed hand to drive the claws deeply into the vampire's gut, but before he inflicted the painful blow, he was knocked off his feet and into the water fountain.

Growls emerged over the loud thrashes in the water. When Jacques rose to his feet, he wasn't alone. Luther stood with him and flailed a mighty fist into Jacques' jaw, knocking Jacques into the air. Jacques' back crashed onto an empty bench, splintering it. He groaned in pain and rolled with the momentum.

"Luther!" Rusk yelled. "What are you doing?"

"What I came here to do," he replied. "Either Jacques yields to me or he dies, but since he's unable to even protect Matilda, it's doubtful he can stop me."

Raginwulf laughed and his attention turned toward Esmeralda.

Rusk growled and headed toward Jacques. "By attacking him before he has slain the vampire, you've proven that you're incapable of *leading* a pack, Luther. You're a mongrel, unworthy of what the rest of us are."

"Hold your tongue, whelp," Luther said. Two more werewolves stood behind him. I assumed they were the ones waiting at the dock earlier in the day. "Or I kill you next."

Raginwulf walked around the corner of the fountain with a nonchalant strut. He was moments from reaching Esmeralda. Since she was already injured, I doubted she had the strength to fend him off.

I pulled my silver cross dagger from its sheath and flung it. The dagger blade pierced through the right side of his chest, inches beneath his shoulder. He winced and turned to the side, trying to yank the blade out. It must have struck bone because he was having difficulty pulling it free. His vest burst into flames where the silver touched his flesh. He patted out the flames but dropped to his knees from the pain. When he tugged at the cross again, his hand singed, but instead of releasing it, he used his pain to his advantage and yanked the blade out.

He turned toward me with hatred gleaming in his crimson eyes. "Hunter, you die for this."

Raginwulf rose to his feet in an almost gliding movement. I held a stake tightly, expecting him to propel forward and attack me. Instead, Albert slinked up behind the vampire.

"I warned you what would happen should our paths cross again," Albert said.

Raginwulf turned with widened eyes. Before he could reply, flee, or attack, Albert bit the vampire's shoulder hard with his gnarled rat teeth. Raginwulf jerked free of the bite and staggered away, slumping to the ground. He fell face forward onto the cobblestone. Black pustules rose on his face and hands, his skin graying. He writhed and rolled. Blood leaked from his eyes, his ears, and his mouth. Seconds later, he burst into flames and turned to ash as though he'd been staked through the heart.

"Let him be, Luther!" Rusk shouted. He ran toward Luther but the other two werewolves grabbed Rusk and held his arms behind his back, preventing him from helping Jacques.

Jacques rose to his feet. Blood dripped from his nose and mouth. Luther struck him in the chest, knocking Jacques to the ground. He kicked Jacques in the stomach several times.

"See?" Luther said. "You're not an Alpha. Yield to me and live."

"Never," Jacques said, spitting out a mouthful of blood.

"Either way, Matilda is mine," Luther said with wildness in his eyes. He hung his long werewolf tongue out and licked the air.

Jacques' eyes narrowed. He went to all fours, trying to push himself to his feet, but Luther kicked Jacques in the side of the head, sending my cousin spiraling into the air. He landed with a hard bounce, but still tried to get up.

Jacques growled. His muscles swelled. He raked his long claws across the cobblestone. Fury darkened his eyes.

Luther grinned at him, taunting him. Jacques rushed Luther, leapt over six feet into the air. He plummeted toward Luther, slashed across Luther's face, and ripping out an eye. Luther howled in immediate pain.

Before Jacques steadied himself, Luther plunged his claws into Jacques gut. Jacques' eyes widened. He gripped Luther's wrists and shoved himself free of the claws. Luther struck Jacques in the face, over and over. Jacques dropped to his knees, clutching his stomach, but holding his head down in defeat.

Luther laughed and extended his sharp claws longer. He walked toward Jacques.

"Forrest!" Rusk said. "Do something! He's going to kill Jacques!"

Luther gazed at me with a devious smile. He showed his teeth and flexed his hands, revealing his sharp claws. "Yes, Forrest, do something. I dare you. It would be nice to have a Hunter in my pack after I kill Jacques."

My jaw tightened, but Father grabbed my shoulder before I could walk toward him. "No, Forrest, all he needs to do is bite or claw you to make you like him."

I jerked free of my father's hold. "I'm aware of that, but he won't do that."

Luther turned toward me with a broader, hungrier smile. "Try me."

I shook my head. An instant later I aimed and fired before he noticed the gun in my hand. The silver bullet struck him in the chest. His eyes revealed the slight moment of fear before he collapsed on the street, dead. I turned and aimed toward the two werewolves holding Rusk. "The bullets are silver. Let Rusk go or which one of you wants to be next?"

They released Rusk and held their hands before them, signifying peace. They walked to Jacques and helped my cousin to his feet. When Jacques stood on his own, both werewolves knelt before him, bowing their heads

Jacques shook his head and walked toward me, holding his stomach with his left hand. He wiped blood from his mouth. "Thanks, cousin, but I was wearing him down."

Matilda groaned, and Jacques hurried to her. Her wounds had healed, at least on the surface, but she was weak and pale. He hoisted her into his arms.

"It's time we get back indoors," he said. "She needs food and water."

I nodded, picked up my silver cross dagger, and walked to Esmeralda who hugged Varak. Albert stood beside me. Her eyes regarded him with great fear. I smiled at her. "I told you that we'd keep the child safe. You no longer have to worry about Raginwulf."

A kind smile appeared on her aged face. "I thank you for doing so."

I studied her for a few moments, wondering what spell she was attempting. I felt magic leap from her toward me, which seemed odd since we had just saved her life and the infant's.

"While it's doubtful," I said, "that another vampire will come to take Varak from you, I'd like to leave a gift with you to help protect him."

I extended my hand, offering my silver cross. Her eyes widened, and she backed against the bench. While she had mentioned she wasn't a Christian other than having to choose a side, I wondered if her claims to magic prohibited her from taking a cross. I held the cross loosely on my palm, but she didn't reach for it. Albert smacked my elbow hard, jarring the cross off my hand. It dropped on her lap, immediately causing her to hand Varak to the nurse.

Esmeralda came at me with her fangs exposed. She was a vampire? How? I had seen her holding a cross weeks before. I had only a moment to grab her by her shoulders and twist her off balance. She fell to the ground on her back, but before she could move, I plunged a stake through her heart. She withered and crumbled to ash.

"Forrest!" Father shouted. "Behind you!"

I turned to see the wet-nurse put the child on the bench. Her face distorted as she gnashed her fangs. She, too, came at me, but Albert bit her, making her suffer the same fate as Raginwulf. Perplexed, I regarded Albert. "They were both vampires? How?"

He shrugged and took the baby into his arms. "It's difficult to say since they're both ash now."

"And you?" I said. "Why did they die after you bit them?"

Albert smiled. "Although the vampires saved me from the plague, I carry it in my blood. I've never known why, but my bite is poisonous to vampires, perhaps due to the curse my former lover had bestowed upon me? After all, she had thought I'd die in prison but when I was cured of the plague, the curse she had placed upon me held untold effects. Maybe because the vampires had saved me she ensured a way they'd never help me again and instead, keep us as enemies for the remainder of my long life."

"And what about the child?" I asked. "Do you think he's the reason Esmeralda became a vampire? And the lady who nursed him?"

"It's doubtful they were turned by this infant. I noticed the infatuation they held for the child, but he's not old enough to turn mortals into the undead. Besides, he doesn't have fangs, *yet*, and they'd have to have partaken of his blood, not to mention be drained by him beforehand."

That made sense. But at what point and by whom were they turned?

The truth behind this secret would probably always evade me. I had seen Esmeralda carry a cross, but not for quite some time. At some point after our first meeting, she had chosen to become a vampire? Or perhaps Trenton had sired the wet-nurse and she turned Esmeralda? But until this moment, I never really thought about the fact we had never seen Esmeralda in the sunlight, only in the night or in the darkness of the tunnels.

Rusk and the other two werewolves hurried from the square down the main street where I suspected they'd find a secluded place to revert to their human forms and sleep until morning.

The rest of us walked at a modest pace down the main street toward Whitechapel.

"With Esmeralda and the lady being vampires, how many of the other Gypsies here are vampires?" I asked.

"Perhaps none," Albert said.

"I never sensed either to be vampires when normally I do."

"Magic can mask many things," he replied. "But as I have already mentioned, the child wasn't the one who turned them. I'd wager they sought out a vampire secretly. He might have mentally projected such a thought upon them."

"Why?"

"To ensure they had the strength to protect Varak."

"She had befriended Trenton. Do you suppose he turned them?"

Albert grinned at the suggestion. "That makes the most sense except she'd have died after Trenton was slain."

I frowned. "That's true."

"Perhaps it was a friend of Trenton though," Albert said.

"After Trenton was killed, we received a reward. It's possible Esmeralda left it."

"Doubtful."

"Why?"

"She didn't have money to offer such a reward."

"Then I wonder who?"

"My guess," Father said, "is Warren."

"The reporter?"

Father nodded.

"Why would he have offered it?"

"Perhaps as an incentive for you to hunt down and slay more vampires."

In a way, that sounded reasonable enough. And since his body was found with the fiddler, both had connections with Esmeralda. For all I knew, Esmeralda had sent Warren with Trenton to study how effective I was as a Hunter, not that any of it even mattered now. What worried me was not knowing how both women had become vampires and who had sired them.

"What should we do with this child?" Jacques asked, carrying Matilda in his arms.

"He will mature into a dangerous adversary," I said.

Albert held the child close to his chest and nodded. "No doubt. His fate of what he is has been sealed. Nothing we do can change that he's a half-blood. Give me through the night to make a decision."

"Are you contemplating to keep him as you have the boys?" I asked.

"Heavens no. I do not wish to have the responsibility of his future terrors placed upon me."

"Then why not kill him?" Jacques asked bluntly. It was a question I had pondered but was too ashamed to ask.

Obvious hurt creased Albert's face. "While such is the most probable thing to do, who amongst you could do such a thing and not go insane? Certainly, I cannot."

"Nor I," Jacques said.

"You think because I'm a rat, I'm capable?"

"No, I—"

"It is why you asked," Albert said softly. "You need to remember. I'm a rat on the outside, but my thoughts and my heart will always be human because that's what I was before the curse. But, I sense the child's undertones, too. He will wreak untold havoc somewhere in the world."

"Then what do you propose?" Jacques asked.

"I will inform you tomorrow."

CHAPTER 41

The sun had hardly risen when someone knocked fiercely upon our door.

With my eyes heavy with sleep, I staggered toward the door and pulled it open. "Constable Shields? Good morning. Come in."

He studied me for a few moments. "That's quite a bruise you have."

I rubbed my jaw. "It was much worse last night." And truthfully, it had been.

Father rose from his chair, shook Jacques and Matilda, and returned to his chair.

"No new murders last night," Shields said. He looked relieved. "I'm hoping you have good news?"

"As a matter of fact," I replied. "The vampire is no more."

Shields cleared his throat. "This . . . *vampire* . . . is the fiend responsible for the brutal murders? You're certain of this?"

I nodded.

Shields looked past me to Jacques. Jacques nodded, but Matilda remained deep in sleep. She might sleep for most of the day after enduring the severe injuries from last night. At least she had eaten well before falling asleep.

The constable took a deep breath and sighed. "I don't mean to sound doubtful, and I truly hope he was the murderer. After all the stress and nights without sleep, it's almost hard to accept it's over."

Jacques offered a reassuring smile. "I understand. It will probably take a few days, maybe even several weeks, before you are more at ease."

Tears came to the constable's eyes. "I don't know that I'll ever be at ease again. Ordeals like these are living nightmares. I cannot imagine anything worse. With your news, I can put in my request for my holiday. I need time away from detective work. And I thank you for offering your services to stop the murders."

He reached inside his jacket pocket and removed an envelope, handing it to me.

"What is this?"

"Reward money, though I offer it in secret," he replied. "I cannot publicly acknowledge you've killed Jack the Ripper since we have no proof of a body."

I shook my head, not taking the envelope. "We cannot—"

He forced the envelope into my hand. "*Please*. You must. I trust you. I know you've never mislead me, and that early on I disrespected your wishes by telling the reporter about what you do."

"All is forgiven," I replied.

"Still, the money is yours. I expect you'll be leaving London soon. You'll need money to travel, especially since you've probably spent a small fortune lodging in this inn."

Father nudged me. "*Take it.*"

"Thank you," I said with an embarrassed smile.

"Have you ever encountered Warren?" Shields asked. "I've not seen him in quite some time."

Jacques glanced at me and then to the constable. "We've not spoken to him in a long time, either."

"Perhaps he's taken holiday," Shields said. "Well, I won't keep you any longer. Do you know where you'll venture next?"

"Matilda and I are sailing to America," Jacques said.

"Father and I haven't made any solid plans yet," I replied.

Shields opened the door and smiled. "Wherever you end up, perhaps you can send me a post now and again. I'd be interested in your endeavors. Thanks for all your help."

Without waiting our replies, he pulled the door closed and was gone.

"John," Jacques said. "Do you mind keeping watch on Matilda for a while?"

"Sure. Why?"

"Forrest and I need to visit Albert and see what decision he's arrived at."

Father smiled and nodded. "Afraid I'll slow you down, eh?"

"No, it's—"

"It's okay, Jacques. Getting there without me is much faster. Besides, Matilda needs her rest. You two hurry. I'll be interested in what news you bring back, and I'm ready to leave London. The sooner the better."

I gave Father a smile.

Jacques grabbed his clothes to dress. "I never imagined you were such a good shot with the gun."

"I've not practiced as much as I'd have liked."

"I didn't realize you had even brought it, but I'm thankful you did."

He stepped into the adjoining room.

About a half hour after we had dressed, we were in the underground tunnels outside of Albert's lair. When we entered his chambers, he sat on his throne with Varak swaddled in a wool blanket. He cradled the child. As he stared at us, he held no emotion on his face.

"Have you decided what we should do with this child?" I asked.

The five were-rat boys were captivated by Varak.

He glanced down at Varak and nodded. "But it requires your help."

"What?" Jacques said.

"You must take him to Freiburg to the Archbishop," Albert replied. "But tell no one what he is, especially *not* the Archbishop."

"You want him taken to a cathedral?" I asked.

"Yes."

"Why?"

"In the hopes that his nurturing under holy guidance with alter his destined path."

"Do you think it will make a difference?"

"Only time will tell. At this present moment, can you offer any solution other than death? We've already stated none of us are willing to perform such an atrocity."

I shook my head. "No. Aren't you afraid that the bishop might discover what he truly is? If he does, he might kill the child."

Albert shrugged. "It's not something any of us could do."

"There's the chance he discovers what Varak is and not kill him. But you know that even within the cathedrals, there are those who do evil deeds and their souls are tarnished by iniquities."

"I agree, Forrest, but with what we know and have decided, we have no other resolution. It's a risk we have to take, for now."

"Matilda and I are journeying to America," Jacques said. He glanced at me. "We're not going that direction."

Albert stared at him for a long while. "I see. And you, Forrest?"

"My father and I can take him."

Albert cocked a brow. "But you don't want to?"

"Necessity overrides my wants," I replied. "We have to place him somewhere safe, and provided the archbishop is the correct person to educate Varak, we will travel there."

"I appreciate your sacrifice, but I insist you and your Father don't make this trip alone. Your father is burdened with his own ailments. It is not fair to ask that you provide the complete care of an infant when you are a child yourself." He handed me a rolled piece of parchment. "The details of where to find her are written on this. Madeline will care for Varak along your journey and make certain his needs are met. You are to keep her and Varak safe to the best of your abilities. Also, a man in London owes me several favors and will provide you with a horse and wagon and a driver, so you won't have to invest your own money for fare."

Albert stood and strolled to me. He held out Varak and placed him into my arms. Holding the child was awkward, but staring into the boy's strange eyes was eerie and sent chills down my spine because I knew what was behind them.

Before I turned to leave with Jacques, Albert said, "It has been a pleasure and an honor to fight by your side, all of you. I expect our paths will cross again in the future, Forrest, as your destiny will no doubt return you to London, perhaps only in passing. And when it does, don't be hesitant to visit. You're always welcome here."

WHEN JACQUES and I returned to the inn, Father was outraged that I had offered to take the child to Freiburg. Well, he was more outraged that he was included in the journey but settled down when he learned we had transportation and a woman to watch Varak along the way.

Matilda had dressed and what few belongings she wished to take to America were already packed. Father and I accompanied them to the ship where Rusk and the other two werewolves were waiting. The man Luther had infected didn't survive the night.

Jacques extended his hand to me. I firmly shook it and pulled him close for a fierce hug. "Never let your guard down, Forrest. As I've told you before, your reputation will continue to expand. You will have enemies who are people you've never met or slighted, but they will want you dead. I wish our paths weren't parting, but destiny calls me else-where since . . . Matilda is carrying my child."

I pulled back and stared into his eyes. He smiled and nodded.

"Congratulations, cousin," I said with a grin.

"If it's a boy, I think Micah is an excellent name."

"Thank you for your guidance and training. I already ache from your absence."

Jacques squeezed my shoulder. "You'll do fine, Forrest. You have your father and Hunter's insight and guidance that's more valuable than anything else I can teach you."

"Can I ask you something?"

He nodded.

"Have you decided to take leadership of the pack?"

"For now. Rusk and the other two, Yuri and Denis, have begged me to be their Alpha. But with a child on the way, I want to put distance between us and any other wolves that might be like Luther. An ocean apart is more comforting than remaining in London."

"Be safe," I said, fighting my burning tears.

Jacques smiled. "Until we met again."

Father and I watched them take their belongings up the ramp to the ship. After they boarded, we walked to the horse and coach. Varak slept in Madeline's arms inside the coach. She was in her forties, slender, with a smile that brightened even my father's darkest mood. Within minutes of being introduced, he seemed smitten by her, asking her continuous questions or telling her funny stories just to hear her laugh.

At times, I seemed invisible, but it didn't bother me. I rather enjoyed time to stare out the window to take in the countryside and think. I was glad to be leaving London since I had no idea what vampire had turned Esmeralda and the child's nurse. The vampire was an enemy, but he never made his presence directly known to me. Since we had slain Raginwulf, perhaps he or she was content with our accomplishment and happy that we were departing.

While I was glad to be leaving, my destiny with Varak displeased me. I didn't feel any urgency to be overly protective of this half-blood. By delivering him to the archbishop, I was only prolonging the inevitable. Regardless of how far our journey was, I didn't see how to avoid my constant worry about how Varak's future and my destiny would eventually reach an unavoidable conflict of epic proportions. Our paths would cross again, and the outcome wouldn't be pleasant.

The innocence in his sky-blue eyes was temporary, and in time, I'd come to discover a ruthless coldness behind those eyes that would haunt me for ages to come, provided I lived long enough.

An ominous feeling overtook me, making my stomach twist. I didn't know if the approaching danger would meet us before we delivered the child to the archbishop or afterwards. But something horrible was coming and Death rode alongside it, seeking me. Jacques was correct. I already had enemies that wanted me dead, and instead of fleeing like a man with commonsense, I was heading toward them.

No one had ever told me that the life of a Vampire Hunter was easy. Of course, I never expected it to be. My plan was to kill the vampires before they killed me, even though I was greatly outnumbered. I'm sure their plans held different end results, but Fate had yet to deal her cards. I never liked to get ahead of the game, but only a fool never planned various strategies for survival. I wasn't one of those fools.

THE END

AUTHOR'S NOTE

Thank you for purchasing this novel. If you enjoyed this book, please check out my website and join my mailing list at www. leonarddhilleyii.com to receive a free digital copy of Forrest Wollinsky: Vampire Hunter.

If you could also take a moment and leave a review, it is greatly appreciated!

Blessings to you and yours.

ABOUT THE AUTHOR

Leonard D. Hilley II grew up a quiet, shy kid with an inquisitive mind. Learning to read at an early age, he fell in love with books. He read every book he could get his hands on and stacks of dark comics about ghosts, monsters, and creepy things that stalk the night.

Like a lot of boys, he caught beetles, wooly bears, butterflies, and had an ant farm. When he was ten, his interests in science increased even more after seeing a professor's insect collection. Soon he set out on his quest to build his own collection. He also learned to rear butterflies and moths to obtain perfect specimens. He learned botany, gardening, and set his goal to become an entomologist.

At eleven, he watched the original Star Wars on the big screen. His imagination soared. Soon after, he discovered Roger Zelazny's Chronicles of Amber. Six months later, he had written the first draft of a novel. A novel he later discarded, but the characters stuck with him. Years later, these characters came to life in Shawndirea, which Hilley intended to be a novella for Devils Den. The characters, however, refused to be ignored and took the opportunity to unveil Aetheaon in their first epic fantasy. Lady Squire: Dawn's Ascension was quick to follow.

Shawndirea was Hilley's farewell to butterfly collecting, and those who have read the novel understand why. He has taken Ray Bradbury's advice to heart: "Follow the characters." He does. He follows, listens, and take notes—often never knowing where they're going to take him, but he's never been disappointed in the results.

Hilley earned a B.S. in Biology and an MFA in Creative Writing to combine his love of science and writing.

Sci-fi Titles: Predators of Darkness: Aftermath, Beyond the Darkness, The Game of Pawns, Death's Valley, The Deimos Virus.

Epic Fantasy: Shawndirea (Aetheaon Chronicles: Book One), Lady Squire (Aetheaon Chronicles: Book Two), Frosthammer (Aetheaon Chronicles: Book Three), Shadowfae (Aetheaon Chronicles: Book Four), and Devils Den.

UF/PR: Succubus: Shadows of the Beast (Nocturnal Trinity Series: Book One), Raven (Nocturnal Trinity Series: Book Two), A Touch of the Familiar (Nocturnal Trinity Series: Book Three)

YA UF/Paranormal: Forrest Wollinsky Vampire Hunter; Forrest Wollinsky: Blood Mists of London; Forrest Wollinsky: Predestined Crossroads.

CPSIA information can be obtained
at www.ICGtesting.com
Printed in the USA
BVHW071455080419
544913BV00010B/1323/P